Lady of the House:

Book Three of the
Forever Divas Series

Lady of the House:

Book Three of the Forever Divas Series

E.N. Joy

www.urbanbooks.net

Urban Books, LLC
97 N18th Street
Wyandanch, NY 11798

Lady of the House: Book Three of the Forever Divas
Series Copyright © 2016 E.N. Joy

ISBN 13: 978-1-62286-751-6
ISBN 10: 1-62286-751-3

First Trade Paperback Printing November 2016
Printed in the United States of America

10 9 8 7 6 5 4 3 2 1

*This is a work of fiction. Any references or similarities
to actual events, real people, living or dead, or to real
locales are intended to give the novel a sense of reality. Any similarity in other names, characters, places,
and incidents is entirely coincidental.*

Distributed by Kensington Publishing Corp.
Submit Orders to:
Customer Service
400 Hahn Road
Westminster, MD 21157-4627
Phone: 1-800-733-3000
Fax: 1-800-659-2436

Dedication

This book is dedicated to my mommy, Joan Ellen Windom. It breaks my heart that the majority of my memories of your life involve you being in pain, sad, miserable, unhappy, and angry. Your life was so hard. If I took every single Divas series book I've written up to this point, the pain, trials, and tribulations each of the characters went through combined don't compare to everything you endured in your life. You lived a story that even the greatest writer who ever lived could never pen; they could never capture your experiences to the degree to which you lived them, survived them, and struggled to overcome them.

Until I sat down to write this dedication, I had no idea why God put it in my spirit to write a book of this nature, which deviates greatly from every other book in the series. With my books usually forcing the characters to visit, marinate in, and get delivered from painful places in their lives, this book allowed my characters and me to reconnect to a happy place that was buried deep within. The fact that it took this book for me to realize that my own happy place wasn't exactly at the shallow end of the pool was a wake-up call that I must not just reconnect, but stay connected to my happy place, or I could end up . . . well . . . like you. And what I know as a mother myself is that we want our children to always be better than we were. The number one thing we want for our children is for them to be happy.

Dedication

I dedicate this book to you along with a promise that I will try my best to live every day of the rest of my life happy . . . for both of us. For all the days of your life that, try if you might, you just couldn't seem to connect to and stay connected to that happy place, I will do it for you.

I love you, Mommy. May you rest, finally, in peace.

Acknowledgment

As an author, I write what I know first, research what I don't know, and then make up all the rest. For all of my other divas books I would DVR reality shows, CNN specials, and countless episodes of *Law and Order* to help me assemble my storylines. I wanted to be in tune with what was going on in the world, as well as what the rest of the world was connecting to. From there, I wanted to build upon that with a spiritual message, plus add a twist from a Bible story. With this particular book I didn't do that.

For *Lady of the House,* I was led to DVR every Hallmark Channel Christmas movie that aired and study them. I found it so odd because God usually had me develop my stories from a place of pain. Everyone has been hurt before and can connect to pain, which allowed readers to connect to my past divas' characters. But for the first time ever in this series, God was allowing me to touch a happy place in my characters . . . in myself. This time, I was able to write about love.

Initially, I was very much on the fence and nervous about this deviation; that was, until I shared my feelings with Reading with Soul Book Club in Columbus, Ohio. When I shared the type of book I was writing, they all practically collectively exhaled, as if this had been the type of book they'd been waiting for me to pen. So I threw doubt out the window, thanked God for using the book club as confirmation for the direction my ghostwriter

Acknowledgment

(the Holy Ghost) was taking me, and I commenced to penning a story that made my soul smile. So thank you, Holy Ghost, for allowing me to take dictation to such a beautiful, fun story. And thank you to Reading with Soul Book Club for assuring me that even if no one else gets and appreciates this shift in my writing, you guys will.

Very special thanks to my writing partner, Nikita Lynnette Nichols, for allowing Lady Arykah to grace the pages of my final Divas series installment. You have literally helped me to move on to a new chapter in my writing career as we jointly bring our readers the Angel series. New journeys in life are always more exciting when accompanied by a sista-friend. Thank you for trusting me enough to throw my character, Angel, the keys to your signature character's car and let her drive. Besides, Angel knows how Lady Arykah is when it comes to road rage. She'd be singing the Ludacris song, "Move, get out the way" . . . the unedited version. LOL!

Chapter 1

"Sister Melanie, did I just see you steal money from the church offering basket?" Doreen stood in the doorway of the church treasurer's office. She didn't want to believe what she'd just witnessed, but what other choice did she have? This wasn't a case of hearsay or it's-not-what-it-looks-like. She'd just seen the church treasurer take one of the white tithes and offering envelopes and slip it into her sweater pocket.

Melanie shot up out of her seat. "First Lady Doreen!" She was in total shock to see Doreen standing in the doorway. "I, uh . . ." Her words trailed off. But that was okay by Doreen. Unless Melanie was about to speak the truth, she didn't want to hear anything she had to say anyhow.

"It's church policy that you don't count the funds without myself, pastor, or another member of the finance board," Doreen reminded the frazzled woman standing before her. "You know what this means, don't you?" Doreen slightly tilted her head forward and raised an eyebrow. She didn't wait for Melanie to respond either. "You're going to have to resign from your position as church treasurer and any other leadership position you hold here at Living Word Living Waters until after you've been delivered from that pilfering spirit."

"But, First Lady—" Melanie tried to speak.

"I love you, Sister Melanie. I can honestly say that you've been one of few people here at the church—heck—

in this town, who has genuinely accepted me since I married Pastor Frey five years ago and became the first lady of this ministry. And although it pains me, there is no way you can continue operating in the same ministry you're stealing from. Now, by no means does this mean you can't continue to hold a membership at the church." Doreen walked around the desk to where Melanie stood. "You know we are a place of healing and deliverance, so you definitely need to be here so we can minister that spirit of theft right on out of you." Mother Doreen gave Melanie a great big Holy Ghost hug. "We love you."

"And I love you too," Melanie said, returning the gesture of hugging Doreen. "That's why I would never—"

"Hey, you two." Pastor Wallace Frey, senior pastor of Living Word Living Waters, entered the room in a rush. "Sorry, I'm late, Sister Melanie." He turned to close the door. "I know it's my week to help you count the money." He turned around to see Doreen and Melanie releasing each other from a hug. Both their eyes were cast downward. He immediately sensed that something was going on.

"If I didn't know any better, I'd say once upon a time there'd been two canaries flying in the room. And either you both ate one each, or you managed to split one poor little fella while the other flew off to freedom." Wallace chuckled. He was always making these quirky comparisons. Everyone figured it was him trying to use modern-day parables like Jesus did in His time. Only thing is, Jesus' were a lot easier to catch on to. "'Cause you both got little yellow feathers hanging out of your mouths." He wiped the corners of his mouth as if suggesting the two women should do the same.

Neither woman responded to his humor.

"What's going on here?" He took a step toward the desk. Neither woman spoke. He was sensing things were far from kosher. "Everything okay?" He reached the chair on the opposite side of the desk where the women stood and stopped.

Doreen and Melanie looked at each other. Their eyes questioned which one would break the news to Pastor. Finally, Melanie relinquished the duty by once again casting her eyes downward.

Doreen exhaled, then spoke. "No, Pastor, everything is not okay." She nodded to the chair her husband stood by. "You might want to sit down for this."

Wallace looked from his wife to Melanie. Worry and fret were plastered across Melanie's face. This deeply concerned him. For the decade he'd known Melanie and the seven years she'd been church treasurer, she'd always been high spirited, donning a smile that could brighten anyone's life. Yet, now, it appeared, from what Wallace could tell, that her eyes had no life in them at all. What had taken place in the last twenty minutes from when service ended and she was out in the sanctuary praising the Lord, to now, where she looked as though God had turned His face from her? This didn't look good. It didn't feel good. He took his wife's advice and sat.

"Honey, I know Sister Melanie has been around and with this church longer than I have," Doreen said. "And like I just told her, she's been one of the kindest and most welcoming people I've encountered since becoming first lady, which is why it pains me to see her have to go."

Wallace hadn't even gotten comfortable in the chair before he shot up right out of it. "What? You can't be serious!" He said, "Sister Melanie, you can't quit. You can't leave us now." He stepped around the desk to her and placed his hand on her shoulder. "Whatever it is, I'll do my best to make it right."

He tightened his lips, shook his head, and then continued. "Although on one hand, I'm grateful that this church has a first lady you felt you could talk to . . ." And Wallace was indeed grateful for that. About 90 percent of the female members of the church still came to him for matters and concerns that his wife, as first lady, could easily handle. In the first year or so, he just figured everyone had always been accustomed to coming to him for prayer, spiritual advice, or whatnot. He hoped that eventually everyone would warm up to and get used to the fact that they now had a first lady they could go to. By year three, Wallace concluded that change was probably taking his church a little longer to adapt to than most. So any other time he'd been 100 percent on board with Melanie having gone to his wife before coming to him, but this, evidently, wasn't any other time. This was a time when the church was losing one of the best treasurers that had ever kept its books. And on top of that, Melanie was a genuinely good person who he'd known over half his life.

"I just don't understand why you didn't come to me with something as serious, drastic, and life changing to the church as you deciding to quit." He stared at Melanie, waiting on a response.

"That's because I didn't decide to quit," Melanie was allowed to say uninterrupted.

"Huh? What?" Wallace was quite confused. "I don't understand. If you didn't quit . . ." He allowed his eyes to travel from Melanie to his wife, the only other person in the room who might be able to offer him up some answers.

"I had to let Sister Melanie go," Doreen said, answering her husband's unasked question.

"But . . . What?" He was truly at a loss for words. In all his years of pastoring the church he had never had to remove anyone from his or her position. Leaders had resigned, others had left the church, some had even, God rest their souls, gone on to glory. But never had anyone been fired.

"Sister Melanie was fired," Doreen said to make it clear.

Wallace shook his head. He couldn't have been hearing things right. He sat back down in the chair. "Hold up, this isn't *The Apprentice,* and you're not Donald Trump," he said to his wife.

If not for the fact Wallace always spoke so calm ly and respectfully, even when he was low-key reading someone the riot act, Doreen might have taken offense to her husband's words. But she knew him well enough to know that his words never came from a bad place. They were always battered in love.

"We don't just up and tell folks, 'You're fired,' especially not folks like Sister Melanie," Wallace said to his wife while sympathetically looking Melanie's way. "And not one who has served as an outstanding member of Living Word Living Waters since I can't remember how many years."

"Seven," Doreen said, then paused. It was obvious she'd been keeping count. She wasn't sure whether that was consciously or subconsciously at this point. Perhaps she was just good with numbers, even in her seventies. Heck, she was good at a lot of things to be in her seventies. She looked good too. Her black definitely didn't crack, not looking a day over sixty-five. And she was as healthy as a horse according to her annual physical she'd just gotten last week. She'd even lost about thirty pounds since marrying Wallace. She was still thick, how he liked her and how she liked herself.

Doreen took several breaths and counted backward from five. She could understand how her husband must feel losing a church leader, but a little part of her couldn't help but wonder if he'd be acting this way had it been any one of the other church leaders. Would he be putting up such a fuss, or would he have simply trusted her judgment and allowed them to pack up and leave?

"Trust me, I am not trying to be Donald Trump," Doreen assured her husband. "And I don't just go around firing folks, that is, unless they're stealing from the church, a church whose mission is to do the work of the Lord, which means if you're stealing from the church, then you're stealing from God." Doreen put some bass in her voice to get her point across to her husband. It felt to her that he was questioning her judgment and her authority as first lady in the church. Just in case he was, she figured she'd get him straight. No, she didn't make it a habit of giving her husband "the business" in front of company, but he'd started it. "It says in the church bylaws, of which I've read front to back cover, that if anyone is caught stealing from the church or in any way, shape, or form manipulating the financial books, then that person is to be immediately removed from any position of leadership they may hold without vote. So you see, *Pastor*, I didn't fire anybody." Doreen let out a harrumph and folded her arms pretzel style.

No part of Wallace believed for one second that Melanie would ever take from the church. He didn't want to verbalize it though. It was already clear to him that his wife didn't like feeling as though she was being second-guessed, whether he was in the capacity as her husband or pastor. So he had to get up out of his emotions and follow the direction of the Holy Spirit instead.

"I'm sorry, Doreen," Wallace said. "I didn't mean for it to sound as though I was questioning your actions in any way. I guess I'm just shocked is all."

Wallace's words comforted Doreen. She was glad to know that his comments had been out of emotion and not that he was questioning her competence on how to handle church business. "It's okay. I was just as surprised myself." She looked at Melanie. "Wouldn't have believed it unless I hadn't seen it with my own eyes."

Wallace's eyes bucked. "You *saw* Sister Melanie stealing?" Any hope he'd had that there was some type of confusion regarding the matter instantly drained.

Doreen nodded. "Took an envelope from the offering just as I was entering the office." Doreen nudged her head toward the pile of envelopes, cash, and loose change that rested on Melanie's desk. There was no specific order. It looked as though Melanie had dumped everything out and was quickly going through the pile. It was a deliberate mess, a mess Doreen was sure Melanie had hoped to have cleaned up before Wallace came to help her count the money.

Wallace looked at Melanie. In that instance, she looked up from the ground and locked eyes with her pastor. He shot her a knowing look.

"I'm sorry, Pastor Frey." Melanie looked to Doreen. "First Lady. I'll clear my things out now." Melanie's eyes darted with nervousness. "I'll go to the supply room and get some boxes." She hurriedly walked to the office door.

With each step Melanie took, Wallace looked as though he wanted to stop her. This didn't go unnoticed by Doreen as she watched it all go down before her. She surveyed the scene and waited with bated breath for fear of what her husband's next action would mean, not only to the ministry, but to their marriage. If her husband stopped Melanie from leaving, then she'd know that this thing was personal and *not* church business.

At the beginning of her and Wallace's courtship, he had not hesitated to let Doreen know that he and Melanie had been a couple long before Doreen had ever been thought of. Wallace and Melanie were former high school sweethearts who'd even been engaged once upon a time. Eventually, Melanie went off to college in another state and their young love couldn't withstand the distance the miles put between their bodies and their hearts. There would be three decades between the two before they'd ever even lay eyes on each other again, partly because Melanie never came back to Kentucky after college. She stayed in Atlanta after graduation from Clark Atlanta University. Her mother falling ill would be what had brought her back to Kentucky. Even when her mother eventually passed away, Melanie remained in the state. It was actually at her mother's funeral when she would see Wallace again for the first time since she'd gone off to college.

Even though Wallace and Melanie hadn't worked out, he'd remained a friend to Melanie's mother over the years. Melanie's mother would always tell him he was the man she wished her daughter had married—a God-fearing man—even though at that point Melanie had married an Atlanta professional football player and had a couple of children under her belt.

By the time Melanie had come back to care for her mother, she was freshly divorced from her husband who couldn't manage to stay faithful. Her children were both grown and off to college in two different states, so she had nothing in Atlanta to go back to . . . And so she didn't go back. She stayed in Kentucky and ultimately ended up attending the church her first love attended. But the sparks, love, and energy between them was no more. No chemistry, no nothing; just the love of Christ. That was the story Wallace had passed on to Doreen, and she'd believed him. Nothing in her spirit told her anything other than what her husband had shared with her. Nothing about Melanie had been a threat to Doreen . . . up until now.

For Doreen, watching Melanie walk toward that doorway seemed to happen in slow motion. Everything else was at a standstill. The world had stopped, but Doreen was certain her breathing hadn't. She could hear her heart thumping loudly in her ears. She could hear her own deep breaths sounding like a gust of wind. And she could hear loud and clear that voice inside her head begging and pleading to her husband to not stop Melanie; that he allow her to walk through that door. A man of God, her husband, wouldn't think twice about letting a church employee go after being caught stealing. A man in love, though, perhaps not. Who was Mother Doreen married to? A man of God or a man in love . . . with another woman? She was now no longer breathing as she inhaled. Her breath was caught.

She watched as Melanie made her way through the threshold of the doorway. The corners of Doreen's mouth raised into a slight smile as she now exhaled. She closed her eyes and thanked God that her worst fear had not come to pass.

Even Wallace's own sister, Jessica, who lived in Oregon, had thought Doreen was a fool for allowing her husband to work side by side with an ex-lover. But Doreen had trusted her husband beyond measure. She'd trusted her spirit of discernment that had never malfunctioned. That trust had just paid off.

However, perhaps Doreen had reveled in that trust a little too soon, as before she could even open her eyes . . . she heard Wallace call out, "Melanie, wait. Don't go!"

Chapter 2

Not even *Sister* Melanie. Plain Melanie. Sister Melanie is how he would have referred to the church employee he was calling back into the office. Melanie is how he would have referred to the woman he had feelings for calling her back into the office. That's how Doreen saw it anyway.

Doreen's heart began to melt—and not in a good way—at hearing her husband call out to his high school sweetheart. *"Melanie, wait. Don't go!"* She replayed the words her husband had spoken in her head.

Why, why, *why* couldn't he have just let her go? Why couldn't Doreen's husband have let his high school sweetheart walk right on out that door so that she could eventually be on her merry way? Any other pastor would have kicked Melanie to the curb the very second they learned she'd stolen from the church. There wouldn't have been any ifs, ands, or buts about it. Miss Thing would have been outta there. That is, unless the pastor had feelings for the thief.

"No, Pastor," Melanie said. She'd stopped in her tracks, but she hadn't turned around to face him. "First Lady is right. I need to be removed from all positions and roles of leadership at the church."

Doreen definitely agreed with that. And in spite of what she'd said before, she now even wished she hadn't invited Melanie to remain a member of the church. How was Doreen going to keep her eyes on Jesus if she had to keep them on a jezebel as well? Doreen quickly repented for that thought. She had no right referring to Melanie as a jezebel. It wasn't Melanie's fault that a married man had eyes for her. That didn't make her a loose goose. It made the man an adulterer. *So a man thinketh, so that man does.* And Doreen could only imagine what Wallace was thinking as he stared at Melanie, pleading with her not to go.

"Let me see it," Wallace asked.

"Excuse me?" Both Doreen and Melanie spoke the same words at the same time.

"See *what?*" This time it was only Doreen who spoke. She wanted to know exactly what it was her husband wanted to see that Melanie had. Boobies? Did he want her to move her long sweater out of the way so that his eyes could marinate on her derrière? Did he want to see her eyes; search them to see if she had feelings for him as well? What? Just *what* in the world was it that her husband could possibly want to see that another woman had?

Not used to Doreen's sharp tone, in the house of the Lord anyway, Wallace raised an eyebrow. "I want to see what Sister Melanie has."

Usually, Doreen was pretty good at being reasonable and keeping her mind stayed on Jesus, but evidently not when it came to men; *her* man in particular. How her mind ended up so far in the gutter after hearing her husband's comment was beyond her. Jealousy had a way of making a woman feel some kind of way no matter how old she was. And Doreen hadn't felt this way since her early days of being married to her first husband, Willie. God rest his soul.

Before Doreen could think about her next words, they flew out of her mouth. "So you're just going to call this woman back into the office and look at her right in front of my face?" She threw her hands on her hips. "I might be the first lady, but I ain't the first lady from *Scandal*, so if you think I'm going to stand here and watch you go googly-eyed right under my nose with Olivia Pope here," she nodded her head toward Melanie, "you got another think coming!" Doreen then said, under her breath, "Got me all twisted," as she rolled her eyes.

Wallace slowly stood as he stared at his wife, wondering *who* this woman standing before him was. He'd never seen Doreen get this sassy, not even outside of the church. Not even when inside the church some of the women threw what the gals today referred to as shade. No, his wife, the first lady, would simply smile, and nine times out of ten, pray for the women. So why now was she 'bout ready to cut the fool?

"I think you're confusing things," Wallace said to his wife. "I want to see what Sister Melanie has, meaning the envelope."

"Envelope?" Doreen said softly, puzzled.

"The money she *stole*," Wallace said with widened eyes, as if he was trying to remind his wife what had started this discussion in the first place.

Thankfully, Wallace's comment and expression rang a bell for Doreen. She was then able to call to mind the whole ordeal about why Melanie was being fired as church treasurer. "Ohhh, the envelope." If Doreen's back hadn't been bothering her so these past few days, she would have bent over and picked her face up off the ground. Instead, she just held her head down in embarrassment. Unlike what she'd just done, her husband would never call her out in front of someone, but once the two were alone, more than likely he'd demand answers regarding her behavior.

Wallace turned toward Melanie and held out his hand. "Sister Melanie, the envelope, please."

Doreen raised her eyes to watch the transaction take place. At least her husband would be able to see for himself that Doreen was very much justified in her actions.

Melanie stood in hesitation. She had a pleading look on her face. "Pastor, please." She slightly shook her head as her eyes darted from him to Doreen.

It was in that instance that Doreen had a strange feeling that the two of them knew something she didn't know, and that they didn't *want* her to know. It pained Doreen to think that her husband had been keeping a secret with his ex-lover. That made Doreen all the more certain that perhaps her intuition was on point; that Wallace and Melanie weren't just keeping secrets, but were secret lovers.

"Sister Melanie, hand me the envelope," Wallace demanded.

At least he was back to putting a spiritual title in front of Melanie's name. Not that that made Doreen feel any less bothered.

Melanie exhaled. "If you say so, Pastor." She slowly and reluctantly removed the envelope from her sweater pocket. She looked down at it, looked up at Wallace, and then handed it to him.

He took the envelope in his hand. He looked down at it, his eyes scanning it from left to right. Next, he opened the envelope and looked inside. He stared into the envelope for a minute, and then said, "Just as I thought." He sighed and looked up at Melanie. "Sister Melanie, that will be all. My wife and I will count today's offering. You're excused. We'll see you at Bible study on Wednesday and at the financial board meeting right before that."

"Wait a minute!" Doreen said to her husband. What did he mean he'd see Melanie at the *financial board meeting?* She was fired. She was a thief. He had the proof in his very hands. If even after all that had taken place

Wallace was going to allow Melanie to hold her position, Doreen would have to seriously consider relinquishing hers—as first lady and as wife.

"I get you being a little perturbed about my attitude," Doreen said to Wallace, "but what I don't get is you being a pastor who sweeps the wrongdoings of his leaders under the rug."

"That's not what I'm doing here, Doreen," Wallace said, still just as cool, calm, and collected as always.

"That's *exactly* what you're doing," Doreen said. She had stopped being cool, calm, and collected about ten minutes ago. Besides, since becoming first lady and dealing with church matters and church folks, those past characteristics of hers had long begun to fade. Doreen looked from her husband to Melanie. "And I will not change my opinion about that, Wallace, unless there is something you two want to share with me."

Both Wallace and Melanie remained silent.

"Oh, okay, I see," Doreen said, nodding her head. "I see *exactly* what's going on here." She glared at her husband. "If you get rid of Melanie, then the congregation will start asking questions. Questions lead to answers. If people find out the church treasurer got caught stealing, they'll be wondering just how long she'd been stealing. Surely this wasn't her first time taking from the church." She looked Melanie up and down despicably. "Just her first time *getting caught*." She turned her attention back to her husband. "This could lead to a church audit and all types of rumors and gossip. So to prevent all that, we're just going to slap Sister Melanie here on the wrist, tell her not to do it anymore, and pray for her." Doreen shook her head and looked at her husband with disappointment. "That's not the kind of man I married." Her eyes became moist.

She'd heard of pastors not being who they said they were. Each time she always said that at least their wives should have known they weren't fully about God's business or living double lives. But in this case, she'd be eating her own words, because not in the last five years had Wallace done or said anything to make her believe he was the kind of pastor—the kind of man—who would allow such a thing to go down in a church he was shepherding.

"Yes, it is the kind of man you married," Wallace said matter-of-factly. "That's exactly who you married, over forty years ago, and his name was Willie. But guess what? I'm not Willie, and I'd appreciate if you didn't treat me as such."

The raised octave in her husband's voice immediately put Doreen in check. The words he spoke penetrated her soul and brought to heart why she was acting the way she was. It was because of Willie. It was because the only man she'd ever loved, had ever been with her entire life before Wallace, had done nothing but cheat on her since they'd exchanged wedding vows. Doreen thought she'd overpowered, knocked out, and buried those feelings forever. But apparently someone knew where she'd buried the bone. That old rascal named Satan knew. It was just like the devil to, in the blink of an eye, take Doreen back to her past. But that's how the enemy worked; tried to keep a person bound to their past because he knows he can't touch their future.

Wallace looked at Melanie. "Have a safe drive home. We'll see you Wednesday." He looked at Doreen, not quite daring her to oppose, but mentally preparing himself just in case she did.

Doreen had had disagreements with her husband over the years. What couple didn't disagree on some things? But what she and her husband didn't have were arguments; loud talking, cussing, and fussing, hands-on-hips arguments. But that's just the direction things were headed and would have ended if Doreen had been able to stay behind the wheel. But that husband of hers had shut it down; had taken control of the moving vehicle and pulled it over to the side of the road before it could take out any pedestrians; namely Melanie.

"Good day," Melanie said nervously as she looked from her pastor to her first lady. She too was preparing herself for Doreen to object. When that didn't happen, she bowed a good-bye with her head, and then hightailed it out of there.

Once the clicking of Melanie's heels could no longer be heard, Wallace looked at his wife. "What in the world got into you just now?" he asked. "You know what? Never mind." He closed his eyes, shooed his hand, and then opened them again. "I know exactly what it was." He walked over to Doreen and put his arms around her. "Remember the one thing we agreed on in our marriage? No kids allowed." He gave his wife a gentle reminder.

"I know, sweetheart," Doreen said regretfully, keeping her arms to her side. "She just snuck up on me. Came out of nowhere."

"Well, I'm about to squeeze that hurt, younger Doreen right out of you." Wallace gave his wife a big squeeze. "That pain-filled little girl inside of you has to go!" he declared with a squeeze.

Doreen didn't return the gesture as she thought about the promise they'd made to each other prior to exchanging vows. Marrying in their late years, Doreen in her sixties and Wallace in his fifties, it went without saying that they each had a life before their life together. They each had a history, a story, a testimony, a past. For most, that past takes root and develops in a person's childhood. So that "kid" inside is always fighting for control. Fighting to be heard. Wanting their pain to be acknowledged and not forgotten. Those are the "kids"—the younger Doreen and the younger Wallace—who were absolutely prohibited to enter their home, marriage, or their lives. The now grown, saved, and sanctified Doreen and Wallace would remain in control. But for one hot second, that kidlike Doreen who once did kidlike things had gained control. Wallace needed to let his wife know that he recognized it and would not hold that moment against her.

It was a little hard for Doreen to receive her husband's instant forgiveness. She was ashamed and discouraged that she'd allowed herself to act like that. Her arms stayed by her side as her husband hugged her and prayed in tongues in her ear.

"Come on, hug me back, baby," Wallace said in-between praying, until finally he'd penetrated the heart of his adult wife, and she squeezed him back and joined him in prayer in unknown tongues.

After a minute or so, the prayers ceased and the couple released each other from their hug.

"Feel better now?" he asked his wife.

A huge smile lit up Doreen's face. "Yes, much better."

"Good," Wallace said. "'Cause that young thug in me was 'bout to rear his ugly head too," he laughed.

Doreen let out a chuckle. "I don't know if I would have seen that as all bad." She placed her arms in front of her, held her hands together and began swaying back and forth as she blushed. "I might kind of like the thug in you. When your voice got deep there for a minute . . ." Doreen said flirtatiously. It just went to show that age ain't nothing but a number. Even in her AARP years and some years into menopause, all the womanly sensations in Doreen could still be triggered by the man she loved.

"Awww, shucks, you better stop it now, woman." Wallace blushed, then got serious as he looked down at the envelope that was still in his hand.

His change in demeanor didn't go unnoticed by his wife, as the two now stared at the envelope.

Doreen cleared her throat. "Honey, please don't take this the wrong way," she said, keeping her eyes on the envelope. "But are you really going to allow Melanie to maintain her position as treasurer here at the church?" she asked. "I mean, forgive me in advance for the comparison, but isn't that like allowing a ho to head the men's ministry?"

Wallace's eyes bucked in shock. "I'm not going to even laugh at that right now," he said, wanting to do nothing but laugh. "Because I know your intention was not to tell a joke, but that, you are, in fact, my dear, deadly serious."

"I absolutely am," Doreen assured him. "And before you get any ideas, I am not jealous of Melanie. For a hot second did the younger Doreen try to come out to play? Yes, and I apologize that for a moment in time, I was thinking things I might have been thinking had it been Willie standing there and not you." There was a time where if Doreen just mentioned Willie's name, she'd draw an invisible cross on her heart and pray that he rest in peace. But the day she married her second husband, she came to grips that Willie had long been resting at peace. It was the young girl who Willie had hurt so badly that hadn't been resting. But the day of her marriage she gave her past life with Willie to God and all that had come with it, and took on a new life with Wallace. "Because the last thing I want you to think is that I'm comparing you to another man . . . Any man. But if you have any kind of feelings for Sister Melanie," Doreen said, "if every now and again that young boy in love for the first time with his high school sweetheart surfaces and you're feeling some kind of way about—"

Wallace placed his index finger on Doreen's lips. "You don't even have to finish that sentence," he said. "No part of me looks at Sister Melanie in that way or feels any type of attraction toward her at all. I love Sister Melanie with the love of Christ, but I lust after my wife and no other woman, so you better know that."

"And I do," Doreen said. She sadly looked down.

"Then why the sad face? Seems like those words would put a smile on your face."

"They put a smile on my heart," Doreen said. "But now that just leaves the question of why. Why on earth would you even think about still allowing her to remain as church treasurer after I caught her stealing red-handed?" She pointed to the envelope Wallace was still holding. "And you have proof positive in your hand."

Wallace let out a deep breath. "Sister Melanie didn't steal from the church offering, Doreen."

Doreen stood there and had to get her mind right, because she had to be losing it . . . for real. Did this man just stand there and say to her that Melanie hadn't stolen anything and was holding the envelope he'd personally confiscated from her that she'd had on her person? This was too much. Doreen had no words, just thoughts that she was going insane.

"See?" Wallace said as he opened the envelope and turned it upside down. Nothing fell out.

Still, Doreen remained silent. She was wondering the entire time why would Melanie steal an empty envelope. A lightbulb went off in her head. "Maybe she'd already taken the money out of the envelope by the time she gave it to you. She had plenty of time to do so. You and I were—"

"Stop it right there, Nancy Drew," Wallace said. "She didn't take anything out of the envelope because there was never anything in it to take." He put his head down. "There never is. It's always just an empty envelope with the same old thing written on the outside."

Now Doreen was more confused than ever. There was definitely a piece of the puzzle she was missing. And it wasn't a corner piece either, which were usually the easiest to place. Sweat beads began forming on her forehead. That was an old trait that hadn't subsided. One that came about whenever she sensed something wicked was brewing. "How come you don't sound so surprised about it?"

"Because I'm not," Wallace answered. "When you mentioned that you'd caught Sister Melanie stuffing an envelope into her pocket, I knew exactly what it was. That and the fact that I know she isn't a thief. She was just doing what I'd asked her to do ever since the first time she found one of these in the offering basket and brought it to my attention."

Doreen swallowed hard. This wasn't going to be good. She could tell. She looked around Melanie's office and spotted the tissue box. She went to grab one, but Wallace handed her the handkerchief from the pocket of his suit jacket.

"Thank you." Doreen took the handkerchief and wiped the sweat from her forehead. Once she was finished she looked at her husband, telling him with her eyes that he could continue on.

"I'll just let you read it for yourself." Wallace extended the envelope to his wife.

Doreen stared at the envelope in her husband's hand for a few seconds before she reached out and took it. For a moment there, she held one end while her husband held the other.

"Go ahead, take it," he urged his wife.

It took Doreen a few more seconds to gain the courage to take the envelope from her husband. She looked in his eyes for comfort as she pulled it to her chest.

He nodded for her to read it.

Holding the envelope in both hands that slightly trembled, Doreen began to read the words written on the envelope. After reading them, her eyes filled with tears and the weight of the envelope became too much for her to bear as it slipped from her hands to the floor. But even then, the words written couldn't escape her as the envelope fell faceup on the floor, and there, written in capital letters, were the words: *BABY KILLERS BURN IN HELL, NOT BECOME FIRST LADIES*

Chapter 3

Mother Doreen wasn't wearing her pearls today, so she clutched the neckline of her blouse instead as she gasped.

"Babe, you okay?" Wallace raced over to his wife who he noticed seemed to be unbalanced by her slight wobble. "Sit down." He assisted her into the chair where he once sat.

Doreen placed her hand over her mouth and nose. She couldn't breathe anyway, so what did it matter? She closed her eyes to hold in the tears, but that only squeezed them out. To muffle the deep breaths that might have eventually turned into a full-blown outcry, she placed her hand fully over her mouth.

"Honey, it's okay." Wallace began rubbing her back with one hand while he rested the other on her shoulder.

Doreen gathered her composure and swallowed her tears so that she was able to speak. "So you say this has been going on for some time now?" she asked.

Wallace nodded. "Yes. Ever since the first Sunday we came back as man and wife after getting married in Malvonia."

"I see," Doreen said, not surprised at all that word about the incident that took place at their wedding had made it back to Kentucky from Ohio before they had.

When the pastor officiating their wedding addressed the guests in the sanctuary and asked if anyone had just cause why the two shouldn't marry, Doreen had never imagined in a million years that someone would actually stand up and speak out. At the time, she had no idea who the Terrance fella who had interrupted her ceremony even was. But as he began to tell the story about his mother, her dealings with Doreen's first husband and his mother's physical encounter with Doreen, she knew then exactly who he was; but not the full depth.

Because of Terrance's outburst, a man Doreen had never met or known about until that day, people learned the story behind Doreen's glory. At New Day Temple of Faith Doreen had been lovingly known as Mother Doreen. She was the church mother indeed. She was the one that everyone, namely the women, went to when they needed prayer, a voice of reason, advice, or just a good old-fashioned straightening out of their behinds. To them, she was like the perfect Christian. Doreen could do no wrong in their eyes because they'd never seen nor heard of her doing any wrong. But no man is perfect. No woman either.

Most elders in the church are looked at as true saints living sinless, drama-free lives. That's exactly who Doreen had been at that time. She was no phony. She practiced what she preached. She practiced what she praised. But that's not who she'd always been. There was a testimony behind the glory in her. But on the day of her and Wallace's marriage, folks got the whole story before there ever was any glory.

It wasn't like Doreen had been hiding her past. With today's technology, folks could have easily Googled her story. Had they, they would have learned decades earlier she'd served time in prison, eleven months and twenty-three days, with five years of probation, for beating the daylights out of her husband's mistress after catching them in bed together. Unbeknownst to Doreen while she was going off on the homewrecker in a violent rampage, the woman was pregnant. The baby didn't survive the assault, and Doreen's punishment was a jail sentence.

Had Doreen committed the act in today's times, she would have served much longer, for she would have been charged with the murder of the unborn child. That law hadn't been in effect back then, though. For some, when it comes to the death of a baby, inside the womb or not, a death sentence is the only satisfying form of punishment. Looked as though someone with that exact concept was a member of Living Word Living Waters.

"I'm not surprised," Doreen said, looking down at the envelope and reading it again. "I mean, I'm not surprised that someone might have felt this way and did this. But what I am surprised about is that they've been relentless with it and are still doing it all these years later." She looked up at her husband. "Can't they see that after five years I'm here to stay, and that no message scribbled on an envelope, as disgusting as it is, is going to run me off? I mean, have I not proved to be exactly who I say I am?" Doreen began to get worked up. "Have I not shown this church I am a true servant of God, that I'm not that woman all those years ago who—"

"Calm down, love." Wallace comforted his wife. He rubbed her shoulders, and then kissed her moist forehead. "Like you said, the devil is relentless."

Doreen looked down at the envelope. "But do you know what hurts the most?"

"What's that, sweetheart?"

"That you and Sister Melanie have been hiding this from me for all these years, and I've been none the wiser." She looked at her husband. "Just makes me wonder what else you and her could be keeping from me right under my nose with me not having the slightest idea."

Wallace pulled away from his wife and stood up straight. "Now, wait a minute. Didn't we just have this conversation about—"

"I don't mean in *that* sense," Doreen said. "I mean, what else are you two hiding when it comes to *this?*" She waved the envelope. "Any threats? Any phone calls? Does this person want to do bodily harm to me? Am I safe? Have I been a walking target all these years?" Doreen began to speak fast, get agitated and . . .

"Afraid?" Wallace said. "You're afraid, aren't you?" He walked in front of his wife and pulled her up. "Woman, you are covered in the blood of Jesus, and don't you ever forget that. You have no reason to be afraid. Jesus is not going to let anything happen to you, and neither is your earthly Lord." He pointed to his chest. "Me. I've got your back, and I've been watching your back. I make sure I pray daily for the strength of the angels God has dispatched to be in charge of your well-being." He flexed his muscles, then to lighten the mood, said, "And I'm in pretty good shape myself. I'm equipped to handle evil principalities with my weapon of the Word and prayer, and can take out a thug or two with *these* guns." He massaged one of the muscles on his arm and laughed.

Doreen looked at her husband for a moment, and then turned away. She couldn't muster up any laughter right now. Her husband had made a good attempt to lighten the mood. But her mind was in too dark a place right now. "When I was in prison, some really bad things happened to me there. Things I've already told you about."

"Yes, I know," Wallace said. It broke his heart just thinking about the fact that one of the things that happened to Doreen in prison prevented her from ever being able to have a child of her own. "I'm sorry those things happened to you, and I'm sorry that I wasn't there to protect you. But if I had been, you best believe, I would have protected you."

A smile revealed itself on Doreen's lips. "I know you would have." She turned to face her husband. "But Jesus was there." Her smile evaporated, and she said no more words. The look in her eyes finished her thoughts for her.

Wallace immediately made his way over to his wife. "Honey, you know that—"

"Everything happens for a reason. God's ways are not our ways. Lean not on our own understanding. God doesn't make mistakes. God was there when something bad was happening to me the same way He was there when something bad was happening to His own Son," Doreen rattled off like it was a script that Christians told other Christians when trying to comfort them. "I get all that. I receive it, and I believe it. But—"

"Then you know that God isn't sitting there allowing something bad to happen to you just for the sake of letting something bad happen to you," Wallace explained. "He's not turning His face far from you, either. But instead, rejoicing in knowing that you, chosen woman of God, would take that thing that everyone else would deem as bad, damaged, and dirty, and use the Master's robe to clean it up and let it shine. That you would allow it to be a shining light of God Himself to draw those in darkness near."

Doreen began to weep at her husband's words. He embraced her as her shoulders heaved up and down. "That's not what I was going to say," she admitted. "And that's not how I always felt or how I always feel. I have continued to keep glorifying God. To keep loving Him. To continue giving Him all the honor and all the glory in my life. But once in a blue moon, such as the one that was just in my dark sky a second ago, I feel that He had forsaken me, if only for just long enough for those bad things to happen to me." She looked into her husband's eyes. "But then something reminds me that wasn't the case." She shook her head. "Like your words were just a true reminder. And then those thoughts go away because God's words, no matter who recites them, will not and cannot come back void. They are true and make anything that does not line up with them a lie. So you don't have to worry. I've been saved long enough to know not to stay in the valley." Doreen sniffed, then smiled. "Unlike some people, I choose not to get comfortable on the rough side of the mountain. I refuse to engrave the words 'Doreen was here,' like it's something I ever want to memorialize."

"That's my girl," Wallace said. "But to answer your question, no, Sister Melanie and I haven't been hiding anything else from you; just those notes."

Doreen believed her husband. "People are going to have their thoughts and opinions, which they are entitled to. But it bothers me that someone can be sitting here every Sunday, professing their love for Jesus, then do something like this." She shook her head.

"Baby, you have to remember that everyone is not a Christian. Not even some of the ones who profess to be, and certainly not everyone who sits up in a church. Some folks come out of habit or because a spouse, parent, or grandparent is dragging them here; not necessarily because they love the Lord," he said. "Some Christians tend to base other's actions on what a Christian would or would not do without considering the fact that not everyone is a Christian. So those non-Christian folks are acting exactly as a non-Christian would and are not doing anything wrong according to their way of life. So what they are drinking, speaking, watching, listening to, wearing, doing, or saying might not conform to the Christian way of life, but that doesn't make what they are doing wrong in the non-Christian's way of life," he explained. "It just baffles me every time when Christians get mad at non-Christians for doing exactly what non-Christians do. What if non-Christians ran around mad at Christians for doing what Christians do?"

Doreen let out a harrumph. "That, my dear, is what the young reality-show folks would call a read."

Wallace raised a confused eyebrow.

Doreen chuckled. "Never mind. Forget about all that. We need to figure out what we're going to do about these evil messages."

Wallace took the envelope from her hand. "Nothing," he said. "Which is why I never wanted you to know about them in the first place. They are just words, not even threatening words. It's simply someone putting how they feel on paper," Wallace said. "Back then, I knew that stepping into the role of first lady would be challenging enough. I didn't want to make it even worse by you having to deal with this nonsense." He placed the envelope in his pocket.

"But now that I do know," Doreen said, "I can't just—"

"You can just let it go, and you will," he said. "You are going to let go and let God. You will not give the devil your energy or time, not one second of it. You are going to continue being the awesome first lady of this church that you have been for the past five years. Sister Melanie will continue to make sure she goes through the tithes and offerings and removes them the same way she has been."

"Sister Melanie!" Doreen exclaimed. "Oh my goodness. I owe her a deep apology." Doreen felt so bad for all the negative thoughts she had about Melanie, both the ones she expressed and the ones she didn't. Especially the one she had about not wanting her to be a member of the church anymore.

"I'm sure she understands how you might have thought what you had."

"And all she was doing was trying to protect my feelings." Doreen stared off in awe. "She was going to walk right up out of here, vacating her position as treasurer and possibly damaging her reputation just to protect me." Doreen shook her head. "Now *that's* someone a first lady needs on her team." She looked at her husband flirtatiously. "Even if she used to be her husband's lady once upon a time."

"That ship has long sailed," Wallace assured his wife. "Sister Melanie has been a Christian long enough to know that what matters most is that her reputation is good with God and that she wouldn't have had to say a word. That He would have used someone else's voice to redeem her."

"And that voice was yours," Doreen said.

Wallace nodded. "Well, now that we've concluded that Sister Melanie is not a thief, what do you say we head home to Sunday dinner? I 'bout wanted to hop out of bed last night when I smelled that roast cooking in the crockpot."

Doreen was old school. She cooked Sunday dinner Saturday night so that all she'd have to do was warm it up good come Sunday after a long day in church.

On cue, her belly grumbled.

"And sounds like you agree," Wallace said. They both chuckled. "Let's get this money counted up, and then head on out of here." He walked over to the desk where the tithes and offerings laid piled up.

As Doreen helped her husband count and log the money, her mind steered away from the entire situation about the message on the envelope. She knew in her spirit that God would handle it. In all her years, God had taken care of any mess that got stirred up in her life.

But there was always a pattern to it. God would have her set her own mess down to go clean up somebody else's. While she was off on what she referred to as an "assignment," God would have someone else take care of the mess she'd left behind. That suited her quite well, because she'd usually be so drained that she needed her virtue to be restored by God before she could even have the strength to tackle her own issues. She was certain that this time wouldn't be any different than the others. God would handle it. So now, all she had to do was wait to see just what assignment God had in store to preoccupy her. During the wait, she would have to make sure to stay prayed up. History proved that these assignments were never corner pieces to the puzzle.

Chapter 4

"You are going to do what?" Doreen spat through the phone receiver as she cleared up the dishes from Sunday night dinner with her husband. Wallace had gone to the master bedroom of their ranch-style home to retire for the night. It had been a long day. Not just dealing with the whole issue of Doreen accusing Melanie of stealing from the church, but the service prior to that incident had been pretty draining as well.

Wallace had preached the roof off of that church, moving four souls down to the altar to be saved. It was a treat having spent the evening with his wife at the dinner table having regular ole talk, not about church and not about the note on the tithes envelope. On the drive home they had reiterated that they would truly let go and let God, which is why they hadn't thought twice about discussing it again at home. Nothing more than a note in the offering basket a few times a year had come about the vindictive acts of whomever was doing it, so their spirits touched and agreed that it wouldn't escalate to any more than just that. There'd be no sticks and stones. Just words. True, the words didn't hurt and bruise Doreen's skin like the sticks and stones would have, but she couldn't say they weren't leaving black and blue marks on her insides.

Still, she was going to trust in the Lord. She was not going to lose one ounce of sleep over it. She'd prayed about it and had given it to God. What sense did it make

to worry about it? That was the same as telling God she
didn't trust Him with her stuff.

Doreen had planned on finishing up the kitchen and
joining her husband in bed for a good night's rest . . . but
that was until her phone rang. And after hearing what
she'd just heard the caller say, she was no longer sure
about that not losing sleep thing. She might not lose
sleep over her own issues, but leave it to God to drop
somebody else's in her lap.

"I've never heard of such a thing," Doreen mumbled,
walking over to the kitchen table and taking a seat. Her
dear friend and confidante should have warned her to
sit down before she shared the kind of news she had just
shared. "A woman of God, not just *a* woman of God, but
a *pastor*—the shepherd of the sheep—going on a dating
reality show to find her a husband? Now, I've heard it all."

"Oh, stop your fussing. Ain't no sin in it," the caller said
in a nondefensive tone, refusing to allow Doreen to get
her all stirred up.

"And ain't nothing biblical in it either, Margie," Doreen
said to her former pastor, now friend and confidante.

"That's where you're wrong," was Margie's comeback.
"You of all people should know that there is nothing new
under the sun that takes place in this world. These dating
reality shows aren't displaying anything new to mankind.
How the heck you think Queen Esther became queen?"

Doreen went to open her mouth for a rebuttal, but she
couldn't. Margie was as right as the hand opposite the
left one. Doreen had turned her nose up at those kinds
of reality shows ever since *The Bachelor* first aired on
ABC. She'd never once stopped to make the comparison
to the book of Esther in the Bible. In chapter one, after
King Ahasuerus's wife, Queen Vashti, defied the king's
commands, she was removed from her throne. King
Ahasuerus then began his search for a new queen to

replace Vashti. All the fair, young virgins were gathered to the palace, and it was decreed that the maiden who pleased the king be queen instead of Vashti. Esther's night spent with the king earned her the position of queen. It soon became official; Ahasuerus had found his wife in Esther.

That last thought gave Doreen just the rebuttal she needed. "Yes, but it was King Ahasuerus who searched for Esther, which lines up with the scripture, *he* who *finds* a wife," Doreen said. "You're talking about allowing some producers to put you up in a mansion for six weeks while ten men will be kept on the grounds in separate quarters, vying to be chosen as your husband. Since when did the scripture get changed to *she* who *finds* a husband?"

Margie chuckled through the phone receiver. "You always have to find a way to try to be right, don't you?"

"It's never about whether I'm right, it's about what God's Word says," Doreen replied. "And the last time I checked, it says 'he who finds a wife,' not 'she who finds a husband.'"

Margie paused. "So you don't think I should do it?"

"Again, it's never about what I think. It's always about what God says," Doreen countered. "So you tell me. What did God say?"

Margie paused before she spoke. "He said to call you."

This time, it was Doreen who chuckled. "I'm being serious here."

"And so am I. After God told me to agree to be on the reality show, He told me to call you up to be on it with me as my advisor of sorts."

"The devil is a liar!" Doreen burst out and said, hitting her fist on the kitchen table. "And I never thought I'd ever say this to you, Margie, but so are you if you think I'm going to believe for one second God told you to, as a pastor, get on television and make all kinds of strange men jump through hoops to try to become your husband," Doreen said and continued on without even taking a breath. "And then call me up to come be your little maiden sidekick? Ha!"

"You can make it sound as secular as you want," Margie said, not the least bit upset about Doreen practically calling her a liar. She knew before picking up the phone to call the person she considered her best friend, that there would be some resistance, but only in the beginning. Margie was certain of what God had told her about the situation. And she knew one thing for certain and another thing for sure: One, God spoke clearly to Doreen, and two, He wasn't going to tell her something different than what He'd told Margie about the same situation. "But you've known me long enough to know that I don't play when it comes to God and the assignments He has in my life. And I've known you long enough to know that you don't either. So do you really think I'd call you up with some nonsense?"

"Five minutes ago I would have given you an emphatic no, but now I'm not so sure. I mean, really, Margie . . . a pastor on a dating reality show to find a husband?" Doreen shook her head. "I can't understand what God could possibly—"

"Do not lean on your own understanding. Now *that's* the Word," Margie said.

"Do not let your best friend get you caught up in any shenanigans. Now *that's* wisdom," Doreen shot back.

Margie couldn't do anything but laugh. "I'm not surprised at all by your reaction. It's exactly what I expected."

"Good, then you won't be surprised when I don't hop on the first thing smoking to Malvonia, Ohio, to be there when you make a fool of yourself on national television."

"Oh, you'll be here."

"Margie, I'm not kidding."

"I'll e-mail you the contract you'll need to look over and sign."

Doreen ignored Margie's comment. "I wish you all the best, but I will not be the Ethel to your Lucy. I won't be the Shirley to your Laverne. The Thelma to your Louise. The Helen to your Weezy from *The Jeffersons*. The—"

"All right, already, I get it," Margie said, sounding exasperated. "I can't box with God, and you can't either. So I'll just let Him take it from here. I just thought, as your friend, I'd drop the bug in your ear that you'll be heading to Malvonia soon. Figured you'd like to get a head start on packing is all." Margie couldn't have sounded smugger. "But if you insist on hearing from God Himself, so be it, although something tells me you knew an assignment was coming your way. Didn't know it would lead you to the set of a reality show, but you *knew*."

Doreen hated that Margie was right. She didn't address that fact though. "The only thing I'll be packing is my husband's lunch, thank you very much." Doreen didn't hesitate to match Margie's smugness.

"If you say so," Margie shot back.

"And I do say so."

"Well, lucky for us both God always has the final say," and with that, Margie ended the call.

"You all packed and ready for your flight to Malvonia?" Wallace said as he walked into his and his wife's bedroom.

"Just about," Doreen replied. She looked around the room to see if she spotted anything that should be in her suitcase.

"Six long weeks." Wallace sighed. "What in the world am I going to do without my wife all that time?" He walked up behind her and put his arms around her stomach. He loved the thickness of his wife. He didn't think he'd enjoy the hugs as much if his hands fit all the way around her and touched. All that meat on her bones aroused him.

"Oh, I'm sure you'll be fine with all you've got going on between the church and your job." Doreen took note of just how aroused her husband was at that moment. She looked over her shoulder at him. "Or maybe not." She gave him a naughty look.

He laughed as he allowed his hands to caress her sides. "I don't think there is enough going on in the world to keep my mind off of you." Unlike some of today's preachers who felt running the church alone was too much for them to work a nine to five outside of the church, Wallace didn't rely on the members of his church to keep the lights on at both the church and his home. Perhaps pastors of megachurches really could afford to put that burden on their members, but Wallace pastored a church with only 200 members, and most of them were living at the poverty level or middle class, still living from paycheck to paycheck, or some even below poverty level. With a good conscious, Wallace wouldn't have been able to sleep at night under a roof members who could barely keep a roof over their own heads were paying for. For this reason, he worked as a general manager of a retail store in addition to pastoring the church.

"Yeah, but I check church and work in at the front door. What's going to keep me busy when I'm here at home?" He kissed her on the cheek and gave her a love tap on her bottom.

Doreen turned and gave him the side eye. "Well, it better be Netflix and TV dinners," she said, and then let out a harrumph.

Wallace chuckled, released his wife, and then sat down on the bed. "I'm going to miss you, but I understood all about your assignments from God when I met you, as you did mine."

Doreen nodded as she walked over to her dresser and gave it a scan.

"So God's got you killing two birds with one stone, huh?" he said.

"Yeah, it looks that way," Doreen replied. "Guess Margie was right. He was going to get me to Malvonia one way or the other. It wasn't a coincidence that no sooner than I got off the phone with Margie last evening did she get that phone call from Lynox about Sister Deborah."

"Yeah, and what a shame." Wallace shook his head. "Let that brotha know that I'm keeping him, his wife, and his children in my prayers. That the whole church will be praying for them."

"I will," Doreen assured him. "Everything is just happening so fast. I'm sitting on the phone one night telling Margie no way am I coming to Malvonia, then the next morning, I'm booking a flight to head out that same afternoon." She let out a gust of wind. "I must admit, there was a chance Margie might have talked me into coming to Malvonia to be on that reality show with her eventually. But there's no way I would not show up to see about my little Debbie." Doreen sighed. "I just hope this whole thing with Deborah isn't because of my disobedience. You know, God using her situation to get me there since I wouldn't go willingly." Doreen had a saying that on the other side of someone's obedience was a blessing. God only knew what was on the other side of disobedience. Doreen wouldn't be able to live with herself if that proved to be the case with Deborah's situation. She had to get to Malvonia and settle her spirit regarding the matter. If it meant Margie had roped her into that reality show along the way, then so be it.

"It's going to be all right. Everything is going to be just fine," Wallace assured his wife.

After giving the room one last once-over, Doreen was all set. "Thank you again for using your lunchbreak to come take me to the airport. I could have caught a taxi, you know."

"But then I wouldn't have gotten to see you off and gotten that last kiss good-bye." Wallace stood. "Or that last free feel in," he winked.

Doreen looked at him. "You are such a dirty old man."

"Who you calling old?" Wallace joked.

Doreen shook her head. She did not want to be away from her husband. She'd miss everything about him, especially that sense of humor of his. Laughing had been the medicine to keep from crying on several occasions during her tenure as first lady. This would be the longest time apart from Wallace since their marriage. He'd gone on several out-of-town preaching engagements during their marriage, but that had only been for a few days at the most. This was *six* whole weeks Doreen would be out of his presence.

"I don't know why God's got me going to help Margie get a man, which means I've got to leave mine at home." She put her fists on her hips. "And I have to help her get a man in such a manner no less. I just don't get it."

"I don't get why you're racking your brain about it. God gets the glory out of everything in life." He shrugged. "Even reality shows, I guess."

"And that's what I'm going to hold onto," Doreen said, "that God knows exactly what He's doing and what He's doing with me. He hasn't led me astray thus far, so why would He start now?"

"Exactly, so quit wasting time trying to understand His ways and get yourself prayed up to help your friend . . . Both of them." Wallace smiled. "Both Deborah and Margie need you."

"You're right," Doreen wholeheartedly agreed. "I guess we ought to get all this luggage loaded up." She picked up her carry-on bag.

Wallace retrieved her large suitcase and her medium-sized one. "Jeez, did you bring your entire wardrobe?"

"I'm going to be filming that stupid show for almost two months. Even though I don't agree with it all and don't really want to do it doesn't mean I'm not going to look good while doing it."

Wallace laughed. "Women," he said as he struggled to get his wife's luggage loaded up.

Doreen offered to help with the smaller suitcase, but he refused, saying, "No woman of mine is going to carry her own luggage when I'm in her presence."

Doreen hated to watch him struggle, but he'd insisted. Unfortunately, as she prepared to head back to the town she once called home, this wouldn't be the last struggle she would witness; not by a long shot.

Chapter 5

"I won't say I told you so, especially at a time like this."

"Then don't," Doreen was quick to say as she gave Margie a hug.

"It's sooo good to see you, friend," Margie said, closing her eyes while she gave Doreen a great big Holy Ghost hug in return. "I just wish it wasn't under these circumstances." She pulled back from Doreen. "I hate to say it though, but I honestly feel that had it not been for this unforeseen incident with Deborah, that you just might not have come otherwise."

That's not what Doreen wanted to hear, and it pricked her soul to hear the words. But there was truth in it. She herself had struggled internally with that very same thought. Was poor Deborah suffering because of Doreen's unwillingness to head to Malvonia on her own free will to help out Margie? Had Deborah been the sacrificial lamb to get Doreen there sooner, rather than later? A bitter moment to sweeten the pot, so to speak?

"Now you know darn well I ain't never not gone where God has told me to go. Our sister needs us right now," Doreen said to Margie, letting her know that if God truly had meant for her to be there for that reality show, she would have been there regardless, even if it meant showing up the day of the shooting. She probably would have been there on her time versus God's, which is why a little nudge may have been needed.

"Thank you for being here for me as well," Margie said. "You could have easily come to Malvonia just to see about Deborah's well-being. But looking at all that luggage you brought with you . . ." She looked at the skycap. He was loading all of Doreen's things into the trunk of Margie's car as they stood on the curb at the CMH airport, which was the nearest airport to Malvonia, "you plan on staying . . . yeah . . . just about six weeks." Margie winked at Doreen.

"Don't go looking so haughty," Doreen said. "I figured since I was going to be here and all, I might as well . . . you know . . . keep you out of trouble with all those men."

"Yeah, right." Margie playfully hit Doreen on the arm. "You knew the price of disobedience. And that's why you've got all that luggage." She laughed as she made her way over to the driver's side of her car.

Doreen gave the skycap a tip while she said to Margie, "Amen to that."

Margie climbed into the driver's seat.

Doreen followed suit and climbed into the passenger's seat.

"Have you been there to see Deborah yet, since, you know?" Doreen asked as they pulled out of the airport terminal.

"No," Margie answered as she drove. "I went up to the hospital. She hadn't come to yet. Her mother was still there when I left to pick you up. I told her I'd be right back so we can relieve her."

Doreen sat quietly for a moment as she thought. "I know what it feels like to want to take your own life," she said. "I just never thought . . ." Her words trailed off as tears formed and got caught in her throat as she tried to swallow them. "I was just a phone call away. Why didn't she call me?" Doreen looked at Margie. "Have I been that distant and unavailable that my New Day family feels they can't call on me anymore?"

"Don't you dare," Margie scolded. "I will *not* let you try to feel one ounce of guilt over this. Of course, we feel like we can call on you. Heck, I called on you, didn't I?"

Doreen sniffed. "Yeah, I guess you did, didn't you? But I didn't make that phone call easy on you. I certainly wasn't a willing vessel."

"What matters most is that you're here now. You've always been there every time anyone has ever needed you. Me, your family, your church family; old and new, I'm sure."

Doreen let out a harrumph, rolled her eyes, and turned her head to look out the window.

"What was all that about?" Margie asked.

Doreen sighed. "Oh, nothing."

Margie wasn't buying that. "Is it the fact that I mentioned your new church family?" She looked at Doreen, and then back to the road.

Doreen bit her lip at first but then spoke. "I mean, at first, like I mentioned to you before, I had the normal issues any new first lady of a church might have had to deal with."

"It's been what, five or six years since you became first lady of Living Word Living Waters? I would say the newness of it all has worn off. So does that mean you are still having problems?"

Doreen shrugged in an attempt to downplay things. "Nothing major, at least that I knew of. But I learned otherwise yesterday at church."

Margie could sense dissatisfaction in Doreen's voice. "What's going on?"

Doreen didn't hesitate to tell Margie what had gone down. Everyone was always spilling into her ears; she should be able to do the same when need be. She would have told Margie the goings-on at her church yesterday over the phone had they had one of their regular girlfriend chats. But Margie had hit Doreen with the whole reality-show thing, making Doreen momentarily forget all about her own ordeal. Then Margie called her back later that night to tell her about Deborah being hospitalized. Doreen then spent all morning and afternoon getting an airline ticket and packing. Now here it was twenty-four hours after receiving Margie's first phone call and Doreen was here in Malvonia. God hadn't left any more room for her to second-guess where she needed to be and when. Give a person too much rope and they'll hang themselves. Give a person too much time and they'll run out of it.

"Apparently, someone at the church feels that baby killers should burn in hell and not become first ladies," Doreen said.

Margie gasped so loud it sounded as if she'd sucked all the air out of the car. "What the . . ." is all she could manage to get out.

"Yep, apparently ever since I became first lady, someone has been writing those very words on a tithes envelope and dropping them in the offering basket. I just found out about it yesterday by accident."

"For all this time?" Margie's tone expressed her sheer shock.

Doreen nodded. "For five whole years, and I've been none the wiser."

"Well, what happened? How did you find all this out?"

Doreen went on to tell Margie the whole situation with thinking Melanie was stealing from the church, when in all actuality, she was just trying to prevent Doreen from being hurt.

Margie was silent for a moment, having taken it all in. Finally, she spoke. "Well, that's pretty honorable of Melanie. But at the same time, your safety could have been in jeopardy."

"That's the same thing I thought," Doreen said. "But thank God, it never went beyond just those cruel words on an envelope in the offering basket every now and then. Wallace assured me of that."

"Thank God indeed," Margie agreed. "But now that you do know about it, what are you going to do?"

Doreen shrugged. "Do what I always do." She looked at her friend. "Stay out of God's way."

"Well, if you wanted me to come all the way from Kentucky to see you, the only thing you had to do was call me. But leave it to you to be so dramatic." Doreen stood in the doorway of Deborah's hospital room. Seeing her young sister-friend so broken and weak looking while lying up in that hospital bed nearly made her knees buckle. But Doreen managed to keep it all together. What would it look like her coming to be the strength that her friend just might need to make it through, and she walked in there and broke down herself? The tables would turn and Doreen would be the one needing strength. Well, she did have strength; the strength of Jesus, and through Him she could do all things. So she set out to do just that; well, at least the thing He'd called her to Malvonia to do in this very hour.

When Deborah broke out crying upon seeing Doreen standing in that doorway, it was hard for Doreen to keep it together, but once again, she called on the strength of her Lord and Savior and stood strong.

"Daughter," Doreen said as her lips parted with a smile. "My little Debbie."

No, Deborah wasn't Doreen's biological daughter, but she was her spiritual daughter. Deborah was the daughter Doreen was assigned to mother and nurture by God Himself.

"Mother Doreen!" Deborah cried out in between heaving tears.

Doreen walked over to Deborah who couldn't even look Mother Doreen in the eyes. She was instead weeping with her face buried into her hands. Mother Doreen took Deborah's head and pulled it right into her bosom. She then wasted no time doing what she'd come to do. She prayed the walls down and the roof off that place.

Learning that Deborah was in the hospital due to the fact that she'd tried to commit suicide by overdosing on prescribed medication, Doreen prayed that God cover, protect, and keep Deborah's mind. Deborah testified and sobbed the entire time.

After Doreen finished praying there was such a peace in the room.

"Thank you so much for coming to see about me, Mother Doreen." Deborah sniffed. "You have this gift to always be at the right place at the right time. You're like my Superwoman. Every time Lois Lane here is in trouble, there you are." Deborah half-sniffled, half-chuckled.

Doreen laughed. "I'm not Superwoman, but I am a woman of God who is always on assignment to do God's will."

"Well, I'm sorry I keep making you have to come all the way from your home in Kentucky to see about me."

"Well, don't feel too bad," Mother Doreen said. "I was probably going to be headed to this neck of the woods anyway. I was going to surprise you." That wasn't a lie as far as Doreen was concerned. When she woke up yesterday morning she might not have planned to be in Malvonia today, but she would have been there eventually all right. She couldn't see God or Margie letting her out of that assignment. No way would she have been in Malvonia and not made a surprise visit to Deborah. She only wished she was dropping in on her at her home and not in the psychiatric ward of a hospital.

"Really," Deborah asked, "what brought you here?"

"Oh, that pastor of yours," Doreen said. "I can't speak on it right now, but oh, you'll find out about it soon enough . . . you and the rest of the world." Doreen hadn't gotten a chance to read the entire contract from the producers, but she had read the section about confidentiality. It was best she didn't mumble a peep, not sure what she could or couldn't say.

"Well, thank you so much for your prayers, Mother Doreen," Deborah said.

"Your help will always cometh from the Lord, but the Lord puts people and sources right here on earth to help us," Doreen said. "Now, let me get on out of here. I'll try to get back to visit you soon," Doreen told her. "I have faith that you can do this, Deborah. But I have more faith that God is going to help you do it."

After sharing a few more words with each other, Doreen exited Deborah's hospital room believing every word she'd said to her friend. She had faith that God was going to see Deborah through her situation. Now it was time for Doreen to practice what she preached and have faith that God would help her through her own. Because God knew better than anybody, when it came to reality shows, there was *always* a situation.

Chapter 6

"I think the church took the news pretty well, don't you?" Margie said as she and Doreen drove back to her place.

Bible study at New Day Temple of Faith had just let out. Since production on Margie's reality show was slated to begin that Sunday, a day she normally would have been teaching and preaching in the church service, she had no choice but to inform her congregation that she'd be missing in action not only for this week's Sunday service, but several Sunday services and Bible studies to come. The producers had agreed to allow Margie to preach a couple of Sundays in the next few weeks, but that was about it. Margie figured they'd only agreed to the Sundays of preaching so that they could get footage of her in her zone. Margie was going to use those two services to her advantage. Something told her they might turn out being the most powerful services she'd preached in her life. That was going to give her the opportunity to take viewers to church who had maybe never been in their life.

Margie had purposely waited until the eleventh hour to share the news about the reality show with her congregation. She had her reasons, and being secretive wasn't one of them. She hadn't wanted to tell them at the time she agreed to do the show. She didn't want the voices of man to be louder or get entangled with the voice of

God. Once she agreed to do the show, which was two
months ago, she still opted not to share the information
with anyone. She didn't want the information out there
long enough to create rumors, lies, and gossip. Of course,
more than likely, all of that would still take place after her
announcement, but again, she didn't want it to infiltrate
her ear gates. And, of course, she didn't want to give the
saints too much time to muster up the courage to try to
talk her out of it.

Margie had to practice what she preached one Sunday,
which was, "It's a known fact that folks can talk you right
out of a blessing. And you hand over the power for them
to do so by listening to them instead of God."

There had to be a blessing in this, some way and somehow. Margie believed that to be true, or why else would
God have instructed her to participate in the show? Why,
of all the single pastors the show could have used, did
they choose her? God was all-knowing, Margie wasn't, so
she had to rely on her trust in Him. What she wouldn't
rely on was what others had to say.

Margie wholeheartedly believed that God often used
man to confirm thus sayeth the Lord, but He never
needed man to validate His word. If God told Margie
to do something, then it was an insult to God to ask
man what he thought about what God had said, or even
worse, to ask if she should actually do what God said.
And even though Margie had a strong opinion and usually managed to stand unwavering in God's Word, she
was still only human. She did not want to willingly jump
into the lion's den to be tested nor tempted. She'd stood
strong even when Doreen had tried to tell her she was
nuts for agreeing to do the show. She just didn't know
how well things would pan out with an entire army of
saints coming for her. So, she decided it would be better
to drop the bomb on them . . . and then run for cover,

which was her home; for now, anyway. In a few days, Doreen's and her temporary home would be a mansion in Columbus, Ohio, overlooking the Scioto River.

"The church didn't have a choice but to take well the fact that their pastor is now on leave to go find a husband on a reality show." Even though Doreen was present and prepared to be by Margie's side during the entire process, it didn't mean she wasn't going to throw her little digs here and there. That would take all the fun out of it. "You told them two seconds before the closing prayer—and then hightailed it out of there," Doreen laughed. Had she not been wearing her favorite girdle, her belly would have jiggled.

"I did not," Margie said, resisting the urge to laugh. She knew darn well she'd practically had her purse and Bible bag parked at the sanctuary doors so she *could* make a run for it. She wasn't going to even go back to her office and risk getting cornered.

"Did so," Doreen said. "I could hardly keep up with you the way you ran out of that church." Doreen laughed harder. "Thought you was going to leave me at the church, but thank goodness, I jumped in the car just in time for you to pull off on two wheels and leave skid marks."

Now Margie couldn't help but burst out laughing. "Why do I fool with you?"

"'Cause you know I'm going to tell you the truth, even if it cuts you deep. But not to worry, I walk around with a boatload of Band-Aids, not to mention our healing balm." She looked upward to the heavens. "Anyway, I didn't hear too much whispering, nor did I see too many side eyes when you made the announcement. I honestly think folks are pretty excited to see their pastor on television," Doreen said. "Even if it's not *The Word Network*."

"There you go." Margie rolled her eyes.

"Seriously," Doreen said. "I don't care what people say, almost everyone watches one reality show or another. Whether it's *Mary Mary*, preachers of this or that, or a reality wives show. There is just something about these shows that resonate with people. I think the members of New Day figure if they are going to watch a reality show, then it might as well be one with their pastor on it." Doreen shrugged. "Gives them a sense of justification, a pass, so to speak."

"Maybe," Margie said, not prepared to dispute that was the reason, or possibly the only reason, her members didn't seem upset that their pastor would choose what would be considered a more worldly platform to be introduced to the world. "Either way it goes, God has spoken, and by this time next week, I could be meeting my future husband."

Doreen got silent, and her body stiffened. This did not go undetected by Margie.

"What it is? What's wrong? You got serious all of a sudden."

Doreen thought for a moment, choosing her words carefully. "You've been my spiritual leader for some time now. More than that, you've been my friend."

Margie agreed with a nod as she continued to listen.

"In all those years, I've never, not once, heard you mention a desire to be a wife one way or the other," Doreen said. "So why now?"

Margie cleared her throat. "Well, I think it goes back to your initial dispute. The Word says he who finds a wife, and not she who finds a husband. So, no, I haven't been out here scouring the earth looking for a husband. I'm not that woman who is ever going to tell a man that God told me he was going to be my husband. If it's meant to be, then my husband will find me and make me his bride. Either way, I'm the bride of Christ, and I'm going to keep doing what He calls me to do."

"I get that, but the way things might appear is that you are, in fact, looking for a husband."

"But on the same token, what if my husband had to travel all the way to Columbus to find me?" Margie could see the lightbulb going off in her friend's head. "Sometimes, we have to forget about what things look like and focus on what things really are. The way something might appear in the natural is not always how it is in the spirit."

Doreen sighed. "Okay, I get it. I get it. You're the pastor, the one who graduated from seminary school. I don't know why I keep trying to question your reasoning. I'm sorry."

"Oh no, please don't ever stop questioning me, and don't ever apologize for doing it. Knowing you will always be there to do just that makes me stay sharp. Iron sharpens iron."

"Amen," Doreen agreed.

"Now, can we at least just focus on the fact that not only is the production company making a generous donation to both our churches, but they are also providing us six weeks in the lap of luxury—at no cost to us?"

"Except for possibly our integrity," Doreen mumbled under her breath.

Margie shot her a look.

"Okay, okay."

Margie pulled in her driveway and stopped. "Pinkie swear." She held out her pinkie finger. "Only thoughts of the glass being half full."

Doreen looked down and poked her lips out. She rolled her eyes in her head, then ultimately hooked her pinkie finger around Margie's.

"That's more like it." Margie hit the garage door opener and drove into the garage once the door was raised. "I can't wait to be poolside sitting under the private cabana they told me about."

"*Poolside?*" Doreen snapped, not sounding too happy about what Margie had just said.

"Yes, why do you sound like that?" she asked, cutting the car off. "Did you not pack a swimsuit? I thought I told you about that. Plus, it's in the contract I e-mailed you."

"Contract? I haven't thought a bit more about that contract since you called me to tell me about Deborah in the middle of my reading it. Matter of fact, I never even put my electronic signature on it and e-mailed it to the producers." Doreen figured she could always print it off for some evening reading and give it to them personally before taping began. "For the couple of days I've been in town, you and I have been like two ships passing in the night. You've been handling tying up some loose ends with church affairs, and I've been out visiting folks." Doreen and Margie hadn't been sitting around hanging out and chatting it up like girlfriends. They were going to have six whole weeks to do that.

"True," Margie said, admitting that she and Doreen hadn't taken the time to discuss the show or even come up with any type of game plan regarding any dos and don'ts. They'd definitely have to let the Holy Spirit order their steps. "Well, there's definitely a pool," Margie said.

"Oh, so now they want to get us on camera lying out in some skimpy little swimsuits? No way. I did *not* sign up for that. All this belongs to my husband, the honorable Pastor Wallace Frey. He's the *only* one who gets to see *this*." Doreen ran her hands down her body.

Margie began laughing so hard.

"What's so funny? I don't blame you for wanting to be all naked by the pool, you trying to get a husband. But this sista right here already has one, and she'd lose him if he learned I was involved in pornography."

When Margie saw just how serious Doreen was, she laughed even harder. "Woman, cut it out," she managed to say as she opened her car door to get out. Doreen exited the car as well. "They won't be filming us in our swimsuits. That, among a few other things, is a clause that was placed in the contract . . . that you *didn't* read. You and I at the pool is off-limits when it comes to taping footage for the show. That's where we have our private time." Margie put her key into the door and unlocked it. She pushed the door open and stepped aside so that her houseguest could enter first.

"You sure about that?" Doreen asked, standing firm on the step, refusing to move until Margie said to her what she wanted to hear.

"Of course, I'm sure."

"Good, because sounds like there are some things I need to make sure are in writing." Doreen gave in and headed on into the house. "No cameras in my bedroom, my bathroom . . . ."

Doreen continued to ramble on while Margie tuned her out. She already knew what was what and had been prepped by the producers that it would only be a matter of time before it felt like the cameras weren't even there. She was certain the same would go for Doreen as well.

The producers expressed how important it was that everything seem natural and that no one was acting for or being obviously mindful of the cameras. It would be a treat, though, hopefully when the cameras weren't around. And that little no filming clause guaranteed those moments would exist. So maybe the cameras wouldn't be everywhere and see everything every time something was done. But there was still one person who would: God.

Chapter 7

After about an hour's drive, the Escalade arrived at the place where Margie, Doreen, not to mention ten bachelors, would reside for the next six weeks. The grand riverfront megamansion was situated on six-point-six acres of land. It wasn't one of those old, spooky mansions either. It was only about twenty-five years old versus a hundred. It was 32,675 square feet of living space split between the main house, where all the men would stay, and the two apartments; one for Margie, and the other for Doreen. There was a total of twelve bedrooms and twenty-one bathrooms. It had a four-car garage. The landscaping was absolutely amazing! There was a man-made pond with a fountain on the right of the front lawn.

"I wonder if I can catch me some bass up in there," Doreen said, nodding toward the pond.

"And since when do you fish?" Margie asked.

"Since my husband asked me to go with him a few years ago when his regular fishing partner wasn't available," Doreen said.

"But I thought I recall you saying how boring fishing sounded to you."

"Heck, when a man asks his wife if she wants to go fishing, watch a game, or anything of that nature, she better jump at the opportunity, regardless of whether she's fond of it."

"But doesn't he have any fellas he can call up and do those kinds of things with?" Margie twitched and scrunched up her nose. "I just hate the thought of fishing.

Putting a squiggly little thing on a hook and the smell of fish in itself would simply repulse me." She put her hand on her chest and shook her head.

Doreen looked at Margie in shock. "The Lord was right. You really *do* need me here. Why He only gave me six weeks to school you on the tricks of the trade of being a wife I'll never know."

Margie laughed. "So *that's* why you think the Lord had me call you up? To teach me how to be a wife?" The car stopped in front of the huge mansion doorway.

"You just confirmed it by making that crazy statement." Doreen huffed and mocked Margie under her breath, *"Doesn't he have any fellas to call up?"* She turned and looked at Margie. "What woman in her right mind would rather not be the first choice when it comes to who her husband wants to spend time with?"

Margie took in Doreen's words. "I guess you're right."

"Sure, I am. And here I thought that was a no-brainer." She exhaled. "So much work to do and so little time." She let out a tsk-tsk!

Margie play hit Doreen's arm as her car door opened and outside of it stood the driver.

Doreen's focus immediately went from her conversation with Margie to making sure she looked presentable. She began primping, starting with patting down her hair.

"Woman, what are you doing?" Margie asked, now watching Doreen dig in her purse, pull out a tissue, and begin patting her face.

"My skin's not too shiny, is it?"

"You look just fine," Margie said, a little confused. "But why are you fixing yourself up? It's *me* who's getting a husband here. Like you said, Miss Know-It-All, you already have one."

Doreen stuffed the tissue back down in her purse. "Child, I'm not thinking about those ten men. I'm thinking about those tens of thousands of viewers that's about to see me for the first time." Once again, she primped her hair and smiled.

"First Lady Doreen Frey, why, I never knew you were so vain." Margie sat there smiling at her friend teasingly.

"I'm not, but I'm not trying to look like no ragamuffin either."

"Well, not to worry," Margie said as she turned her body to exit the vehicle. "They'll be no cameras getting us arriving. Cameras will get the *men* arriving to meet *me*."

Doreen let out a gust of wind, and then relaxed her body. "Oh, shoot, why didn't you just say so?" She turned sharply toward her own door.

"That's why you should have read the entire contract and not just put your John Hancock on it," Margie fussed.

"Oh, come on, let's go, then," Doreen pouted, hating that she'd only scanned the contract. Her eyes had gotten too heavy to read it in full, so when the producers insisted she fax it, she just went ahead and did it. She figured if her friend, mentor, and former pastor didn't have a problem with the contract, then she wouldn't either. "Had me sucking in my stomach, holding my breath, can't hardly breathe, about to die before my debut television appearance, and ain't even no darn cameras to catch us arrive." She shuffled and scooted out of the car. "What kind of darn reality show is this? A reality show with no cameras. Just janky."

Margie laughed as she listened to her friend fuss while getting out of the vehicle herself. "So, is this another lesson?" Margie said to Doreen as she walked to Doreen's side of the car, which was facing the mansion's doorway. "How to sound like a complaining and nagging wife?"

Doreen shot Margie an evil glare.

Margie burst out laughing, and then looped her arm through Doreen's. "Come on, friend. Let's go take a tour of our new home."

Doreen wriggled her arm from Margie's. "Naw, don't try to make nice now. I'll show you nagging." Doreen took steps toward the house as she continued fussing under her breath.

All Margie could do was shake her head. She then looked up to the sky. "Lord, we might not make it into heaven, but we're about to make some great TV."

"Pastor Margie," a woman said excitedly after flinging the front door open before either Margie or Doreen could make it up to the door. The woman, wearing black khakis and a tan shirt whisked past Doreen and ran straight to Margie. "It's such a pleasure to see you again." She shook Margie's hand vigorously. "Thank you, thank you, thank you so much for agreeing to be the subject of our reality show. When we read your submission application, we just knew you were the person we were looking for."

"Submission application?" Doreen said, surprised and confused. If she recalled correctly, Margie said that the producers had come to her, not that she'd submitted an application to them.

"Yes," the woman replied to Doreen, but still shaking Margie's hand. "The audition video that—"

"You don't have to keep thanking me," Margie said, eager to cut the woman off. "I'm glad to have been chosen to be a part of your vision."

"Your vision?" Doreen looked the woman up and down and let out a harrumph with a raised eyebrow. Then she looked at Margie. "Her *vision?* I thought this was *God's* vision."

"Well, that too," the woman said, releasing Margie's hand, and then turning toward Doreen. "By the way, I'm Fatima Swanson. You must be First Lady Doreen." It was now Doreen's hand Fatima was shaking to death. "It's such a pleasure to meet you. I heard so much about you. The way Margie spoke of you and the insight she gave on you, there was no way we could do this show without you. Not to mention Margie wasn't going to do the show without you. We told her we had a team of producers and staff she could consult with when need be, but she insisted on consulting with only you. So, in a sense, I guess we couldn't be doing this show without you or Margie." Still shaking Doreen's hand she said, "So thank you for agreeing and getting that signed contract faxed to us."

Doreen didn't have time to reply one way or the other as Fatima released her hand, and then went back to address Margie.

"So, we've pretty much gone over everything that will be taking place over the next few weeks, but we'd like to do a recap with the entire crew." Fatima spoke just as quickly as she'd shaken their hands. "But first, Anya is going to give you guys a tour of the mansion, then take you each to your respective apartments." Fatima nodded to a woman who had stood almost invisible in the doorway.

"Hi," the soft-spoken, timid girl who Fatima had referred to as Anya said and waved.

Fatima waved her over. The young protégé came out of the house and was introduced to both Margie and Doreen. Unlike Fatima, Anya shook their hands sternly while staring them in the eyes as if they were about to make a deal as serious as a corporate takeover.

"I'm going to get with the crew and go over setup," Fatima said. "But you guys are in good hands." She then raced off into the house.

"Well, ladies, shall we?" Anya said. She was just the opposite of Fatima who was bubbly and high-energy. But after a few puffs of Fatima, one needed to come down off their high with a more laid-back type of personality.

"Yes, we shall," Margie said as she took steps toward the door.

"Video audition," Margie heard Doreen mumble as she walked by her.

Margie ignored Doreen. All she wanted to do right now was get a tour of the beautiful home. By the time it was over, if God was on her side, Doreen would be so mesmerized by her current living situation, she'd forget all about the whole business of an audition video.

"First, let's start with the grand foyer," Anya said as she led both women through the huge wooden double doors into the marbled floor foyer.

"My God!" Doreen said as she looked around. "This is just a foyer? My first house could have fit in this space alone."

"My current apartment can fit in it," Anya said.

Margie looked up at the seven-tier chandelier. "What beautiful crystals," she remarked.

"Diamonds," Anya said with a stoic face and dry tone.

"*What?*" both Margie and Doreen shouted.

Anya nodded proudly as if it were her home. "Diamonds, ladies."

Doreen walked straight-ahead to the pond that sat in the middle of the foyer. "It's like the one outside."

"Just smaller," Margie said, walking over to the pond and standing next to Doreen. She looked into the pond, then at Doreen. "I guess if you can't catch bass out there, you can catch them right in here."

"Amazing," Doreen said softly as she watched the variety of colorful fish swim around.

Margie turned her attention from the pond to all the beautiful paintings decorating the walls of the circular foyer. "Feels like when I took that European vacation and visited the Vatican."

"As it should," Anya said. "Some of these paintings are originals done by some of the artists whose work you'd find at the Vatican." It was clear that Anya had been well versed on the details of the home. "Shall we see the rest of the house?" Anya didn't wait for a reply as she escorted the women out of the foyer into what looked like a sitting room. It was modernly decorated, and again, massive in size.

"I can only imagine how much it's costing to rent out this space," Margie said as she walked over to the wall of windows and looked into the garden area.

"Well, actually, the owners had just listed the home for sale when we approached them," Anya replied. "By the time all was said and done, they agreed to donate the use of the home to us in hopes that it would help sell the property that much quicker. And, of course, some free advertisement for the owners has been included in on the deal as well."

"What's the asking price of a place like this?" Doreen inquired.

"Almost $5 million," Anya said.

Doreen whistled.

"And from what I've seen so far," Margie said, "I bet it's worth every penny."

Anya escorted them out of the sitting area and back into the foyer, where, once again, the indoor water feature made both Doreen and Margie breathless. It was just truly hard to wrap their head around the fact that the same pond with a fountain they'd seen outside in the front yard, had a baby version that sat in the middle of the foyer. They honestly didn't need to see too much more of this home to know that they'd be temporarily residing in the true lap of luxury. Of course, they excitedly continued on with the tour, which led them to the kitchen.

Once in there, Doreen didn't want to leave the state-of-the-art chef's kitchen. She wanted to whip up a meal for them right then and there. She verbally made that known.

"That won't be necessary," Anya had said in a staid tone at Doreen's offer to do just that. "You are a guest in this home and absolutely anything either of you need will be provided. You name the meal you desire, and it will be prepared for you. We only want you focusing on aiding the lady of the house here." It was clear that this Anya character was all business.

"But I can bake a mean—" Doreen started, just itching to utilize the tools in that kitchen.

"You heard the girl," Margie interrupted.

"But not even one of my famous pound cakes?" Doreen said, looking around the kitchen regretfully.

"For once in your life, let somebody take care of you." Margie paused, and then continued. "While you help take care of me," she laughed.

"You're right about that," Doreen said. "Probably gon' lose my appetite and not even have the strength to eat after fooling around with you, let alone stand in here and cook a full-course meal."

"Oh, it won't be that bad," Anya said to Doreen as she headed toward the kitchen exit. "This is going to be fun." That was hard to believe coming from someone who sounded as if they had no clue about what the definition of fun was. "There are so many others who wish they were in your shoes right now. I mean, we went through hours of audition tapes."

Margie thought it ironic they were in the kitchen, seeing Doreen shoot her a look as if she wanted to cook her goose. *That darn Anya*, Margie thought. Here she was supposed to be getting Doreen's mind off the whole audition tape thing by wooing her with the grandness of the estate. Now here they were back to square one. "I thought I read something about there being an outdoor pool," Margie said, changing the subject and racing behind Anya. She was willing to suffer a twisted ankle versus finding herself alone in that kitchen with Doreen.

Doreen reluctantly followed behind. Margie should have been a mind reader, because Doreen absolutely wanted to cook her friend's goose all right. From the sounds of things and this whole audition tape business, Margie had left out a few details regarding her involvement with this reality show. Doreen would let her off the hook . . . for now. She didn't want to act up in front of company, aka Anya, but if she waited too much longer, she might end up acting up in front of the whole world via a camera lens.

"Of course, there is a pool," Anya said. "What mansion wouldn't have an outdoor swimming pool?" She hustled down a long hall, bypassing rooms they hadn't gone into yet. She stopped in her tracks and turned to face the women just as she got to the double glass patio doors. "Well, this one has *two*." She smiled and eagerly turned back around and pushed the doors open. She then stepped aside and raised her hand high in ta-da mode. She looked like one of the girls on *The Price Is Right*, only she wasn't showing all thirty-two teeth with a beautiful smile.

Doreen was taking note of Anya's character more so than Margie. Margie was too busy hoping to distract Doreen. The fact that it seemed like Anya had nothing to smile about in life was a distraction for Doreen indeed. She wondered why a young girl who looked to be about in her twenties was so serious and practically afraid to part her lips into a smile.

Hmm, maybe Anya is my true assignment, Doreen thought. God was a God who would absolutely go through all this trouble just to tend to one of His sheep. Doreen knew that to be true after hearing the testimony of Unique, a former member of New Day Temple of Faith. Poor Unique had driven to one of her baby daddies' place of business, which happened to be a crack house he hustled out of. She decided to leave her three sons in the car while she tried to get child support from one of her sons' father. It just so happened that the police raided the place while she was in it, knocking her out during the raid and hauling her off to jail unconscious. Unique was thrown in jail for drug trafficking, along with everyone else in the house, but when they found her sons dead in the backseat of her car as a result of being left in that car for hours on the hottest day of the year, they charged her with their murders as well. They didn't even allow her to go to the funeral.

It was a long, dark trial for Unique, indeed. But not only did God keep her while incarcerated and fight for her on the outside until the truth of the entire situation prevailed and she was released from jail, but He used Unique to save her cell mate's soul. Upon hearing that testimony, Mother Doreen immediately knew that the struggle wasn't even about Unique. God hadn't placed Unique in darkness for her own sake. He'd placed her in darkness to be a light for someone else, and in doing so, the saints and angels rejoiced upon gaining another soul in the kingdom. People on the outside looking in may have thought that testimony was a testament to what God did for Unique, but in all actuality, it was a testament of what God did for Unique's cell mate. How God will do whatever He has to do to go see about that one sheep.

Margie and Doreen stepped out onto the cemented patio that circled around a huge swimming pool that was shaped like the figure eight. There were lawn chairs and patio tables surrounding it. Standing nearby was a private cabana that had a fire pit in the middle of it. It looked more like an outdoor pool one would find at a resort versus a home.

Doreen was really starting to be glad she'd agreed to be a part of what she felt would be a mess of shenanigans. In spite of that, though, she was going to make the most of it, and when she wasn't watching Margie's back, she'd be lying on hers out by the pool.

"Is there a Walmart nearby?" Doreen asked Anya.

"Uh, I, uh . . . I'm not sure," Anya stammered, wondering what in the world Doreen could need a Walmart for when everything she could possibly need was right there on the grounds. "Why?"

Doreen looked at Margie. "I guess I'm going to need that swimming suit after all."

Margie smiled. "Umm-hmm, I told you."

"Yeah, yeah, yeah." Doreen shooed her hand at Margie. "No need to gloat."

"We can absolutely get you a swimsuit," Anya said. "That won't be a problem. Like I said, whatever you need, don't hesitate to—" Just then, Anya's phone rang. She pulled it out of her pocket, looked at the caller ID, then held her index finger up. "Excuse me for a second, ladies. I need to take this call."

Both Doreen and Margie nodded as Anya turned away and proceeded with her phone call.

"This is even more beautiful than I imagined," Margie said, staring off at the pool.

"Guess they left a lot of the extra little pertinent details out when they told you about this place," Doreen said.

Margie nodded. "They sure did."

"Good," Doreen snarled. "Then you're reaping exactly what you sowed."

Margie swallowed hard with nervousness. "Wha . . . What are you talking about?"

"Oh, you know *exactly* what I'm talking about, Pastor Margie. I'm talking about you leaving out the fact that God didn't send these people to you to be a part of this show. You went to them. An audition tape, Margie? Really?"

Doreen's voice got louder the more she spoke. Anya had even briefly turned her attention away from her phone conversation to see what all the noise was going on behind her.

"Shhh," Margie said. She looked to see that Doreen had caught Anya's attention. She then took Doreen by the elbow and began walking around the pool. "It's not what it seems like, and I wasn't trying to keep information from you. I already knew what your reaction was going to be to all this, and I didn't want to make it any worse."

"So you lied about it?"

"I didn't lie about nothing," Margie protested. "I just didn't tell you everything. Besides, it's not relevant. What's relevant is that we are here. For some crazy reason or another, God wants us here. Do you or don't you believe that to be true?"

Doreen exhaled. She knew darn well they were right where they were supposed to be, even if in the beginning she had come kicking and screaming. Why her flesh kept trying to fight it she had no idea. Maybe it was because she truly would have rather been at home with her husband. And at the same time, she wouldn't be telling the truth if she said that situation back at her church didn't drop in on her mind every now and then.

Doreen reckoned that was actually probably one of the reasons God scooped her up out of Kentucky as quickly as He did. The whole incident with finding out about the vicious notes being left in the offering basket was just too new. Too new for her to be standing before the congregation and not giving them all the side eye trying to figure out who the culprit was.

She would have just loved to have been at her church come Sunday morning and pinpoint who was behind it all. What she'd do once she got them cornered, only God knew. That is probably another reason why He'd made it so that no one would ever have to find out outside of Himself.

"I know it's true," Doreen admitted. "But what I don't know is how you even heard about this show."

"It was one of those instances where the clock struck four in the morning and God woke me from my sleep," Margie started to explain.

"Lord have mercy, I know how that goes," Doreen said, having been awakened by God at that very hour more times than she could count. "What is it about the whole four a.m. thing with God?" she chuckled.

"I don't know," Margie shook her head, "but I got on up after God nudged me, and I turned on the television. Some entertainment news show was on, and they were talking about a reality show in the works, and they were seeking a pastor to be a part of it. They didn't give many details, just a Web site to go to for information. I paused the television and wrote down the Web site. I had planned on going back to sleep, and then looking into it in the morning."

Doreen busted out laughing because she already knew what Margie was about to say next.

"But you already know God is not one to sleep nor slumber, so when He's got an assignment for you, He ain't gon' let you do it either."

"Amen," Doreen laughed.

"So, of course, He wouldn't let me get any sleep until I powered up my computer and went to visit the site. So I did just that. When I began to read the information on the Web site, I got really confused. It stated that they were looking for male pastors who were bachelors and they were looking for women who wanted to be first ladies, hence—"

"*Lady of the House!*" Doreen shouted out. "I at least read enough of the contract to know the name of the reality show."

Margie chuckled. "Yes, but initially the full name was *Lady of the House of the Lord*. I immediately got confused. God had already called me to be a pastor. I was already the lady of a house. Not saying that being a first lady of a church would be a demotion, because I know of plenty of first ladies who run their husband's church behind the scenes."

"Amen and amen," Doreen said. She didn't run her husband's church, but she was the brainchild behind a lot of what went on in the ministry.

"But at the same time, I just couldn't see God, without warning or sending His Word beforehand, removing me from the position of a pastor to that of a first lady."

Doreen nodded her understanding.

"As I continued trolling the Web site, I kept hearing God tell me to submit. I'm thinking, 'Lord, I always submit to you.'"

Doreen laughed.

"But, of course, He was telling me to submit an audition tape, but not to be one of the ladies on the show, but to be *the* lady on the show . . . the *only* lady . . . the lady of the house."

Doreen nodded and smiled as she listened to Margie. It always tickled her how God got His way in spite of man.

"So by five o'clock that same morning, in my pink fluffy robe with matching pink fluffy house slippers, I recorded my audition tape on my cell phone and uploaded it to that Web site."

Doreen frowned. "Well, did you at least do your hair?"

"And pink fluffy rollers."

"Oh, Lord Jesus!" Doreen shouted. "You didn't!"

"I did. I figured if this was the Lord's will, then whether I was in my pastoral garb, a two-piece suit, or my pj's, His will was going to be done."

"I hear you." Doreen couldn't disagree with that, but being the black woman that she was, if nothing else, she would have made sure her hair was done right.

"Need I tell you by eight o'clock in the morning I was awakened again?"

"By God?" Doreen asked.

"No, by my cell phone ringing with the producers on the other end of the phone."

Both Doreen and Margie laughed.

"Well, technically, it was God," Doreen said. "He was just speaking through the television crew."

"Yeah, I guess," Margie agreed. "All I know is that the Fatima lady on the other end of the phone was pretty much instantly sold. In just hours, they revised their entire vision around the one God had given me, and the rest, as they say, is history."

"Huh, you mean *history in the making,*" Doreen huffed.

Margie stopped walking and looked at Doreen. "So do you forgive me for not telling you about the audition tape and all that good stuff?"

Doreen stopped walking. "Of course, I do. But I don't forgive you for thinking that you couldn't tell me all of that in the first place."

"It was hard because the minute I mentioned the whole reality-show thing, you were already shooting it down. I honestly don't think it would have mattered much what I said at that point," Margie said. "Plus, in the end, I knew you'd be game."

"Yeah, well, that still doesn't mean I'm going to stop giving you the blues about it."

"I'm sure it doesn't," Margie replied. "God has a sense of humor, so we ought to have one as well. Even Anya assures us it's going to be fun."

Doreen let out a harrumph of doubt. "Not that I've got the impression that she's an expert on fun."

"Speaking of Anya, I think she's waiting on us."

Margie nodded to Anya, and Doreen's eyes followed. When Anya saw that she had the women's attention, she waved at them.

"Yep, looks that way," Doreen concluded.

Both women headed back over to Anya who finished up the tour of the main house, showing them where the men would reside and where much of the taping would take place. Next, she showed them Margie's apartment, and lastly, Doreen's. They truly were full-size luxury apartments, and they each had the most elegant Egyptian décor.

"So, ladies, I know it's been a long day, and the days are only going to get longer," Anya said as they stood in the living room of Doreen's apartment. "Get comfy; your luggage has already been delivered, so get changed. You can order dinner, eat it wherever you like even in the dining room at the main house, because the men won't be arriving until the day after tomorrow. Or you can just dine individually or jointly in one of your places. It's up to you."

Doreen and Margie looked at each other.

"We'll play dinner by ear," Margie spoke for both of them, and Doreen nodded.

"Sounds good," Anya said. "Then, I guess I'll leave you two ladies alone to do what you need to do. But remember, tomorrow, we will go over everything, then the day after that, it's showtime," Anya confirmed in the tone of a drill sergeant, and then headed to the door.

"Thanks again for everything, Anya," Doreen said, giving her a salute behind her back.

Margie shook her head, and Doreen dropped her arm down to her side.

"The pleasure was mine," Anya said, opening the door. "I look forward to working with you two." On that note, she exited the apartment, closing the door behind her.

"Well, I guess we have our marching orders," Margie said.

"Yes. I can't wait to go experience that Jacuzzi tub in my bathroom," Doreen added.

"You and me both," Margie agreed. "Because after today, our work begins. We probably won't even have time to enjoy all of the amazing amenities this place possesses."

Doreen looked around. "Yeah, you're probably right, which means, before things really get started and we get all wrapped up in this show, there's something I need to do first. Someone I need to see."

And Margie knew just what and who Doreen was speaking of.

Chapter 8

"The Laroques have a beautiful home," Doreen said after being led to Deborah's living quarters by Reo and Klarke Laroques' house manager. Deborah was staying in the guest house of a couple who were mutual friends of both Deborah and Lynox.

Doreen hadn't gotten the full details, but the state child protective agency was somehow involved in Deborah's family affairs with her husband and children. From what Doreen did know, Deborah's suicide attempt was a result of such interference. Doreen had no intentions on prying or picking. She didn't need to know all of somebody's business in order to pray for them in general. Sometimes knowing exactly what to pray for was a plus, but her only concern right now was making sure her spiritual daughter was getting well mentally.

"This is my temporary home for now," Deborah said. "I'm not allowed to live under the same roof as my own children at this time per the state's orders. So Lynox and I decided it was best, it was easier, if I uprooted, and he and the children stayed at the house." Deborah closed her eyes and tried to shake off the thought of not having her children near her as well as her husband whom she loved with all of her heart. She so desperately wanted to change the subject, so that is what she did. "But I hear that you have a temporary home as well. Both you and Pastor." Deborah sat on the couch in her borrowed living room.

"I guess news travels fast," Doreen said, joining Deborah on the couch.

"Well, you know I was in the hospital trying to get myself together when I first heard about this whole reality-show business," Deborah told Doreen. "And they thought I was the crazy one." She took her index finger and twirled it about her temple.

Both women laughed.

"I just couldn't imagine for the life of me why my pastor would ever consider doing such a thing. Lynox records and watches reality shows all the time. He studies them as a resource for his novel writing." Deborah shot Doreen a look. "But what I really want to know is how Pastor Margie managed to drag *you* into it as well."

"Well, you know me, I might not be all the way on board with this," Doreen said, "but I'm going to have Pastor's back. You know that."

"Oh, I figured as much. You have everybody's back."

Doreen smiled at the compliment. Little did Deborah know, had it not been for her being hospitalized, forcing Doreen to hop on that plane ASAP, there is a slight chance the size of a mustard seed that Doreen might not have had Margie's back. She'd like to believe with all her heart that she would have been obedient and loyal, but at the end of the day, she was human and only God knew for sure what lay ahead in any situation.

"But on second thought, you know I guess I shouldn't be too surprised about Pastor Margie agreeing to do the show. Not when you think back to that time when half the congregation was making a big hoopla about her being a single, female pastor."

"Yes, and then someone even trying to set her up with their cousin, uncle—somebody." She threw her hands up. "Just madness!"

"Right, so if being on this show is going to shut those church members up, then so be it," Deborah said. "And who knows? She just might get a husband out of this, then maybe the people who practically drove her to this will get off her back."

Doreen felt a smidgen of conviction at Deborah's last comment. "Well, you know that once upon a time I felt the same way as some of the other New Day members . . . But only for a hot second," Doreen was quick to add. "I mean, she was a female pastor always going to preach at other churches, mainly churches where men were the pastors. And then, of course, when the male pastors would come here to preach as guest pastors, she'd have to entertain them. I just felt that it would be nice to have a man covering her, you know."

"Oh, I know," Deborah agreed. "I'd see the side eye some of those pastors' wives would give Pastor Margie." Deborah laughed. "Especially the sistas."

Doreen knew that Deborah had a point. To prove Deborah's point, Doreen recalled the occasion that Margie had a private dinner in her home set up for the visiting pastor and his wife. Doreen couldn't remember their names, but she'd never forget that dinner. As a matter of fact, it was a dinner that a former member of New Day who used to own a catering business had prepared the food for Margie. The caterer has since gone on to be with the Lord, but her signature macaroni and cheese still lives on. And it was that macaroni and cheese that started the whole tiff that took place at the dinner that night.

"I hope you all enjoyed the macaroni and cheese," Margie had said to the pastor's wife.

The pastor had excused himself to the bathroom while Doreen had carried some dishes off to the kitchen.

But Doreen had heard Margie's inquiry as she exited the dining area and headed into the kitchen.

"You can't get mac and cheese like that just anywhere," Margie had added.

The first lady, who had been all smiles and pleasant during the entire dinner, immediately let her fangs out once she was alone in the room with Margie. "My husband gets macaroni and cheese just fine at home—among other things." She spoke loudly and sharply.

Doreen, who just happened to be holding the pan of leftover macaroni and cheese, stopped in her tracks and listened at the door.

"Oh," Margie said. Her tone revealed that she was a little taken aback by the first lady's response.

"You think I didn't see the way you were staring at my husband the entire time he was preaching?"

Margie sat a little dumbfounded and speechless. Her silence gave the first lady an invitation to keep it coming.

"And I know you are not going to just sit there and deny it."

"Well, no, I won't. I probably did watch your husband the entire time. The entire congregation—everyone in the room—was watching him. Clearly except for you. Obviously, you were watching *me* instead."

"I *know* you just didn't." The sound of the four legs on the first lady's chair scooting back on the tiled dining-room floor sounded like screeching nails down a chalkboard.

Doreen could tell by the sound that the first lady had come out of her chair. That let her know that she needed to come back into that dining room. When she reentered the dining area, she saw the first lady leaning over the table and pointing at Margie.

The first lady didn't care who had come in the room, as she continued going in on her host. "You are not much to look at, so don't flatter yourself."

"Hold on now. Wait just a minute," Doreen said as she laid the pan she was carrying back down on the table. "We are all grown women here. Not just grown women, but women of God. There is no way we should be throwing insults at one another."

"Well, these white women kill me," the first lady said in her defense as she glared at Margie, the *only* white woman in the room. "They always thinking they can run up on our men and try to take them from us. I'm a Christian, but I think those Muslims who think white people are the devil just might have something there."

Margie shot up out of her seat and a gust of wind escaped her mouth.

But more than wind escaped Doreen's mouth. "Get the hell up out of this house right now!"

This time, Margie seemed to have sucked the gust of wind right back into her mouth . . . And choked on it. She'd never, *ever,* in all her years of knowing Doreen, heard her even almost or accidentally cuss. And the expletive she'd just let roll off her tongue was definitely on purpose.

"When I say get the hell out of this house, I mean it, literally," Doreen explained. "You brought hell up in this house, and now I'ma need you to get it out of here. You can stay, but the hell that's brewing inside of you must go in the name of Jesus!" Doreen shouted, then lifted her right hand up, silently rebuking the devil that she felt was using the first lady.

"What's going on in here?" the guest pastor asked as he entered the dining area after coming from the bathroom. He looked at his wife and immediately went to her side, as he should have, her being his wife and all. It was clear there was tension in the room and as her protector, he needed to go protect her. And from the way both Margie and Doreen were glaring his wife down, oh, she needed protecting all right.

"What's going on is that I watched this so-called pastor stare you down the entire time you were in the pulpit," the first lady said to her husband, nodding toward Margie. "Then she invites us over here with this soul food." She spread her hands over the table, then spoke to Margie. "Why didn't you make Alfredo or some other white people stuff? I have white friends, and we've had dinner at several other white pastors' houses, and ain't not nary one of 'em ever had macaroni and cheese, collard greens, candied yams, grits and shrimp, fried chicken, catfish, and mashed potatoes with gravy made from the leftover frying grease."

Doreen was impressed. This woman knew her gravies from scratch, that's for sure.

"Just so you know," Doreen interjected, not meaning to overtalk Margie or speak for her, but something told her that the words she spoke would be much kinder, more diplomatic, and Christian-like than the ones that would have flown out of Margie's mouth. The last thing Doreen wanted was for this first lady to say that Margie was a fake Christian who, behind the scenes, got real ratchet. She was already prepared to say that she was loose. "Pastor Margie had this dinner catered especially for your husband. Your church secretary e-mailed our church secretary your husband's favorites, as well as any food allergies."

The guest pastor cleared his throat. "She's right, honey. I was tired of eating foods I'd never heard of when we're dinner guests of hosts from the Caucasian persuasion." He looked to Margie. "No offense, I hope."

"None taken," Margie said. "There was a time when I didn't know how much more chicken smothered in hot sauce and fried cabbage with smoked turkey or ham hocks I'd be able take either. So it's always refreshing when allowed input into dinner preparations."

The guest pastor laughed. His wife shot him a sharp look. Guess she didn't want him laughing at white women's jokes either.

"First lady," Doreen said to the woman. "We meant no harm or disrespect, but—"

"You don't have to say 'we' like you're her house Negro," the first lady snarled at Doreen. "I don't have an issue with you. You weren't the one staring my husband up and down all through church service."

Doreen took a deep breath while she said a three-second and three-word prayer to herself, *Lord, help me.* Here she was calling herself saving Margie from looking a fool and going off on this woman, and yet, she was five seconds away from doing it herself.

Doreen looked at the first lady. Her flesh absolutely 100 percent wanted to address the first lady about her reference to a house Negro, but Doreen's spirit saw to it that the bigger issues that took precedence were addressed instead. So even though Doreen wanted to pull out an outdated can of butt whoopin' on that first lady, her spirit woman prevailed.

"Everyone has a backstory, a past, a testimony, something they've overcome or are trying to overcome," Doreen said. "I can tell by your actions today that even though you've overcome some things, you're still a work in progress, and that's okay. We all are." Doreen was trying her best to make sure the first lady knew she was not trying to single her out to make her feel bad. "Yes, Margie may have been looking at your husband along with other members of the congregation. I know for a fact I couldn't take my eyes off the man of God while he was delivering the Word."

The first lady's eyes bucked a little. Was Doreen, who was a single woman herself at the time, standing in front of the first lady telling her she had eyes for her husband? Not when the first lady had just watched that episode of *Mob Wives* when one girl told another girl's boyfriend that he smelled delicious . . . and expected not to get laid out on the floor.

"But it wasn't the man, your husband, that had us all in a trance. It was the God in him. When God speaks, everyone listens." Doreen got real intense. "Sister, I know you know what I'm talking about." Doreen balled her fist and let it bounce up and down. "I'm talking about when the voice of God commands His children's attention. And that is the spiritual gift your husband has; to be used by God mightily. And since God chose you as your husband's helpmeet, then both God and your husband have to be able to trust you to recognize and understand that power."

The first lady, drawn into Doreen's words and the passion with which she spoke them, nodded her head in agreement as her eyes began to moisten with tears. "Yes, God," she said in a humbling tone.

"You have to embrace that gift and power," Doreen told her, "not be jealous of it. 'Cause God can absolutely give it to somebody else's husband . . . a man whose wife knows what to do with it and how to respect the God in him."

"Oh no," the first lady said in fear. God giveth it, and God taketh away, but she did not want her husband to have to pay the price for her actions. "I wouldn't want that." She hugged her husband. "Do you know how many blessings I'd be the cause of so many people not receiving? How many souls I'd be responsible for not getting saved?"

The guest pastor turned to wipe the tear that was rolling down his wife's face.

The first lady looked up to him. "I'm sorry, honey."

"I know, Cheeks," he said to his wife, apparently calling her his nickname for her. He kissed her on the forehead, then the nose, and then the lips.

Margie cleared her throat, reminding the couple that they had company. Heck, *they* were the company.

"Oh, I do apologize," the pastor turned and said to Margie and Doreen. "But when you have the most beautiful wife in the world . . ." His words trailed off as he and his wife looked all starry eyed into each other's eyes.

"Well, looks like you two need a room," Margie said, and then chuckled. "And thank goodness you have one since you're from out of town."

Everyone else chuckled as well.

The first lady turned away from her husband and walked over toward Margie. Doreen turned her body toward the first lady and subconsciously balled her fist.

"Down, girl," the first lady said jokingly to Doreen. "I come in peace."

Doreen, realizing she was looking like Margie's bodyguard, loosened up and stepped aside.

The first lady went and apologized to Margie, and then to Doreen. She shared with the women that just recently she'd dealt with, a woman who had tried to steal her husband from her right up under her nose. She still had her guard up and regretted treating Margie as if she were that woman.

Now, more than ever, Doreen understood how one could hold the act and sin of someone against another person. She'd done the same thing to her own husband that day in the office with Melanie. But this wasn't about Doreen. This was about Margie and her outlandish idea to be on a dating reality show. No, perhaps it wasn't something Doreen would ever do, nor would she have dreamed of taking part in such a production. She didn't want to. God knows she didn't want to. But the same way Margie had needed Doreen there that evening to jump in, or rather intercede on her behalf with that first lady, she needed her there to do the same during the filming of this reality show. Not that Doreen had doubts about being there or thought she might have heard incorrectly from God, but more confirmation never hurt a saint.

"Well, I just wanted to come over and check on you," Doreen said to Deborah, rising up off the couch. "I have to head to Walmart to get me a couple of swimsuits, then make my way back to the mansion."

Deborah stood up and smiled. "Oh yeah. That's right. They usually do tape those shows at great big ole houses. Is it just as lovely as the ones that are on television?"

Doreen stopped and turned to Deborah. "Child, better." She let out a jolly laugh.

"I bet," Deborah said, walking Doreen to the door. "Well, thank you so much for checking in on me before you get all wrapped up in TV Land."

"No problem. I didn't know how much free time I'd have once we started taping this show, so I at least wanted to make sure I laid eyes on you again."

"I appreciate that, Mother Doreen. I appreciate you." The two women hugged when they arrived at the door.

"You take care now." Doreen stepped to the side while Deborah opened the door. "And call me if you need me. We can't have our cell phones on, but you can leave me a message on my cell phone. There is a house phone there I can check my messages on and call you back. I can't remember the number to the house phone, but I'll text it to you before I shut my phone down."

"Wow, so you all are pretty much at their mercy when it comes to communication, huh?"

"Can't even watch television," Doreen said. "We can get on the computer and all that, but you know me, I'm not into all that technology. Margie is, but I'm ten years her senior. This aging brain of mine ain't sharp enough to comprehend all those features and functions that change every day. Heck, some people change their phones every other month. Took me six months to learn to use the one I got. Why would I want to go changing it up? I still have the very same one I got with my Verizon plan when I signed up."

Deborah paused. "Mother Doreen, please don't tell me you're still using a flip phone."

"My phones are just like my cars, I ride 'em until the wheels fall off."

Deborah shook her head. "I hear you, Mother." She gave Doreen another hug.

Doreen continued to speak as she shuffled out the door. "Like I said, call me if you need me. I'm about to be cut off from the outside world. It feels like . . . like a juror sequestered during the O. J. trial."

"With all the craziness going on in this world, that just might not be a bad idea. I love you, and I'll talk to you later," Deborah said.

"Love you too," Doreen said, and then made her way back to the waiting Escalade. It was nice having a car waiting for her. It's what awaited her once the show got rolling that gave her concern. And it wouldn't be long before she would find out.

Chapter 9

"Are you nervous?"

Margie took in the question Doreen had posed to her, and then exhaled as she sat in a chair in the nice-size bathroom of her apartment. It was nice enough in size where the makeup artist and hairstylist had each set up a chair and station to do what they needed to do to get Margie camera ready. And there was still enough room for Doreen to be present as well.

"I know my motto is usually stay ready, be ready, and you won't have to get ready." She turned and looked at Doreen as the hairstylist tried to assure not a hair was out of place. "But how in the world do you prepare yourself for something like this?" Margie was gripping the arms of the swivel styling chair. Her nerves were really getting the best of her.

She felt like doubting Thomas at the moment. It wasn't that she was doubting God, but there was definitely an internal battle going on within her. *A reality show.* There was the potential for her to be before the entire world. Would she come across fake and phony? One moment would she forget the cameras were rolling and do or say something others might feel a pastor shouldn't do or say? Would that turn them off from her, from church, and most importantly, from God?

Margie wasn't the first pastor to appear on a reality show by far. But she'd heard some of the things people had to say about those who had been. Some of those pastors had turned people off completely from wanting to get the Word of God from a church pastor. She did not want to risk having that type of blood on her hands. Souls were at stake here. It felt like too much for her to bear. It was too much responsibility it seemed, but what could she do about it?

Well, one thing she could do was to get up out of that chair and make a run for it. If she got up and walked away from the show before it ever started, the weight of the world would be lifted from her shoulders. But in her heart—in her spirit—she believed that getting up and walking out on that show and its producers would have been like walking out on God as well. She'd already said yes. Her soul had said yes. Her spirit had said yes. There was no other option but to press through.

"With lots and lots of prayer is how you prepare and stay prepared for this type of assignment," Doreen said. "And I prayed all morning for you."

"Well, if you prayed for me, then I know I'm ready to take on the world." Margie turned her head back straight so the gentleman doing her hair could do what he needed to do. "Or at least ten hunky men."

"Honky?" Doreen said. "Did you really just say that? And what if they aren't white? What if some are black, Hispanic, Asian—"

"Mother Doreen!" Margie said in shock. "Did you really think I meant it as in the derogatory term for white?"

Doreen shrugged. "Well, didn't you?"

Margie laughed. "No, I meant *hunky,* as in a hunk of a man. Fine. Built. Good looking."

"I thought you meant *honky* like George Jefferson meant it." Doreen was referencing the character on a sitcom played by the late Sherman Hemsley.

"I can't even believe you think I would use such a degrading word," Margie said. "Especially with *me* being white. Why would I use such a word to refer to my own race?"

"Black people do it all the time," Doreen said.

"Say the word *honky?*" Margie asked.

"No, they call one another the derogatory N-word all the time."

Margie didn't look too surprised. "Yeah, I hear it in a lot of rap songs, and I've seen it done in movies, as well. In the movies, some black people call each other the N-word, and then smile and bump fists."

"For some black people, though, hearing the N-word ain't nothing but another Tuesday. But for others, typically the older ones like myself, the word makes us cringe because we can't associate it to anything good, let alone use it as a term of endearment."

Margie nodded her understanding. She wasn't black so she couldn't even begin to imagine how a black person of any age felt about the N-word. She didn't like the word. It was a disrespectful word that upset her whenever she heard it, but again, that wasn't the same as the effect the word might have on an actual black person.

"I hear black people say that the word lost its power when they began to use it on themselves," Doreen said. "Kind of like the fat kid making fat jokes of himself so that when the skinny kid tries to crack on him, it's not funny anymore." Doreen stared off.

"I take it you don't agree with that," Margie said.

"Nope. That word still has the power of a bullet from an AK-47. It will cut right through you, and it burns. Just tears your insides out." She looked at Margie. "You know what I mean?"

"I don't know, my sister. I can only imagine. And even that makes my soul weep."

There was silence in the room as if the two were at a funeral, mourning. "If only that word could be put to death. And I guess they can bury the word *honky* right next to it," Doreen suggested.

"Yes," Margie agreed, then looked at the hairstylist and makeup artist. "Even though I hope everyone knows that is absolutely not what I meant when I said the word."

"It was an honest mistake on my part," Doreen said. "I hope I didn't offend anyone." She looked at the makeup artist who was African American. But that still didn't mean she couldn't be offended by the comment.

"Not at all," the makeup artist said in regards to being offended.

Doreen looked at the hairstylist, who was Caucasian. She wanted to make sure that she'd not offended anyone with her misunderstanding.

The hairstylist looked up from Margie's hair to see Doreen was waiting on a reply. "Oh no. I'm good," the hairstylist said. "Besides, I'm Irish."

The makeup artist sucked her teeth. "Irish, Italian . . . Child, you *white*," the makeup artist shot.

The hairstylist was quick to snap his neck back. "I'm *Irish,* thank you very much. The same way I'm sure you are proud to be black, I'm proud to be Irish."

"Actually," the makeup artist waved a tube of lip gloss she'd been about to put away, "my mom is 100 percent Haitian and my daddy is black. But do you hear me running around talking about," she began mocking her coworker, "I'm not black, I'm Haitian"? She then snapped out of her dramatics and spat, "I'm black, and, honey, you're white. How 'bout that?" She continued packing away her products.

Margie frowned her face up and looked at Doreen. "Lord have mercy, what was that?"

"That's what us black folks call *a read,*" Doreen said to Margie. "And apparently, that's what Haitian folks call it too."

Everyone in the room couldn't help but to laugh at that one. That was a good thing, because the sound of laughter immediately broke up the tension. It even made Margie forget all about her inner turmoil.

"Voilà!" the stylist said, after putting the final touches on Margie's hair and spinning her chair around to face the mirror.

"Oh, wow!" Margie exclaimed as she stared in the mirror, slowly rising up out of the chair. "Who is this person? My God!" She turned to Doreen. "I don't even recognize myself." She turned back to the mirror. "My hair! It's not blond anymore." Her once-blond hair was now darkened as were her eyebrows. This was her first time having seen her hair and makeup done. She'd hopped from the makeup chair right to the stylist's chair. "This makeup . . ." She went to touch her face but stopped herself. "My God." Margie looked to be in awe.

"Well, I hope that's a *good* thing," the makeup artist said, having gathered all of her items.

"You like it?" the hairstylist couldn't help but ask.

"I . . . I *love* it," Margie swooned. "I'm just so used to looking like—"

"A pastor," Doreen jumped in and said.

Margie nodded and laughed. "Yes, a pastor."

Doreen walked over to Margie. She stood next to her and put her arm around her while they both looked at Margie's reflection in the mirror. "Underneath that robe and collar is a woman. A divine, an inspirational, a virtuous, anointed woman. And do you know what the acronym for that is?"

"No, what?"

Doreen turned Margie to face her. "*DIVA!*" She then held her hand up for Margie to give her a high five, which she did.

"Pastor Margie," Anya stuck her head into the bathroom and said. "We need to get you dressed. The first gentleman will be pulling up in less than forty-five minutes."

Margie looked at Doreen. "I guess it's just about showtime."

"I guess it is," Doreen answered.

Margie looked to the cameramen who had been filming all this time as a means for Margie to get used to them. It wasn't footage they were going to air, just a little test run to see how natural Margie would be in front of the camera.

Margie took Doreen's hands into her. "Thank you for doing this. Having you here, knowing someone who truly has my back and my best interest, not to mention who is praying down the wall of Jericho, makes this that much easier to go through with. Because I'll tell you, just five minutes ago, I was about ready to hop out of that chair and find my way back to my home."

"You a runaway bride and don't even have a fiancé yet," Doreen laughed.

"I know. But I'm here, and now there's no turning back."

"Then I guess we need to get the show on the road, sit back, and see what God makes of it."

Margie looked at the door where Anya impatiently waited. She looked back at Doreen. "I sure do wish you could be there when I meet these men."

"Now, I *know* it's been a minute since you've dated," Doreen said, "but you know darn well don't no man want to go on a date with a woman when her friend is a third wheel."

Margie laughed. "I know, but the dates haven't started. I'm simply meeting them tonight."

"But once all the men have arrived, you will be mingling with them for a while," Anya interjected.

Margie ignored her and continued speaking with Doreen. She took in a breath, and then let it out. "I'm about to be the only woman in a room full of men."

"With a room full of cameras, so everything is going to be all right. They'll be no funny business going on around here." Doreen looked to the door. "Right, Anya?"

Anya was antsy. "Pastor Margie," she looked down at her watch, then back up to Margie, "we really need to get going."

"Okay, okay," Margie said, not in a tone as if she was being aggravated by Anya, but in agreement. She gave Doreen a *"Here goes nothing look,"* and then headed over to the door.

"That's right," Doreen called out, "go get your man!"

Margie stopped, did a half turn, and threw her hands on her hips. "Honey, it's the man who has to get me." She winked, and then exited the room.

Less than an hour later, Margie was standing at the end of the walkway from the front door of the mansion. Fatima had been right. The cameras and lights set up around her didn't bother her at all. Perhaps it was because Margie was used to being watched. Week after week, hundreds of eyes stayed glued on her every move. For her, this really wasn't that much of a difference. In some ways, she felt it was better. At least in this case, she couldn't see the faces that were watching her. There'd been plenty of times where Margie had been preaching and looked out to see someone looking at her like she had two heads. Others would be frowned up. Some looked as if they had attitudes, while some were even sleeping. She didn't have that distraction in this instance. She appreciated that and found the eye of the camera to be much more comforting.

When Margie saw a black limo coming up the drive-way, she let out a deep breath. Among all the other emotions she was feeling, she had to admit that she was excited. She honestly couldn't remember the last time her interest had been piqued by a man. She always had ministry on the brain, never taking a moment to really figure out what her own needs were. She was always consumed with the needs of those around her. Ironically, she'd still be somewhat consumed about others' needs; *ten* others, to be exact, but who's counting? And if she was the woman they needed in their life.

When the car stopped in front of Margie, she just about thought her heart would stop beating as well. The limo driver exited the car, and then walked around to the back passenger door facing Margie. He opened the door and within seconds, Margie saw two shiny shoes hit the ground. Her eyes scrolled upward, about six feet and two inches upward, until her eyes met with a pair of piercing green eyes. She couldn't have kept the smile from covering her face. She couldn't recall having seen a man so handsome ever in her life.

A minor concern of hers when Fatima had gone over all the details of the show with her was that she wouldn't have any part in picking the ten bachelors that would be part of the show. Margie felt she should have at least had some say in the persons she would be spending the night in close proximity with; the men she would have to go on dates with, hold conversations in the garden with, and whatever else.

Fatima had told Margie that they didn't want her to be biased and choose the men based on their looks. They wanted this to be a win-win situation. Yes, they wanted great ratings, but they also really wanted Margie to find true love. The producers tried to make it seem as though they had Margie's best interest at heart, but she knew they needed some type of validation for the show, and even a wedding spinoff show like so many of those other reality shows had. For Margie, all she wanted was what God had for her, and if He was paying attention, right now, she wanted this fine hunk of a man who was heading her way.

"Pastor Margie," he greeted, stepping to her, as the limo driver got back in the car and drove off.

"Please, call me Margie," she insisted. Right about now, with her having the thoughts that some might think a pastor shouldn't be having, the last thing she wanted was to be reminded that she was, in fact, a pastor. Nope. She'd rather stand right there and marinate in her natural, womanly thoughts.

"Okay, Margie," the man agreed. "I'm Clayton B. Farmers. The B is for Benton. It is truly an honor to be in the presence of a powerful woman of God such as yourself." He did a slight bow, and then handed Margie the rose he was carrying with both hands.

"Thank you. You're so beautiful."

Clayton's huge dimples formed in his cheeks.

He's got dimples too! Margie screamed in her head.

"A woman who doesn't bite her tongue," Clayton said. "I like that." He dropped his head and blushed.

That made Margie's belly flutter with butterflies taking off. She still had it to the point where she could make a grown man blush; who knew?

"I appreciate the compliment," he said, looking back up at her with his piercing eyes. "Not many women have just come out and told me I was beautiful. But you are beautiful as well." He leaned in to Margie. "If you don't mind me returning the compliment."

It was almost as if Clayton was on a five-second delay with Margie. She'd watched his lips move, but it took a moment for the words he'd spoken to register. And once she was able to string his words together in a coherent manner, it sounded as if he was acknowledging the fact that she'd just called him beautiful. She'd thought the words as clear as day, but had they actually escaped her lips?

"I . . . I . . ." No way could Margie recant what she'd said to him on camera. That would come across as just plain rude. Besides, she did think he was beautiful, but she hadn't meant to express it verbally. What she'd meant to say was that the rose was beautiful, so she decided to say that too, and hopefully, it would get her past the awkwardness she was feeling inside.

"The rose is beautiful," Margie said. "And how beautiful and kind of you to bless me with it." She accepted the rose and sniffed it. "Beautiful gesture indeed." Margie felt confident she'd cleaned that up real good. She smiled proudly at her ability to be quick on her feet. She turned to the glass vase that sat on the pedestal next to her. She'd already been instructed to place the roses she was going to be presented with by each man into the vase.

"You deserve far more than just a rose," Clayton said with much confidence. "And if you keep me around long enough, I'll make sure you get everything you deserve, and then some." His tone became more sensual.

Margie maintained her composure, praying to God that her cheeks didn't reflect how warm Clayton was making her inside. "Oh my." She began to fan herself. She was becoming a little flustered. Even Clayton's voice was beautiful, and it was penetrating her soul. Was this man really all that, or was it simply that it had been so long since Margie had actually paid attention to a man in this kind of manner? All she knew was that he had her speechless. No words being spoken wasn't good for television.

"Cut!"

Both Margie and Clayton turned toward where the voice had come from. Walking past Fatima, who had yelled out "Cut," a man in a black tuxedo walked up to Margie.

"Pastor Margie," the man said with an English accent. He stopped in front of her. "You're doing quite well, but remember, you have to keep things engaging. Ask him where he is from, what he does for a living, why he's here, etcetera. Just be your natural, wonderful self." He pepped her up as if she needed coaching. "Can you do that for me?"

He sounded condescending, but Margie knew that wasn't what he was trying be. She'd met the man for the first time right before they'd begun taping this evening. He'd been introduced to her as Lincoln. He was the host of the show, the narrator and mediator between Margie and the men. He'd gone over what his role was and let Margie know that she was the star of the show, and he was just there to coach things along.

"I got it, Lincoln," Margie said to him. "I'm sorry."

"Oh, you do not have to apologize," he said. "Like I told you, you're doing fine. I know this is kind of an oxymoron, but while ignoring the cameras, be mindful of the fact that the camera is rolling, so keep things alive and moving and, of course, interesting,"

"Got it," Margie said. She patted down the lovely red skirt suit she was wearing. It was a long skirt that went down to her ankles. The suit jacket was embellished with some gold gems. The producers had asked that she wear a large brim hat. They felt it would give off a regal look. Margie informed them that it would be disingenuous for her to do so because hats were not her thing. And besides that, had they stuck with the original reality-show theme, the bachelorettes would have been vying to be first lady, so the hats would have been more understandable. But most importantly, wearing that

hat would hide Margie's new hair makeover. She was quickly getting used to being a brunette.

When they'd asked that she wear her ministerial robe, she shot that down as well. She felt that would intimidate the men, and they'd see her only as a woman of God and not what she was first and foremost; the plain ole woman God had created her to be. Ironically, it seemed like Margie was the one feeling intimidated by the men; at least this first one anyway.

"Quiet on the set!" Fatima called out. She nodded her approval of Lincoln's discussion with Margie to him. Then she took her place back by one of the cameramen.

The cameraman yelled out, "Marker!"

Some fella, a little on the grungy side, placed one of those black and white clipboard thingies in front of the camera.

The cameraman spoke. "*Lady of the House*, meeting the men, scene one, take two."

The grungy fella clamped the handle on the clipboard down, the cameraman thanked him, and then Fatima called out, "Action!"

Five seconds after the word "Action" was called, just as she had been taught, Margie resumed her conversation with Clayton.

"So, Clayton, where are you from?" Margie asked him.

"I was born in England," he said.

"Oh," Margie said. "I didn't hear an accent."

"That's because I don't have one," he replied. "My parents moved to the United States before I was even a year old. My father is an engineer. His job is responsible for the move. So he, my mother, my five sisters, and I have called the good old U. S. of A. home since I can remember."

"Oh, wow, five sisters!" Margie exclaimed.

"Yes, I'm the youngest and the only boy."

"What was it like growing up the only male, besides your father, of course?"

"Let's just say the great thing about it was that I didn't get forced to wear any of my older siblings' hand-me-downs."

Margie burst out laughing while Clayton gave off a deep, hearty laugh and was able to cut it off instantly, without allowing for his laughter to die down. So just like that, it was only Margie's roaring laughter that could be heard. With the sound of her own voice ringing in her ears, it sounded as if she was trying way too hard with Clayton. It reminded her of "that girl" who laughed too hard at her date's jokes just to make sure he was aware that she found him interesting.

"Sooooooo," Margie said, allowing her laughter to fade, "five sisters, huh?" She tucked her lips and nodded her head.

"Yes, and in spite of what most would believe, I loved it. I love women, and after spending so much time with them, how could I leave home and not understand them? How could I be raised by a woman and with five women and not know what a woman wants, what a woman needs, and how to make her happy?"

"Right, yes." Margie nodded, hanging onto his every word. Right about now, she wished she'd practiced this whole conversing with a man thing on subject matters that didn't involve ministry before doing it on camera. "So, just where were you and your sisters raised here in the States?"

"Philadelphia," Clayton said, "so you know what that means."

Margie waited for his reply.

"Means I'm a fighter. Means when I want something, even if it's not meant for me to have,"—he looked Margie up and down—"I'll fight for it anyway."

Margie couldn't stop her eyelids from rapidly flutter-ing, nor could she stop her cheeks from turning red. "I see," was all she managed to say, then she found a few other words. "You said that your father was an engineer. Is it safe to say that you followed in his footsteps?"

"Pretty much. I too am an engineer," Clayton said. "Matter of fact, you know that company that brought my family over here to the States?" he asked, then continued on before Margie could even answer. "Well, I now own it."

Margie was truly impressed. But the fact that he was so impressive put up a red flag. He seemed *too* perfect; like one of those men she'd seen in a Hallmark channel movie. They were all fictional made-up characters. So if that's who he was, then that meant he was nothing more than a big ole fake.

"Clayton, I know I haven't known you but five seconds," Margie said, "but my discernment when it comes to people seems to be quite on point."

"Oh yeah? And just what is it that you are discerning about me?"

"That you are a pretty decent guy."

"Then why do I sense a hint of worry behind you saying that?" he asked.

"Because it makes me wonder why you're not settled down with a woman, why you're here looking for one. You just don't come across as the type of guy who would have to get on a reality show to find a wife. Seems to me women would be throwing themselves at your feet. And if they're not, then clearly you've never been to the New Day Temple of Faith Singles' Ministry." Margie chuckled. "So, again, it just makes me wonder if there is some other reason why you're here besides to find a wife."

Clayton took a deep breath as he looked down. It was a dead giveaway that Margie must have hit the nail on the head. Her discernment was definitely on point; she could tell by his reaction.

Clayton gathered his words, and then began to explain himself. "I've never been married before, but I have been in love. As a result of that love, I have two amazing twin sons who are both in school for their doctorates. I'm not that into superstition, but I think it's a bad idea to talk about exes when you first meet and are trying to get to know someone, but I was madly in love with my sons' mother. She just couldn't say the same about me. My focus for a really long time was my education and my career. Yes, I'll admit, even though I was in love with her, I was already married." Before the full look of horror could plaster itself across Margie's face, he added, "To my job. I'd promised to marry my children's mother eventually, but not until after I'd accomplished all my career goals, because it wasn't until then I'd be able to give her all the attention that she needed . . . that she deserved." Sensing Margie was connecting with his words he added, ". . . That any woman deserves from someone calling themselves her husband."

Margie listened intently. Her eyes darted from his eyes, to those dimples whenever they popped up into his cheeks, to his full lips.

"Unfortunately, she decided she was worthy of more than playing second fiddle to my dream, and I agreed." There was a look of both hurt and regret in Clayton's eyes.

The vulnerable side of him was even more appealing to Margie.

"She left and went back to New York where she was from," Clayton continued. "I pursued my happiness and dreams. Unbeknownst to me, when she'd gotten back to New York, she learned that she was pregnant. She kept that a secret from me, not wanting to delay or put a damper in what I'd been so focused on achieving. My boys were five years old by the time I learned of their existence."

"Oh my," Margie said. "I can't imagine how you must have felt missing those beginning stages of your children's life."

"Words can't describe it. I mean, I'd always felt as though there was some kind of void in my life. Like there was just one thing missing, besides my ex, of course. Come to find out, it was two." He smiled. "Their mother sacrificed a lot for me, both before and after she left."

Margie nodded. "For as hard as it was for you to have not been there for the first five years of your boys' lives, it had to have been that much harder for her to not have you there."

"Exactly," he said sincerely. "It's kind of like you." He looked into Margie's eyes. "You're kind of like a single mother."

Margie tilted her head for him to explain.

"Well, you take care of quite a bit of God's children," he said. "And you do it all by yourself." He took Margie's hand into his. "But not for long . . . if I have anything to do with it." He placed a soft kiss on Margie's hand as he stared into her eyes. "I'm here because I'm ready. I'm ready to make something—someone—more important than my life's goals." He looked into Margie's eyes. "Seems like you're ready too, or else you wouldn't be here either."

Margie let out a slow exhale. She had to force herself to keep breathing, for everything Clayton seemed to say made her breathless.

"*Are* you?" Clayton asked in a smooth, deep voice.

"Am I what?" Margie said, melting into his eyes, causing her to have short-term memory loss on what all he'd just been talking about.

"Are you ready?"

Margie had been so caught up in everything physical about Clayton that she still wasn't quite sure what he was asking her what she was ready for. Not wanting to reply to something she was ignorant of, she slid her hand from his, cleared her throat, and then said, "Well, Clayton, it's been my pleasure meeting you and learning a little bit about you."

"And I hope to learn more about you," he said. "And I will, if I have anything to do with it."

Margie smiled and blushed.

"I'll see you later on in the house."

Once Margie met each of the men individually, her next step would be to go inside and mingle with them all together. But she had to admit, it was Clayton she definitely wanted to mingle with inside.

"Absolutely," she announced.

Fatima was off camera biting her lip as she watched the evident chemistry and attraction between Margie and Clayton. She looked over at Lincoln who gave her a thumbs-up and a you-sure-can-pick-'em nod.

"Then I'll see you inside," Clayton said to Margie as he walked off and headed toward the mansion's front door.

Margie stood looking straight-ahead. She pictured that he was looking at her over his shoulder as he walked away. She sensed it. She tried to fight looking behind her to confirm whether he truly was, but the temptation was too much, and she ultimately gave in. When she looked over her shoulder, her eyes instantly locked with his. It was electric. An energy, a volt, shot through her that was completely different than the one that hit her when she was preaching in the sanctuary or filled with the Holy Ghost.

She quickly turned to look straight-ahead. That's when the headlights of the limo returning caught her attention. Until that moment, Margie had forgotten all about the fact that she had nine other men to meet. She couldn't imagine any of them comparing to the one that had just awakened senses in her she hadn't known existed. But a deal was a deal. She'd signed the contract, and there were rules to be followed. But something about Clayton told her that he would be willing to break them all in order to be the last man standing.

Chapter 10

"I hope I didn't come across as desperate with Clayton," Margie said to Lincoln. This was her first time getting a break during taping since ending her conversation with Clayton and moving on to the next four men. Even though Clayton had been the first man she'd met and those who followed were charming and good catches as well, Clayton was fresh on her mind as if he'd been the last.

It wasn't just Clayton she was concerned about having come across as desperate to, but what about the viewers? She did not want to look like some loose female pastor pouncing on a man the first chance she got.

"You were fine," Lincoln assured her. He looked to see the limo driving up. "Okay, time for the next half."

Margie let out an exasperated gust of wind. Getting through the first five men had been enough. Each came across as the perfect gentleman. In Margie's opinion, those five alone were plenty for her to get to know over the next few weeks. As far as she was concerned, they didn't even have to include the other five in the show at all. There were good pickings in the five she'd already met. But if these last five gave off as good of vibes as the first batch, then it was only going to make things that much harder for Margie to get down to her final man. Thinking ahead made her head spin.

"Here we go," Lincoln said, walking out of the camera shot. "You're doing good, Pastor Margie. Just continue to be yourself."

Margie nodded, then mentally prepared to take on the final five. Within moments, out of the limo stepped man number six. Just like the first five, he was equally as attractive, smart, and kind. As the evening went on, so were the next four men. To say that Margie felt like a kid in a candy shop was cliché, nor did it suffice how she really felt. Even though Clayton had made a huge impression on Margie, each man had a trait about him that really interested her.

The second man Margie had met, Rayshawn, a retired NFL player, was outgoing, talkative, and just had a certain spark about him. Not being on the field anymore hadn't kept him from keeping in great shape. He had biceps for days!

Then there was José from the Dominican Republic who serenaded Margie with a song in Spanish. And even though she didn't understand a word he'd said, the emotion in his eyes, in his voice, told her that the lyrics had been passionate and sincere.

Cleveland was hilarious. His sense of humor was to die for. And just when she thought a man couldn't get any more handsome than Clayton, here comes Alexander. Alexander wasn't as suave as Clayton and stumbled on his words here and there due to a slight stuttering issue, of which Margie was sure his nerves only made worse. But she didn't mind. It felt good with the tables being turned and her making someone else nervous instead. Besides, his good looks pardoned where he lacked in communication.

Margie wasn't shallow. The person she got into a relationship with had to have more than good looks. He had to have substance as well. From what she could tell, every man she'd met had substance. Even though initially it looked as though Clayton was going to be a shoo-in, Margie truly wanted to get to know each of these men better.

"I'll see you inside," Margie said for the tenth and final time that evening after having met Brandon, who happened to be a preacher as well. What Margie liked about Brandon is that he didn't keep announcing that he was a preacher in an attempt to increase his chances of connecting with her better. As a matter of fact, he'd only shared such information after she'd asked him. There was just this anointing all over him that hinted he was a man of the cloth. It was the way he spoke and carried himself. It just goes to prove the saying that if a person is a Christian, they don't have to go around announcing it and wearing it on their sleeve. People will just know.

"I can't wait to see you inside." Brandon nodded, and then headed toward the mansion door.

"And cut!" Fatima called out, and then walked over to Margie. "Well, how did we do, as far as picking out ten prospective future lifetime mates for you?" Fatima stood there eagerly rocking from one leg to the other. She looked so proud that she really didn't need Margie to confirm what she already knew.

"You did excellent," Margie informed her. "These are some amazing men, and one is from right here in Malvonia," she said in regards to Cleveland. "I can't believe our paths have never crossed."

"It's all about timing," Fatima said. "All about timing." She gleamed with pride figuring that was a sign that it was perfect timing for a show of this nature as well.

"Amen to that," Margie agreed. "So do I head inside now to socialize with all the men?"

"In about a half hour." Fatima looked at her watch, and then back up at Margie. "We've got to get you back to hair and makeup to get you touched up, then you'll be escorted back to the main house. There, you'll spend about an hour with the men. There is no agenda. Whatever happens, happens."

Margie snapped her neck back and raised an eyebrow. "What do you mean by whatever happens, happens?"

Fatima laughed. "Nothing like what you're thinking, according to that look on your face. I mean, there is no particular man you have to talk to or converse with. If you end up doing a one-on-one conversation, then so be it. Just do what you feel comfortable doing."

Margie nodded her understanding.

"So let's get you back to your apartment." She looked over her shoulder. "Anya?"

"Yes," Anya said. She'd been off to the side discussing things with other members of the crew.

"We need to get Pastor Margie back to her apartment, then she needs to be escorted back to the main house," Fatima said. "I'm going to head inside the main house and go over some things with the men, so I'll catch up with you guys later."

"Gotcha," Anya said. She then looked at Margie. "Can we get you anything? Something to drink or eat?"

"No, I'm fine."

"Good. Then let's hop on the cart and get you back to your place."

Anya assisted Margie onto the golf cart that was waiting to drive them to Margie's apartment. That's just how huge the property was. Walking was doable, but not when they were on the clock, which they happened to be.

A few minutes later, Margie found herself back in the stylist's and makeup artist's chair.

"They told me you were taking a break. How did it go?"

Margie looked up to see Doreen entering the bathroom.

"Were the men nice looking?" Doreen asked.

"Nice looking is *not* the word."

"Oh, let me guess . . ." Doreen said, walking over to Margie. "Were they hunky?"

Both women burst out laughing.

The stylist and makeup artist simply shook their heads and smiled at the cackling women.

"Oh, they were hunky all right," Margie said. "Heck, after I met the first man, I was about ready to tell them they were going to have to figure out how to turn six minutes of footage into six weeks of taping. I was sold on the fact that man was heaven sent. They could have let the other nine stay home."

Doreen chuckled. "He was all that, huh?"

"Clayton was *more* than all that." Margie looked off starry eyed. "He was *everything*."

"Ummm, look at you looking all googly-eyed." Doreen examined Margie's face. "And are you blushing or is that the makeup?"

Margie giggled.

"And giggling like a schoolgirl too! Oh, I gots to meet this man."

"And you will," Anya entered the bathroom and said. "Later." She looked at Margie. "But for now, the men are eager to make your acquaintance . . . again."

Margie hopped up out of the chair with quickness.

"Well, I can't wait until later," Doreen said. "If they've got her jumping out of her seat like her britches are burning, I have got to see these men now. I mean, look at her." Doreen threw her hand in Margie's direction. "She's acting like a woman in love after only five minutes."

Margie paused when she realized she had moved as fast as lightning. "Is it obvious that it's been that long since I've had male companionship that I'm willing to practically break my neck to get back to them?"

"Yeah, something like that," Doreen said and laughed. She shooed her hand. "But that's all right. Woman, go on and get your groove back. Maybe you can tell me about the rest of your evening over breakfast."

"Ehh, ehh, ahh," Anya said, shaking her head. "Come morning, two of these men will have the pleasure of having breakfast in the garden with Pastor Margie."

"Oh, okay," Doreen said, slightly disappointed. "Then maybe lunch?" she said to Margie, sounding a little more hopeful.

"Nope, we have to shoot Pastor Margie describing what she was feeling during introductions with each man," Anya said.

Margie looked to Doreen with a look of disappointment on her face as well. "We can always do—"

"Dinner is out of the question as well," Anya stated.

"Well, heck, I could have stayed in Kentucky," Doreen said. "I'm here for my best friend, but you guys won't let me anywhere near her."

"Now, now, Doreen, it's nothing like that," Anya said. "You are a big part of Pastor Margie's life, so your opinion will play a big part in her decision making. It's just that in the beginning, we want to make sure Margie forms a relationship with, as well as her own opinion of, these men without any outside influence. So these first few days will be a little tight, but then, I promise, it will get better. You'll have plenty of girlfriend time discussing the men that we'll get lots of footage of. Okay?" Anya was using her fake cheery voice just to keep the peace.

Doreen exhaled doubtfully. "If you say so, Anya." She began shuffling back to the door. "You have fun, Marg . . . without me."

"Oh, stop it," Margie said. "Listen at you sounding all pitiful, like you've lost your best friend."

"I'm not just sounding pitiful, I *am* pitiful," Doreen clarified. "And it feels like I *have* lost my best friend.

This was supposed to be like a vacation with you. I didn't know I was going to be Whoopi and you were going to get to be Angela Bassett, just out kicking it without me."

Several people in the room laughed, including Margie. "Oh, you are too much, woman. Get on out of here so I can go, as you would say, get my groove back." Margie did a little twitch in her hips.

The stylist whistled and the makeup artist cheered her on.

"Look at you," Doreen said. "Ain't known them men a full twenty-four hours and already they got you hot in the pants."

Margie play tapped Doreen on the shoulder. "Stop hating."

Once again there was laughter in the room.

"You two are a riot," the stylist said, chuckling.

"Yes, they are," Anya interrupted. "And as much as I hate to interrupt your Lucy and Ethel routine," she went over and put her hands on Margie's shoulders and began escorting her out the door, "this one has got to get going before Fatima comes looking for us."

"Well, have fun," Doreen told Margie, "even though something tells me you need very little encouragement. But I'ma pray for you. Lord, am I gonna pray for you!"

"Then that ought to keep you nice and busy," Margie said, "because I'm going to need a whole lot of prayer." Margie, led by Anya, headed out the door. "Pray for the strength of my flesh." Margie was just joking with Doreen. In her years in ministry, she'd been up against more demons than she could count, and she'd slayed them all. So surely, she could handle her own among mortal men. She'd find out sooner than later.

***

"Pastor Margie, do you mind if I steal you away for a moment?"

Margie looked up from the couch she was sitting on, a man on each side of her.

She wasn't surprised to see Fred standing over her with his hand extended. He'd come across even more confident than Clayton. His didn't come across as natural as Clayton; more like he'd worked on it for some years. Not only was he confident, but he was assertive. He wasn't the aggressive type, but the type who didn't beat around the bush, nor did he wait for someone else to dance a jig around it. Margie had gathered as much about him from their initial introduction as well as the way he'd politely taken over the conversation among all the men during this evening's gathering.

"I don't mind," Margie answered, "but something tells me these other fellas will." She chuckled and looked at all the men around her.

"No disrespect to my fellow contestants," Fred then leaned down to Margie, "but I don't care about these gentlemen right now. My only concern is stealing a moment with the lovely lady of the house."

Margie didn't even give the men around her the proper departing words such as "Excuse me for a moment" or "I'll be back." She simply extended a hand to Fred, who took her hand into his, then pulled her up.

The two stared into each other's eyes as they walked, off hand in hand, out of earshot of the other men. It was a wonder they hadn't tripped and fallen. The way those two were mesmerized by each other, they wouldn't have even seen a black bear had it been in their path.

"So, how does it feel to be the center of attention?" Fred asked Margie as the two entered the library/den of the house.

"I hope this doesn't sound vain, but I'm usually the center of attention every Sunday." Margie let out a laugh.

"Oh yes, how could I forget?" Fred said, smiling. He looked toward the sitting area that had a small old-fashioned couch patterned in flowers and a coffee table in front of it. "Shall we sit?" He extended his hand toward the couch.

"Certainly," Margie said with a nod, and then allowed Fred to lead the way.

Once seated, Fred continued. "Allow me to reword my inquiry. How does it feel to be the center of attention among a house full of men? Men hoping they might be ever so blessed to be the one who walks away with the one thing we are all here for?" He let out a breath. "Whew, that was a mouthful."

"I'll say," Margie agreed. She got serious for a moment once something Fred said registered in her head. "Thing?" Margie said. "The *thing* you all are here for?" She wasn't too fond of being referred to as a thing, if she, in fact, was that *thing* he was referring to.

"Yes, that thing called love," Fred said. He watched the sour look on Margie's face vanish. "Oh, wait a minute. You didn't think I was calling *you* a thing, did you?"

"Well, no, I, uh . . ." The last thing Margie wanted to do was start off a relationship on a lie; any lie, be it big or small. "Yes, I did. Made me feel like a piece of meat, if I'm being honest."

"Oh, you can be honest," Fred assured her. "Matter of fact, I hope we can be honest with each other from here on out. I mean, we don't know each other from Adam, so not telling the truth wouldn't benefit either one of us at this point. We aren't vested in each other," he quickly looked at Margie, "yet . . ."

Margie smiled.

"So we have nothing to lose, but as time goes on, we'd have each other to lose." He put his hand up. "I'm not trying to rush things, I'm just, to bring this thing full circle, being honest."

Margie still had a smile on her face. "I get exactly what you are saying," she said, but her spirit was discerning that Fred wanted to say more; he was just warming her up a little.

"Good, because I think there is something you might want to know about m—"

"Don't you think you've had the lady all to yourself long enough?"

Neither Margie nor Fred had heard José come up behind them. They were stunned to find him standing behind the couch.

"Oh my goodness," Margie said, clearly startled. "I didn't hear you approach."

"Neither did I," Fred said, almost through gritted teeth. It was safe to say that he was not the least bit thrilled about José interrupting his moment with Margie. And his timing couldn't have been worse. "Gotta be careful of the sneaky type."

"Touché," José said, then gave Fred a knowing look.

Fred's coffee-served-black complexion couldn't cover up the redness of his cheeks.

José ignored Fred's reaction, then turned to Margie. "Do you mind if I steal you away from the . . ." He cleared his throat, then gave Fred the side eye, "gentleman?" He turned his attention back to Margie. The crabby look he'd just given Fred turned into a smile.

Something was going on here that Margie wasn't privy to. She knew the men had a little friendly competition going on, but whatever was taking place between Fred and José went beyond that. It almost sounded personal. Since the men had had a chance to converse with one another before Margie had arrived that evening, without a doubt, she figured words had been exchanged between them. For some of them, Margie knew that even though their heart might have been in the right place when they initially signed up for the show, it would turn out to be nothing more than a pissing contest for them. She was certain she'd be able to see right through them and weed the phonies out eventually, once she got over the initial shock and flattery of it all.

The night was still young, not to mention it was the first night she'd met any of the men. It would take a little time for her to be able to read them, especially since she was draped in her womanly flesh for the most part. But once she set the natural aside and was able to view things in the spiritual, she might find that it was better to have kept her fleshly blinders on, because it was going to be too much for even her spiritual eye to handle.

"Pastor Margie, you've had a chance to meet all ten men individually," Lincoln said as they all stood around the fireplace that was lit, even though it was the middle of summer. Everything was for the cameras. "And we noticed that a couple of the men even pulled you to the side for some brief one-on-one conversation. But right now, we're going to ask you to choose, between all the men, who you would like to have dinner with your first night."

Now things were getting real. Margie had basked in the company of such fine gentlemen. She'd made them smile at one point, as they had made her smile. But now came the time where only one man would end up with a smile on his face this evening.

"So, Margie, who is it going to be?" Lincoln asked.

All of a sudden, Margie felt as if Lincoln was pressuring her. He'd put her on the spot. Even though she was well aware that sending the men home one by one was part of the agenda, making someone feel left out—like a loser—it was going to be much harder than she thought it would be. Her look of disinclination was written all over her face.

"Pastor Margie, this is just the beginning. It's only going to get harder after this."

Lincoln was right. It shouldn't have been this difficult to pick which one of these fine men she wanted to spend the next hour with. If she was having this much trouble keeping one, how in the world would letting one go affect her?

She had to look at this thing as a glass half full. It could have been worse; they could have been asking her to kick someone off the show. That final thought gave Margie just the burst of elation she needed to choose one of the men. Based on her contact with them, any one of them would make for a fine dinner date. But per Lincoln's instructions, she could only choose one.

"I've gotten a chance to meet with you all," Margie started, "some I spoke with longer than others."

The couple of men who had found a way to monopolize a good portion of Margie's time smiled mischievously and/or victoriously.

"I truly enjoyed the conversations and can't wait to speak even longer with you all." By this time, Margie had looked to Clayton, Fred, and José.

Each of the three men Margie had just eyed were feeling real confident. Clayton even popped his collar.

"And something tells me I'll get that opportunity," Margie said, "but for now, I want to have dinner with Franklin." Margie looked to one of the men who had pretty much just been flying under the radar. He wasn't as bold or assertive as some of the other men, but when he did speak, he held Margie's attention. There were moments she could have listened to him speak even longer, but had been torn away by one of the other men who didn't mind raining on another man's parade.

Some of the other more confident men were surprised in Margie's choice, as shock was written on their faces. They hadn't seen that coming. That made Margie feel good. It meant she wasn't predictable. That would make it a tad more difficult for any players in the game to try to play her. Her strategy was to always be one step ahead of the men. And, well, maybe, if there was one who could keep up with her, perhaps he was the one meant to reign by her side.

"Franklin, I guess you're the lucky man tonight," Lincoln said.

Franklin nodded and smiled. A couple of the other men gave him a congratulatory pat. Margie was almost certain she'd heard a *thump,* which meant one of the men had maybe given him a slightly harder pat than they'd intended.

Or maybe they had intended.

Even though it momentarily wiped the smile off of his face, Franklin shook it off and went back to smiling. "It ain't luck, Lincoln. It's a blessing." He winked at Margie, who blushed.

"Well, dinner is set up for you two out in the garden," Lincoln announced.

Franklin walked over to Margie and took her hand. "Thank you for choosing me. I can't wait to spend the evening getting to know you better." He gave the other men a playful glare. "Without interruption."

There was laughter in the room.

"Like I said, a beautiful dinner has been prepared this evening for you two," Lincoln said, "so please enjoy while the other men, well, I guess, get to know each other better."

"Thank you," Margie said as she and Franklin began to walk away to go share their much-anticipated meal.

"But, uhh, wait a minute, Pastor Margie," Lincoln called out, stopping Margie in her tracks. "Before you go enjoy dinner, there is one more thing we need you to do."

"Sure," Margie said with a nod. "What is it?"

Lincoln paused long enough for Margie to notice the upper corners of his mouth raise as if he was the Joker. Instantly in her spirit she felt this last little thing he wanted her to do couldn't be good.

"Before you and Franklin go, one of these men needs to go as well," Lincoln said.

"Oh?" Margie said, sounding a tad confused. "So, I'm going to be having dinner with two men tonight?"

"Oh no," Lincoln said. "I didn't mean that one of these men needs to go with you two, I meant one of these men needs to go—period . . . from the house."

Margie gasped, and the men looked terrified, with the exception of Clayton, Fred, and maybe José. They still looked as though they had this thing in the bag.

"But, I just met them," Margie protested. "I haven't known any of them long enough to determine if I'm compatible or not. That doesn't seem fair."

"Pastor Margie, I'm sure you know that life isn't fair," Lincoln said. "Sometimes we just have to follow our heart, or even better, follow the direction of the Holy Spirit." There was just a hint of sarcasm behind his last statement. The left side of his upper lip raised to form a subtle smirk.

Margie frowned. She could sense that Lincoln was trying to be funny. One thing she would not do on this show was make a mockery out of God, nor would she allow Him to be mocked, not in her presence. That was a sure way to get under Margie's skin; to make fun or insult her Heavenly Father.

"Cut!" Margie called out, then turned to Fatima who looked as if someone had just stepped on her toes.

"Pastor Margie, what are you doing?" Fatima snapped. "It's *my* job to call cut. *I'm* in charge here."

It was then when Margie realized that she had indeed stepped on Fatima's toes; figuratively. Just that quickly, she saw a side of the producer she hadn't seen before. And just seconds before, Lincoln had revealed that little snide side of him he'd obviously had tucked away. Margie's spirit instantaneously became vexed. She smelled a setup. She smelled a rat. The nice, sweet crew who had catered to and wooed her, and had her thinking she would have a voice in the show, seemed to be turning on her. Was it possible they had some kind of hidden agenda?

Through her peripheral vision, Margie could see a couple of the cameramen drop their cameras from their faces. Clearly, they didn't care who hollered out *cut*.

"I understand that you are the producer," Margie said to Fatima, "but I'm the subject, the lady of the house . . . remember?" She threw her hands on her hips. "But in addition to that, I'm a woman of God, and what I won't stand here and do is allow you guys to make a mockery of my religious beliefs." Margie was on fire for God, because she was definitely ready to light things up around there.

"We respect your religious beliefs, and we respect you, but this show isn't about God. Granted, it's about a woman of God in search of perhaps a man of God, godly man, or whatever, but we're not here to preach to the viewers or shove God down their throats. We're just here to entertain them."

"Well, the show can both entertain and minister," Margie said. "Do you know for a lot of artists their craft is their prayer? A poet's poem is their prayer. A painter's painting is their prayer. A singer's song, a photographer's picture, an author's writings—"

"Yeah, yeah, I get it," Fatima said. "But right now, you have a man to get rid of. You signed up for this. You agreed to do the show and what was asked of you."

"Well, maybe I shouldn't have," Margie declared. "And maybe I should fix that problem right now." Her eyes threatened to walk off that set right then and there. Her head wanted to carry the threat out, but her heart didn't want to devalue her word. And she'd not only given them her word, but she'd signed a contract.

Fatima let out a harrumph. "You call yourself a Christian, right? Well, Christians aren't supposed to lie. And aren't pastors held to an even higher standard than the average Christian?" Fatima was on a roll as she continued to try to use Margie's status in the kingdom against her.

Margie didn't know what to say. Fatima was standing there reading her like some chick on the street, or some chick on one of those reality shows. Then it hit Margie. *She* was a chick on a reality show. The Bible said when Paul was in Rome he should do as the Romans do. So if Margie was among a ratchet reality-show diva, then it was time to go toe to toe with her and do what she did.

"Listen here," Margie said, pointing her index finger at Fatima, "I don't know what kind of game you're trying to run on me here, but don't let the collar fool you."

Fatima's face frowned up. She was confused about what Margie meant by *collar*.

"My *minister's* collar," Margie clarified.

"Oh, *that* collar," Fatima said, then stood while Margie continued.

"Yes, *that* collar," Margie said. "And regardless of whether I'm wearing that collar, I will still represent God."

"So is that what you're doing now by being insubordinate? Representing God?" She poked out her lips and wobbled her head on her neck. "Wonder what He thinks about that."

"Insubordinate? I don't work for you."

"Oh, but you do," Fatima said. "You are being paid for your services in the form of a nice donation to your church. Oh, wait a minute. Let me guess. That's not your money, that's God's money." Fatima let out a wicked laugh, and the cameramen chimed in with laughter of their own.

Margie was fit to be tied. She was steaming. They were clowning her, but even worse, they were clowning her God.

She looked around the room, remembering that ten men had their eyes on her. She'd been so consumed with Fatima and her trickeries that she'd forgotten all about them. But they certainly hadn't forgotten about her as they were watching her every move and action. So not only was Fatima clowning her, but she was clowning her in front of the men. Not wanting them to think she was some weak woman, she was going to stand her ground and stay holy while doing it.

"Look, Fatima," Margie said, lowering her tone but being firm all the same, "I will keep my word and do what you asked me to do, but this wasn't part of the so-called agenda you showed me. And if you guys are pulling stunts like this now, then no telling what else you've got up your sleeves. And like I told you before, it might be a show for you, but it's my life. I don't want to be manipulated into doing anything that would make Jesus cringe or my mother roll over in her grave. So I'd just appreciate it if you'd give me a heads-up, but more importantly, if you would be mindful of not coming off as condescending when referencing God or my religion. Period. I don't joke when it comes to that, and I don't play games."

Fatima stared at her for a moment. "Are you done?" she asked.

Margie thought for a moment. "Yes, as a matter of fact, I am."

"Good," Fatima said, then burst out laughing.

Margie couldn't imagine what in the world Fatima found to be so funny. But the more Fatima stood there laughing, the hotter Margie got under the collar, and not her ministerial collar, either.

"I understand an unexpected curve ball was thrown," Clayton stepped up and said to Fatima, "but all is well now. Just show the lady some respect." He nodded toward Margie.

"I show people respect who deserve it," Fatima shot back.

"And are you saying that she doesn't deserve respect?" Rayshawn stepped up and said.

Margie watched proudly as one by one the men stepped up and defended her . . . all but a couple. She made a mental note of that.

"Well, looks like you've really made an impression on these men," Fatima said. "They all seem to think you are worthy of stepping up to the plate and going to bat for. Cute, but we've got a show to do, and your dinner is getting cold, and I'm sure Franklin is starved by now, aren't you, Franklin?" Fatima looked at Franklin, who was standing off to the back of the room, behind the other men. He was one of the men who hadn't come to Margie's defense.

Margie looked at Franklin, then looked at Fatima. "Fine, let's do this then, and let's do it right now," she said. "You want me to send a man home, then that's exactly what I'll do." She walked over toward the men. "Each and every last one of you seem like wonderful men, and I thank you all for taking the time from your lives to come get to know me. But you heard the producers, someone has to go." She walked over to Franklin. "Fatima said you're probably starved. Is that so?"

Franklin rubbed his belly. "Well, I guess you could say that." He smiled.

"Then I guess you're going to die of starvation, because you, Franklin, are going home."

Everyone in the room was surprised to hear Margie's words.

Franklin's mouth dropped open. It took a moment for the words to rise up out of his throat, but eventually they did. "But I thought you picked me to have a one-on-one dinner tonight."

"I did . . . initially," Margie said. "Until I realized that there was no need to waste my time or yours. The man I welcome into my life is going to be a protector. You would have stood there all night and let them jump all over me." She pointed to Fatima and Lincoln. She then turned and looked at the other man who had failed to speak up on her behalf. "You all might as well send him home too." She pointed. "If I'm in a fix, I need to know that the man I'm with is going to have my back, and unfortunately, you didn't," she said to Franklin. "So I'm sorry, but you are the one I choose to leave the house tonight." Margie turned and walked back over to Fatima. "So there, happy?" she asked, raising her arms, and then letting them drop to her side. Margie began walking toward the door to exit the room.

"But what about dinner then?" Lincoln called out.

"Oh well, guess I just lost my dinner date. Looks like I can call it a night then. I seemed to have lost my appetite anyway."

"But we've got more taping we need to do tonight," Fatima called out. "You were supposed to pick someone to have dinner with and—"

"And that's exactly what I did," Margie said. She let out a sarcastic snicker. She hated to play tit for tat. God knows she should have turned the other cheek, but being in the situation she was in made it hard to practice what she preached. "So I guess I've fulfilled my obligations for the evening. I'll see you in the morning." Margie turned to the men to bid them a farewell. "Gentlemen," she said with a nod, and then continued her trek toward the exit. She didn't feel the least bit guilty either. She'd done exactly what she'd committed to. She picked a dinner date, and she sent the first man home. It's not her fault they didn't get it on camera. And thank God too. She'd put on a little show, but it was one not meant for the world to see. What kind of pastor argues back and forth throwing verbal jabs at another woman? That wasn't the message she wanted to relay to the world. But she was almost certain she'd made her point to those whom it mattered most.

"Cut! We got it!" Fatima said, clapping her hands as if she was a coach and her team had just scored the winning touchdown on Super Bowl Sunday. She walked over and pet one of the cameramen on the shoulder. "Great job, Danny."

Margie stopped in the doorway as her stomach began doing flip-flops. She could have been mistaken, but from the sounds of it, Fatima was hollering "cut," which meant someone's camera had still been rolling the entire time she was throwing her hissy fit. She turned on her heels.

Margie looked to see Fatima high-fiving one of the cameramen, presumable Danny. That's when Margie realized that when she'd yelled "cut," ole Danny boy hadn't stopped filming.

"What do you mean, 'we got it'?" Margie asked, swallowing hard. "You, you weren't recording that, were you?"

"It's a reality show, Pastor Margie," Fatima said in the same respectful tone she'd been showing Margie up until five minutes ago. "We record everything. That's what we do." She walked over to Margie. "But don't worry, it was great footage. And about all that sassin' I did." She shrugged her shoulders. "Sorry about all that. It was for the cameras. You have to know that I wholeheartedly respect you. I'd never try to make fun of who you are and your love for God, but this is television, so I had to get you to push the envelope a little bit, you know what I mean?"

"Actually, I don't," Margie said. "And I can't allow you to use that footage."

Fatima paused. She gathered her words before she spoke again. "Pastor Margie, I'm a PK, a preacher's kid. I understand how it goes. My dad was the head minister of a church for twenty-seven years before he retired. Everything he did he felt had to be for the Lord. And I get wanting to glorify God in everything you do, but in order to minister to people, everything doesn't have to have a religious tag or genre attached to it. Isn't that what being a vessel of God is all about? Figuring out how to reach those outside the four walls? Figuring out how to reach those who are unreachable, meaning those who don't go to church come Sunday morning?"

Margie heard what Fatima was saying, but that still didn't mean she was okay with being portrayed any other way than how her congregation had seen her for years. "I was totally unaware that the cameras were still rolling. I was unknowingly being recorded, so I'm forbidding you to use that footage."

"I really don't understand what the big deal is." Fatima shrugged her shoulders while simultaneously opening her hands flat. "So you got a little hyped, it's not like you cussed anybody out. So there was a little tension between us. So what? The viewers are going to love that."

"What kind of viewer wants to see a pastor arguing with someone?" Margie begged to differ. "I might be here for more than one reason, but my number one reason is to honor God. And to, I don't know, maybe somehow save a few souls while I'm at it. Or maybe in all honesty, I don't know why I'm here at all." Margie was becoming exasperated. Usually, at the end of the day, everything she thought she was doing for God seemed worth it. She wasn't convinced He'd feel the same about this one.

Fatima allowed Margie to get everything off her chest, then once she saw that she was done, in a calm, understanding voice, she spoke. "Pastor Margie, you asked what kind of viewer wants to see a pastor arguing with someone. The kind of viewer who wants to see that a pastor is simply human. That viewer who needs to see that a pastor is not some flawless, blemish-free, sinless saint walking the face of the earth, but is merely just a vessel used by God. A vessel who can pop off and stand their ground when and if need be. Someone who can stand up and whoop the devil's butt."

Fatima continued. "Do you know how many folks I've heard over the years say that they stopped going to church because the pastor did this or because the pastor said that? The pastor gambled, the pastor drank, cheated, fornicated, committed adultery, or even molested a child! And you know what I have to say to that? Good, let that pastor go to hell then. That's between that pastor and God, but because I read the Bible and know that Paul was a murderer and one of the biggest sinners in the book, yet God still used Him to speak to His people, that God can, will, has done, and will continue to use those same kinds of people in the current days.

"I have great respect for you, Pastor Margie, and that's because I thought you were different. I thought you'd be the perfect person to, in spite of all the trash that's on television now—especially when it comes to reality television—show the world who God is *and* who you are. What does it look like when you're in the flesh and not under the direction of the Holy Spirit? What are the consequences? Some pastors are always so quick to tell folks the consequences of their actions when their actions don't line up with the Word of God . . . Well, how about showing them?"

Margie stood there listening because the words Fatima were speaking, as harsh as they seemed to be, were the gospel truth. Maybe seeing someone not trying to be so holy that they were no earthly good is exactly what people needed.

"I still do respect you, Pastor Margie," Fatima said, "but not if you're standing here trying to tell me that you only want the world to see what you look like in obedience and not out of it. Because you're not perfect. And if half the people out there in this world would stop people-worshipping and stop looking for the actions of pastors for their salvation instead of the one who hung, bled, and died for them, then maybe we can get some of them who are not in the church into the church, and those who have strayed from the church back in the church. Not to mention the ones on the verge of leaving the church." By now, Fatima had tears in her eyes and her chest was rising. Clearly, she had a hidden agenda, but maybe it wasn't quite exactly what Margie had thought it was.

Yes, Margie was probably right in thinking that Fatima was trying to get her to get out of character, snap, and blow up. But her reasons weren't to make a fool out of Margie . . . or God . . . but to show the real side of her, the human side. That none of us, twenty-four hours a day, do what Jesus would do.

Margie had heard many a people say at one point or another how ignorant, ratchet, or ghetto some of the cast members on the reality shows are because of the way they pop off if pushed to a certain limit. Well, everyone was capable and had it in them to act in such a manner. It was just a matter of how much self-control they had.

Now that Fatima had finished reading Margie the riot act, Margie gathered her composure, and then spoke. "Respect is a priceless jewel. The last thing I want to do is to make you lose respect for me," she said. She cleared her throat, and then continued speaking. "Although I don't appreciate the method you used to try to get your message across to the viewers, I can see how passionate you are about your mission. I want to work with you, Fatima. I'm going to be as real as possible, but being backed into a corner is not playing fair."

"I agree, and I apologize," Fatima said.

"And I apologize for trying to do your job. Hollering *cut,* telling you what footage to use or not use . . . You're right. This thing is going to be what it's going to be. I just have to trust God that the right message gets to the right people. And so do you, missy." Margie gave Fatima a playfully stern look.

"And I promise that I will trust God to order the steps of this program from this point on," Fatima said. "No more interfering and trying to get you or any of these men to act a certain way." She waved her hand toward the ten men standing off to the side. Some were sipping on the champagne that had been provided to them. Some were even eating from the fruit and cheese tray. Guess that was their version of eating popcorn during the main event. Margie and Fatima had provided quite the entertainment.

"Deal," Margie said.

Fatima extended her hand out to shake Margie's.

"Young lady, please," Margie said, and pulled Fatima in for a hug.

"Whew, this was one rough first day of taping," Fatima said as she and Margie pulled apart from the hug.

"I'll say," Margie said and chuckled.

"We're going to call it a wrap," Fatima said to all in the room. She looked at Danny. "Did you happen to get any of . . ." She pointed from herself to Margie a couple of times.

Danny shook his head. "You yelled *cut,* so I cut."

It was clear there was only one person Danny took his orders from. It was also clear that Margie was forgetting who she took her orders from. Surely God was just as upset as Fatima had been when Margie stepped on toes. Hopefully, God had some pretty big feet, because this was just the beginning of Margie losing focus. Hopefully, God's feet were pretty tough too, because she was about to stomp all over them.

Chapter 11

Doreen raced inside Margie's room to find her in bed with the covers pulled up to her neck and her head buried in a pillow. Doreen couldn't even see her face.

"What's going on?" Doreen made her way to Margie's bedside. "When you called it sounded as if you were . . ." Doreen's words trailed off as Margie removed the pillow from her face and turned to look at Doreen, "crying." Doreen frowned at the sight before her. Margie's makeup was smeared all over her face and the pillow. "My God, what happened? Did all the men end up turning out to be that bad?"

"No." Margie shook her head and sniffed. "It was me who turned out to be that bad."

"Oh, Lord. Let me go put on some tea." Doreen turned to exit the bedroom.

"No, no, thank you. I don't want any tea. I need an ear. Can you just come sit and talk?" She pulled the covers down as she sat up and scooted over to make space for Doreen.

Doreen eyeballed Margie up and down. "I *know* you are not lying up in this bed fully dressed."

"Didn't have the strength to change my clothes," Margie informed her, sniffing.

"Umpf, umpf, umph." Doreen sat. She took a deep breath, and then looked at Margie.

"It was just awful." Margie burst out crying, grabbed Doreen's arm, and rested her head on her shoulder.

Doreen looked at Margie peculiar. Never had she seen her former pastor so vulnerable and emotional. Usually, Margie was the one trying to get someone else to pull it together. But now, here she sat on the flip side of the coin. Doreen didn't know what to say, so she said nothing. Hopefully, the Holy Spirit would kick in any minute now and begin to direct her path.

Margie cried and sniffled for a few moments before, all of a sudden, she stopped and looked up at Doreen. "Well, aren't you going to say something? Anything?" Margie sounded upset.

"I, I honestly don't know what to say. I've never seen you like this before. Usually you're—"

"The strong woman of God standing before all to pray for all, to minister to all, to lay hands on all, to be an example of what a virtuous woman looks like to all. I know, I know!" Margie slammed her hands down on the bed.

"Well, yeah, I guess that's just about what I was going to say."

Margie sighed. "Well, for once, before I leave this earth to go be with the Lord, for one lousy time, can I just be a woman? Not a woman of God. Not a woman of the cloth, but just a woman? One with feelings, one who makes mistakes, and one who sometimes falls short of God's glory? Please?" Margie's shoulders began to heave up and down with stifled sobs.

Doreen put her arm around her friend and just let her get it all out. Clearly, plenty of tears had been stored up in Margie, and now the dam had broken. Doreen was glad that she'd been there to make sure Margie could release and not drown in it all, even if it meant Doreen had to get a little wet . . . literally.

Margie had to have cried for five straight minutes. Doreen just sat there grateful that she'd been present for the release. It felt like it was just the two of them alone in the room. The crew was right; before they knew it, they wouldn't pay those cameras any attention. It would almost be like they weren't even there. But they were there.

When Margie's tears finally subsided, she lifted her head. This allowed Doreen the freedom of movement to grab a tissue from off the nightstand. She handed it to Margie.

"Thank you," Margie said, taking the tissue and blowing her nose with it.

"Now do you want to tell me what happened?"

Margie pulled herself together while she relayed the evening's events to Doreen.

"Wow, I guess the night was full of surprises for everybody, huh?" Doreen said. "Just goes to show that we can plan all we want. We can have a schedule or an agenda laid out to the tee, but God's plan is the only one that will ultimately prevail."

"You'd think me of all people would know that," Margie said. "How did I get caught up in this mess?" By the time Margie had gotten back to her apartment, the devil had already been in her ear telling her that no matter how righteous she and Fatima may have been in their logic behind "keepin' it real" on the set, her congregation—viewers everywhere—would raise an eyebrow at her behavior.

The devil whispered things to her like, "You were a grown woman acting like a big baby throwing a tantrum. You're a pastor; you're supposed to have more self-control than that."

But what especially got underneath Margie's skin was when the devil said, "You can't even handle the tricks of a reality-show producer, so what will make people think you can handle the tricks of the enemy?" Then when the devil spewed out a wicked laugh into her eardrums, she spewed out tears.

And now, once again, even more tears spilled from her eyes. "Maybe it was my own voice I was hearing, pushing me to do this and not that of God's."

"Oh no, you won't sit here and get to sounding like the serpent in the Garden of Eden." Doreen was defensive. "Don't you question the voice of God." She wagged her index finger in Margie's face. "So you jumped bad with the show's producer. Sometimes folks need to get told off. But from the sounds of it, she told you off right back."

Margie nodded in the affirmative. Fatima had told her a thing or two about herself. "But people might expect that from Fatima and not even care," Margie said. "But I'm the pastor of New Day Temple of Faith. Do you know what the congregation is going to think of me if they ever see that footage?" she asked. "The person always preaching about turning the other cheek?"

"They're going to think the one thing about you that they haven't been quite sure of in some years now," Doreen said.

Margie twitched her nose up in confusion.

"That you are human," Doreen clarified.

Margie rolled her eyes. "Oh, there you go sounding like Fatima." She paused. "Wait, is this part of a script? Are you playing along with Fati—"

"I'm gon' cut you off right there. You know darn well I don't live life scripted or planned. Heck, I enjoy life's surprises. Besides that, do you really think I'd ever set you up for the okeydoke? That's just craziness now." Doreen sucked her teeth.

"I'm sorry," Margie said. "I can't believe I just almost doubted you. Even though it was only for one hot second, I was wrong."

"As wrong as the day is long," Doreen said, not about to let Margie off the hook and tell her it was okay. It wasn't okay that Doreen was giving up six weeks of her life for Margie and here Margie thought she was going behind her back with the producers.

"It's just that for years, as a pastor, I haven't had many friends. You know that. Outside of you and Sister Naomi, there really aren't too many people I call friend. It's just hard to trust people," Margie said, "church folks included."

Now the show even had her doubting the honestly and loyalty of her best friend. That was something Margie had never done. So this was definitely a trick of the enemy, Margie surmised. Perhaps because God wanted her on this show, the devil was going to come against her with all he had, even if it meant coming between her friendship with Doreen. Things were going from bad to worse, it seemed. Just when Margie got past one moment of uncertainty, here came a boatload more. She was drowning in it all. Had she felt like she was drowning in problems before? Yes, but usually they weren't her own, so she could dog-paddle back to shore if she'd wanted. But now that she was in her own pool of doubts, she was finding it real hard to keep her head above water.

"Just know this," Doreen said, "I may fail you someday, Naomi may fail you someday, but you can always trust God. He is a God who cannot and will not fail."

"Amen! Hallelujah!" Margie shouted out, raising her right hand. "You just preached right there."

"Good, now pass the collection plate and let me head on back over to my apartment." Doreen stood up.

"So you think I overreacted?" Margie asked Doreen.

Doreen stopped and thought for a second. "Nah. Push my buttons and wind me up long enough, and Jack's gonna pop out of my box too."

Margie chuckled.

Doreen laughed, and then said, "But seriously, you signed up for this. You signed up for ministry. A lot comes with the territory. You know what we say. It's easier to be a Christian and all saved when you're up in the church, then it is in your home. And it's even harder than that in the world. But you just have to remember one thing, woman of God." She looked at Margie knowingly for her to finish the sentence for her.

"I may be in this world, but I am not of it."

"Amen, God bless you and good night." Doreen headed back for the door, throwing Margie a good-bye wave over her shoulder.

Margie nodded her head and smiled. She didn't know what she would've done without Doreen being there. Probably pack her bags, void her contract with the production company, and pay back any expenses she might have incurred thus far. But God had her there for a reason, she'd have to keep telling herself that. But even if she forgot to, at least good ole Doreen would be there to do it.

Margie climbed out of bed and went to shower and get her bedclothes on. When she returned to the bed, both her mind and her body felt fresh and renewed. But knowing she had to get up in the morning and face the cast and crew, in the back of her mind existed the fact that this feeling would not be long lived. Something in her spirt told her that things were only going to get more challenging.

"Well, Pastor Margie," she said to herself as she reached to turn the lamp off, "I just hope you are up to the challenge." She cut off the light, then lay down, thinking she might have signed up for something her flesh possibly couldn't see through. But it went without question that her spirit man was ready for battle.

***

"How darling," Anya said to Margie when she arrived at her apartment to escort her to the area they would be filming first today.

"Thank you," Margie said with a frown.

"What's a matter, you don't like it?" Anya circled Margie. "I think your little tennis outfit is cute."

"You just said the key word right there," Margie said. "Little." She looked down at the short, white skirt.

"What? That's what tennis skirts are supposed to look like." Anya looked Margie up and down, and then whistled. "You're putting Serena to shame."

"Oh stop it." Margie shooed her hand as her cheeks turned red.

"If I had those legs . . ." Anya let her words trail off as she shook her head.

"That's the thing," Margie said. "I haven't shown my legs since I can remember. I'm always in my robe at church, and underneath that is usually a pant suit. And if it is a skirt suit, then it's practically down to my ankles. No way would I ever show this much flesh."

"But this afternoon's taping is on the tennis court," Anya reasoned. "What would people expect you to wear for a game of tennis? Besides, you're wearing more than Serena Williams wears, and she *does* play tennis!"

Margie thought back to that December 2015 cover of *Sports Illustrated* that had the well celebrated tennis star on it. From a distance, and at first glance of the magazine while standing in the grocery store line, Margie had thought an adult men's magazine had accidentally been placed on the rack. She'd mistaken the athlete for a stripper instead of an athlete. But even if Margie had a body half as good looking as Serena's, she'd still feel uncomfortable in what she was now wearing.

Still frowning, Margie checked herself out from front to back. "I don't know. Don't they have tennis shorts to go with these tennis shoes?" She stuck her foot out. She was wearing all-white Keds with some ankle Nike socks.

"We don't happen to have any tennis shorts in wardrobe," Anya informed her. "But if you want us to wait a minute while you go change into your pastor's robe, that won't be a problem." Anya kept the same straight face she always had. She wasn't being sarcastic, just being herself. But as far as Margie was starting to notice, Anya's self could stand to loosen up some.

"I'm gonna pray for you and your fresh mouth, young lady," Margie said, letting out a little snort. "You know darn well I'm not going to go play tennis in no dang robe."

"Well, you can't say that I didn't ask," Anya replied. "Anyway, are you about ready?"

Margie sighed. "As ready as I can be I suppose."

"Look at it this way, just be lucky we're not shooting on the beach or something, then wardrobe would have definitely put you in a bikini."

"Over my dead, wrinkled, white body," Margie said and busted out laughing.

Anya simply stood there and waited for Margie to stop laughing at her own joke.

"Oh, come on here and let's go," Margie said, realizing she was not going to get a laugh out of the young woman. Margie headed out the door. "Got me in here acting simple." She looked around outside. "And thank God Danny and his camera weren't around to capture it this time."

Anya let out a harrumph and pulled the door closed behind them as she and Margie got in the waiting golf cart.

Anya prepped Margie on what was about to go down as they drove through the grounds. Margie tried to stay focused and pay attention to what she was telling her, but she was too busy pulling her skirt down. It wasn't like anyone besides Anya could see her in it. She simply was not used to wearing short skirts, especially one that short.

"You're gonna be fine," Anya told Margie as they got out of the cart, only for Anya to see Margie just a tugging at her skirt. "If you keep pulling that thing down, something more private than your legs are going to get shown."

Margie gasped and covered her mouth with her hand.

"I'm serious," Anya said. "Now head over to the court like the attractive, confident woman you are. The skirt is just fine and totally acceptable for the sport you are about to engage in. And on top of that, you have the built-in Spanx just in case you bend over to hit the ball and the camera catches a nice shot of your derrière."

Once again, Margie was horrified. "Was that your pep talk to make me feel better? That's it. I'm going back to change." Margie stormed back to the golf cart.

"Oh, Pastor Margie, I was just joking with you. Couldn't you tell?" Anya stood there with a stoic face as always.

"No, not really," she said.

"Well, I was," Anya confirmed, then said under her breath, "Jeez, don't you Christians have a sense of humor?"

The nerve, Margie thought to herself.

"Should I expect there to be no laughter in heaven?" Anya asked.

Margie opened her mouth as if offended, but then thought about what Anya had said. Maybe she was being way too serious about this whole tennis skirt situation. She also recalled Fatima's mission in all this. It wasn't about Margie only being a woman of God, but a woman. Period. With that thought, Margie wanted to reflect that women should absolutely treat their bodies as temples, that not just any Tom, Dick, or Harry could get a day pass to take a tour of. Some things needed to be kept secret and sacred. But maybe Margie was going just a little overboard with the whole legs thing. If showing a little leg in a tennis skirt where she was clearly on a tennis court gave some folks the impression that she was a jezebel, then the devil was a liar.

"You're right," Margie told Anya, once again heading back toward the tennis court. She walked with authority and power. She was woman; hear her roar . . . in a tennis skirt.

Anya continued prepping Margie until they were halfway to the court. Cameras were rolling by then, and Margie was on her own.

She walked up to see all nine remaining men dressed in their tennis wear as well.

"And here is the lady of the house right now," Lincoln said, smiling and welcoming Margie to the set with open arms. He kissed her on each cheek, then gave her the once-over. "Don't you look just lovely?"

Clearly he'd gotten over his and Margie's little tiff from last evening. He was acting as if she was his best friend. Sure, he was probably doing it for the cameras, but one thing Margie agreed she wouldn't do for the cameras was be fake. So if she was going to proceed with things properly, she had to clear the air between her and Lincoln and not just sweep it under the rug for the time being.

"Thank you for the compliment, Lincoln," Margie said. "But before we move on, I'd just like to apologize for my snappy behavior last night."

"It's water under the bridge." He swished his hand over his shoulder. "I get it. This is not my first time at the rodeo." That comment reminded Margie that she had seen Lincoln host another reality show. "Having cameras in your face twenty-four seven can make anyone testy. You're only human, right?" He leaned in jokingly to Margie. "Unless God gave you some extra superhuman powers just because of those hot legs of yours."

The men agreed with variations of chatter and head nods.

"Thank you." Margie blushed. "But, no, no super-human powers here. Just the power to say that I'm wrong and hopefully you have the power to forgive me, because that can sometimes take a whole lot of power, if you know what I mean."

"I do, Pastor Margie," Lincoln said. "I both know what you mean, *and* I forgive you. No harm, no foul. Like I said," he shrugged his shoulders, "you're human, and so am I. So are all these men here." He ran his hand past the men.

"Amen," Margie said, then turned her attention to the men. "And, gentlemen, I hope you will forgive me for making your first night at the mansion an unexpected eventful one. But seeing that," Margie stopped and counted to herself while pointing at the men, "all nine of you are still here," she laughed, "I guess I didn't run any of you off with my less-than-acceptable behavior."

"I'm not going anywhere."

Of course, Clayton would be the one to speak up.

"Well, since we've taken a head count and everyone is here," Lincoln said, "why don't we pair up for a game of doubles?"

Lincoln picked up four rackets that were lying on the ground and began handing four of the men rackets.

"Let me forewarn everyone," Margie said, "I do not play tennis, so I hope no one expects me to hit a grand slam."

Several of the men chuckled while Lincoln tried to contain his laughter.

"Pastor Margie, a grand slam is something that deals with baseball," Lincoln told her.

"Oh." Margie looked confused.

"I think you might be referring to The Grand Slam tournaments," Lincoln told her. "It's the four most important annual tennis tournaments, also called majors."

"Oh, well, maybe that's where I heard it from," Margie said. "See? Told you I knew nothing about this game."

"Then that's just fine," Lincoln told her, "because it's actually the men who are going to sweat it out in a game of doubles. And while the four men are on the court, you and the other five men will be observing, cheering them on, and maybe chatting it up a little."

"Oh, okay." Margie was a tad bit disappointed. Here she'd agreed to wear that stupid short tennis skirt, and she wasn't even going to be playing tennis. How would she now justify wearing that little piece of material? Oh well.

"So it looks like Cleveland, Richard, José, and Rayshawn are going up first," Lincoln said, looking to the four men holding rackets.

Margie was glad Richard was one of the first men to go. He had a tendency to douse himself in just a little too much cologne. Perhaps he'd wear off some of it in a game of tennis.

"So that means the remaining five men, as well as you, Pastor Margie," Lincoln continued, "can get comfortable right over in that shady spot over there." Lincoln pointed to an area that had an oversized tent set up. There were about a dozen chairs. There was also a table set up with lemonade and other refreshments dressing the table.

"Oh, wow," Margie said, admiring the setup. "I wasn't expecting that."

"Well, I'm glad this little twist is to your liking." Lincoln raised an eyebrow.

"Well, I was willing and ready to get out there on the court," Margie said, "but I'm not going to complain about not having to." She laughed.

"I figured as much," Lincoln said. He then went on to run down how things would work. "We'll be keeping score, and the first pair that loses will be eliminated.

Then another four men will play. The losers from that match will be eliminated as well. The last two men left will play the winners of the first match. Those winners will then go against the other two remaining men. With Franklin having gone home, we have an odd number, so one of the losers from the first match will stand in for another match to make the teams even. The last two men standing will then enjoy a relaxing evening with the lady of the house." He looked among the men and Margie. "Everybody got that?"

Some of the men nodded while others verbalized their understanding.

"Not quite," Margie said, "but since my only role is to sit in the shade and drink lemonade, I guess it doesn't matter." She laughed.

"Well, that's all you have to do . . . for now anyway." Lincoln shot her a knowing look.

"Oh, Lord. Here we go again," Margie sighed.

"So, gentlemen, you may all take your places," Lincoln said.

The four men set to play against each other first headed toward the courts while the other five men and Margie headed for the tent.

"Please allow me to do the honors," Kent said, extending his elbow for Margie to grab hold of. He too had been one of the men flying under the radar.

Kent had seemed really interesting to Margie. When she first met him he informed her that he'd been a high school teacher in the Chicago Public School system for the past twenty-five years. Chicago had been in the news quite a bit lately for the number of killings that had been taking place there. Margie was eager to hear more from Kent about how he dealt with that and his take on things.

"Absolutely," Margie said to him, looping her arm through his.

With Kent having escorted Margie to the tent, he was guaranteed a seat next to her as he walked her to a chair, and then simultaneously sat beside her. He wasn't about to give any of the other men a chance to slip in and get close to her.

"Thank you, Kent," Margie said.

"Anything for the lady," he replied.

"Can I get you something to drink?" Brandon asked, figuring he'd get Margie's mind off Kent by catering to her.

"Probably in a few," Margie said. "Right now, I'm fine."

"I'll second that," Alexander said, who was probably the most flirtatious man in the bunch. Margie noticed that when he was flirting was usually when he was less nervous. She could tell because he didn't stumble on his words as much. Margie took that as a sign that he had no trouble spitting it right out when he saw something he liked. He didn't do the Hokey Pokey around it at all.

Margie had chuckled thinking about if she did end up with Alexander, she'd at least know when he was lying if she asked him if she looked good in an outfit. Kent didn't know it, but his stuttering to her was like Pinocchio's nose growing when he lied. It would be quite beneficial in a relationship based on truth and honesty if you asked her.

She giggled. With no mirror in front of her right now, she was completely oblivious to the fact that she was a woman in her early sixties. She felt like a schoolgirl, not being courted by just the captain of the football team, but the whole darn football team. Margie was fortunate enough to still pretty much wear the same size she'd worn in college. She'd kept in shape over the years, and with all the fasting she'd done for members of her congregation, the church, herself, and even strangers, she had no issue with eating excessively and gaining weight. As a matter of fact, being offered three round meals, plus anything she wanted in between for the next few weeks was exactly what she needed. She hoped to even walk away with a few extra pounds. She'd feel even healthier with a little more meat on her bones.

Margie cleared her throat. Whether or not she wanted to think about it, she was a sixty-some-thing-year-old woman. Figuring she looked pretty ridiculous sitting there in that little skirt like she was the cheerleader cheering the football team on, she gathered her composure and turned to have a more serious conversation with Kent. She knew she needed to hurry up and do it before one of the men tried to steal her away like Fred had done yesterday during the meet and greet.

"So, Kent, you said you teach high school back in Chicago," Margie confirmed.

"Yes, ma'am." He nodded. "I got offered early retire-ment to make room for some of the new jack teachers that are coming out of college. I passed, though. My kids need me."

"Is that the excuse you are using to keep from letting the job go?" Margie asked. "I have a couple of friends who took early retirement, only to find themselves going back to work part-time, going to work full-time at an entirely new job, or even going back to their old jobs full-time."

Kent held up the palm of his hand while shaking his head. "No, ma'am. I assure you I'm not making excuses. Those kids really do need me, and not just for education. I get who they are. I get who they aren't. I know who they are. I know who they aren't . . . because they are me. Those kids who walk through those schoolhouse doors used to be me. I lived and still live in their neighborhood, neighborhoods where over a holiday weekend over eighty murders can take place." Kent stressed his statement by holding up his index finger. "On one single weekend."

"Umpf, umpf, umph," a couple of the men said.

The men were so engaged with Kent's story, they didn't even bother to interrupt. Just like Margie, they wanted to hear more.

Margie stared straight at Kent, urging him with her eyes to continue.

"And you know what bothers me most?" he asked. He continued on without pausing for an answer. "So-called activists and conscientious people will charter buses to other states to go see about one dead black boy shot down in the streets so that they can rally and march. But they could come to the streets in Chicago every day to do it, and they don't. They get mad at Donald Trump and storm his rally, but won't use that same anger to form their own rally against all the violence in Chicago." He shook his head and let out a tsk.

"Wow," Margie said. "I never looked at it that way."

"If people don't see it on television, see it in a movie, or hear it in a song, it's like it doesn't exist," Kent said. "I mean, I love rap music because some of it really does tell the story of what's going on in the streets. But when the story gets drowned out by a bangin' beat, bling, and a catchy hook, the real story gets lost in the midst."

Margie wasn't a huge rap fan, so she couldn't wholly relate to what Kent was saying.

"I live and teach on the West Side of Chicago."

"Whoa wee," Rayshawn said. "That's the roughest part of Chicago. Had a brawl or two in that area back in the days I'd go out after a game with some of my teammates."

"It is," Kent agreed. "I have young men in my class who have spoken to me regarding their peers trying to get them to join a gang. Gang members harassing them, trying to make them part of the gang. I was able to give this information to their parents. In addition to praying that God build a supernatural barrier of protection around these children, their homes, and their families, I was able to work with the parents in staying aware and watching for signs that the kids might be caving in to the pressure. Some of the parents and I communicate. We find ways to keep the kids busy, even if it means me giving them a boatload of homework and projects. Even if it means the kids staying after school for tutoring and me taking them home, or me going to their home to tutor them. If gang members are waiting for them at their bus stop when they get off the bus, then I take them home or I communicate with the parents for family members to transport them. I'll even buy them a public transportation pass. Whatever it takes to save them."

"Wow. That's just . . . It goes beyond what one might think a teacher is supposed to do. It goes beyond teaching," Margie said.

"Yeah, but it's no different than what you do, right?" Kent said. "I can only imagine that some of the things you have to do for some members of your congregation goes beyond what one might think a preacher is supposed to do. It goes beyond preaching." He winked. "Your ministry is not confined to a church house, and mine isn't confined to a schoolhouse."

Margie smiled. "Amen to that," she said. She appreciated that Kent recognized that being a pastor went beyond a one-day workweek of Sundays, or a two-day workweek if Wednesday Bible study was included. At least if they did end up together, they'd both understand one another's calling without complaint.

"When I decided I wanted to become a teacher," Kent said, "it was because I had parents who didn't really drill the importance of education in me. I honestly couldn't remember coming in from school, my mom checking my book bag to see if I had homework, or even just asking me if I had homework. And if I did have homework, I definitely don't recall my mom sitting down at the table and doing it with me. I couldn't remember them going to parent-teacher conferences. I couldn't remember my mom or dad going to a PTA meeting to see what was going on in a classroom. To this day, I still don't understand how a parent can send their children somewhere for so many months out of the year, and yet, they themselves never step foot in the place."

"Ha!" Margie said. "Sounds like back in the day when the parents would send their kids to church every Sunday like clockwork, but would never step foot in God's house themselves."

"So you know what I'm saying?" Kent laughed.

"I guess I know a little something about it," Margie said, then ceased her laughter. "But not as much as you, of course. It's just hard to imagine parents wouldn't want to know the faces of the people who are partnering with them in their child's education."

"It's supposed to be a partnership, but some parents are still under the impression that teaching their child is all up to the teachers; after all," Kent said mockingly, "we get paid to do it." He used his fingers to put his last statement in quotation marks. "I don't have any children myself, but from what I've heard, aren't parents supposed to be a child's first teacher?"

"I don't have any children either," Margie said, "but I've heard the same thing." Another thing the two had in common, Margie thought. Kent was moving further and further up the ranks with her. Talking to him was so easy. The conversation wasn't forced, and he wasn't talking to be talking. He actually had something worthwhile to say. He was definitely at the top of the list now.

"So how do two people who don't have children know this, yet, I encounter so many parents who do not?"

"Well, I might beg to differ about you not having children," Margie said. "From the sounds of it, you have lots of children. I mean, look at how much time you dedicate to your students. You're not just concerning yourself with their education, but with their well-being altogether. You want them to make it. You're nurturing them. You're teaching them. In some cases, you *are* the parent."

"Now that you put it that way," Kent said, "I guess you might be right."

"You're being modest. Of course, I'm right," she said. "You're just so involved that you don't see it."

Kent thought for a moment while he stared off, taking in Margie's words. "Those kids truly are my life. I wake up every morning, excited to see them. Heck, sometimes I don't even go to sleep at night. I'm too busy doing lesson plans or planning how to save the next child. No, I haven't saved them all, but I don't stop trying. The one who makes it encourages me and gives me strength to stay in the game because there are many more to save. So early retirement? Ha! They're going to have to drag me out of that school kicking and screaming." He shook his head, looked up, and smiled. "I don't have any children, but yet, I'm a father to so many." Now he nodded with a look of pride on his face. He turned to Margie, that same huge smile still spread across his lips. "I probably would have never realized that had I not decided to be on this show."

"And here you thought you were doing this show for one reason and one reason only," she said. "Look at God."

"Yeah, look at Him," Kent said while staring at Margie with true admiration in his eyes. He took her hand into his. "Thank you, Margie. Thank you for helping me to see that. I may not have come here simply to end up being your husband, and maybe you won't choose me. But I already know in this very moment that I will not regret having come here."

Margie nodded and smiled. She was deeply moved by Kent's sincerity.

"And believe me when I say it was a very difficult decision to leave my kids to take part in this process, but I just kept feeling this pull, you know, this tugging of my spirit, that I needed to be here."

"Oh, you are preaching to the choir." Margie let out a small laugh and pet Kent's knee with her hand.

Some of the other men noticed what they called a little love tap. Several men had to hide their jealousy.

"Maybe God sent me here just for this very moment. For you to show me how much my life is starting to make sense."

"Come again?" Margie said. Kent had lost her at that point.

Kent shifted in his seat to get as comfortable as he could while facing Margie. "When we started this conversation, I mentioned how much those kids need me." He looked straight-ahead and smiled as if he'd just had a revelation. He then looked back at Margie. "But after talking to you, I realize that wasn't a completely true statement. I need those kids. It's my life that means something if they are in it, not the other way around. They may look back years from now and not even remember me and my efforts. As far as they are concerned, I might just be doing what a teacher is supposed to do. I may not add a single thing to some of those kids' lives I encounter. But that doesn't mean I won't stop trying. It gives me hope. It gives me joy, and that is what keeps my heart beating every single day. Wow." Kent shook his head in amazement.

"Wow is right," Margie agreed. "What a wonderful revelation, Kent."

Kent now took both of Margie's hands into his. "And I owe it all to you."

As Lincoln headed over to inform the next group of men that they were up on the court, most of them felt their efforts of breaking a sweat would be in vain. With Margie and Kent sitting there looking all sparkly eyed, as far as the other men were concerned, the game had already been won.

Chapter 12

"I got it! I got it!" Margie shouted as she pounded on Doreen's door. She was dang near out of breath and hunching over trying to catch the little bit of breath she still had left. She'd run all the way from her apartment to Doreen's, which was on the opposite side of the main house from Margie's. A golf cart was always available for Margie to call upon to be transported, but when the spirit had hit her, she didn't have time to wait on a golf cart. She'd jumped up from her knees where she'd been kneeling at her bed saying a bedtime prayer before climbing into it.

For Margie, prayer wasn't a one-sided thing where she did all the talking, closed out the prayer in Jesus' name, and then said, "Amen." No, for her, prayer was a conversation. She was mindful to always give pause and allow God to speak if He had something to say. In doing so, this time around, God did actually have something to say, and it just so happened to be the answer of the main question she'd had when going into this whole reality-show thing.

"Doreen, open up." With her bathrobe on and rollers in her head secured by a headscarf, Margie couldn't have cared less that a camera was hot on her trail. She was being filmed banging on Doreen's door like she'd stolen something and was running for cover to someone she knew would hide her from the PoPo.

"What in the world?" Doreen said, swinging the door open, and then stepping back in order to get out of Margie's way, who breezed right in.

"Why, yes, Margie, please come in at ten o'clock at night," Doreen said sarcastically. "I was just about to play a board game and maybe do a little yoga. The night is still young, after all." Doreen slammed the door closed once the outside cameraman had entered. There'd already been one set up inside her apartment in the living room. He'd actually been packing up to leave since Doreen had already gone to bed and was calling it a night. "Woman, why are you banging on my door like you're running from a bear?" Doreen looked behind her at the door, and then back at Margie, who was still huffing and puffing, trying to catch her breath. "Wait a minute. Is there a bear out there?"

"No, crazy," Margie said.

"Crazy? You calling *me* crazy, and *you're* the one standing there looking like a white Aunt Jemima. Tuh! Anyway, have a seat 'fore we have to hit this show with a lawsuit from you dying on the set. Let me go get you a glass of water." Doreen started walking toward the kitchen.

"No, I don't need water," Margie said, not gasping and carrying on as much as she had been at first, but still huffing and puffing no less.

Doreen threw her fists on her hips. "Then what can I get you? An oxygen mask and tank?"

Margie managed to laugh while catching her breath. She stood up straight and exhaled. "Whew wee."

"Are you okay now?"

"I'm better than okay," Margie said with a smile. "I get it. I got it, Doreen!" She walked over to her friend excitedly and threw her arms around her.

The happy energy Margie was feeling inside transferred into Doreen's spirit. She instantly started smiling and patting Margie on the back as she embraced her. "Well, praise God." She pulled out of the hug and looked at Margie. "Now, are you going to let me know what *it* is?"

Margie nodded, unable to speak. Not because she didn't have the breath, but because she was so overwhelmed with joy. Tears began to fall from her eyes.

"What is it?" Doreen said, seeing that Margie had gone from overly excited to now crying. "I got a decade on you, and if I ain't started having weird outbursts and crazy mood swings, you shouldn't either." Doreen tried to lighten the mood while Margie gained her composure. "You ain't got that disorder Danny Glover be talking about on that television commercial, do you?"

Margie shook her head, sniffed, wiped away her tears, and then spoke. "You know how I once said that the greatest Aha! moment a person can ever have is when their life begins to make sense?"

"Yes," Doreen said with a nod. "Umm-hmm."

"Well, my life makes sense now." Margie hugged Doreen tightly and began jumping up and down.

Doreen hugged Margie back, but was looking as confused as all get-out.

Margie pulled out of the hug and continued talking. "For so many years of pastoring, not trying to put myself on a pedestal, but I've always felt like so many people needed me."

"Well, so many people *do* need you," Doreen said.

"Yes, but not nearly as much as I need them," Margie said excitedly. "Isn't that wonderful?" she squealed in excitement.

"Woman, do you mind telling me what the heck is going on? And let's go sit down while you do it." Doreen headed over toward the couch. "I'm getting worn out just by looking at you move about like you've got ants in your pants."

Margie followed her over to the couch, and the two women sat.

"Today, the men and I played a little tennis," Margie proceeded to explain. "Well, they played tennis, and I watched." She thought momentarily. "You know what? I can't even say that I watched. While the men were playing, I mostly sat talking to the men who weren't playing. And in doing so, I had a conversation with one of the men named Kent."

"Just what did this Kent say that has you all wound up?"

Margie spent the next ten minutes or so relaying her and Kent's conversation to Doreen. By the time she was finished, she was still in just as much awe and simply emotional.

Margie sat stiff in her seat. She didn't even blink. She knew if she blinked the tears that had filled her eyes would go running down her face. She was on camera and felt she'd done enough crying on the camera for the night. Try as she might not to try to come off as something she wasn't but to just be herself, she was mindful that a preacher bawling in every scene might look weak. But having heard herself repeat Kent's words again and claiming them as her own had truly hit home.

"I do get it, honey," Doreen said, grabbing a Kleenex off the table and handing it to Margie.

Margie accepted the tissue and began to wipe her tears away. Doreen continued to speak.

"For all of your years of pastoring, I've witnessed in part you dedicating so much of yourself, so much of your time. I've watched you officiate weddings, perform christening ceremonies, officiate funerals, visit and pray for the sick and shut-ins. I've watched you provide counseling on so many levels. You've taken phone calls in

the middle of the night and prayed for folks. You've spent
hours at hospitals. You preach on Sundays and teach
on Wednesdays. Let's not even talk about what it takes
to prepare those preachings and teachings." Doreen
thought for a moment and nodded. "I can see how you
could make the comparison with what Kent does to what
you do."

"Yes, his ministry goes beyond the classroom the same
way as mine goes beyond the church. God confirmed that
after I prayed tonight," Margie said. "Everything we do
for the Lord is supposed to go beyond four walls. I mean,
I've always known that; it's just tonight it hit me like a
ton of bricks."

"Well, being on a reality show is definitely outside of
the four walls," Doreen agreed. "And the box."

Margie continued. "And it's all Kingdom work. And it's
not about me at all. Every single member of that congregation can go on with their lives regardless of whether
or not I play a role in it. But one thing is for certain and
two things are for sure, I can't go on with my life without
them, not if I'm to live a purpose-driven life. Nor would
I want to, and neither will I ever, at least not as long as I
have breath in my body. Without you, without New Day
members, and every other single person God places in my
path to minister to, would my life have purpose? Would
there be meaning to my life? Would it make sense?"

A happy tear slipped from her eye and passed over her
smiling lips. "My life is not mine any more than Jesus'
life was that of His own. We all are each other's heartbeat.
Kent helped me to see that. I was supposed to be here
today at that very moment to receive that very revelation;
he and I both. I know this because God confirmed such in
my spirit after I prayed tonight." Margie couldn't help it;
the tears began to fall from her eyes. "Oh, Doreen, my life
makes sense. Hallelujah!" She pumped both fists.

"Then to God be the glory," Doreen said. "So, tell me this. Since it was Kent who brought about this revelation, does that mean he's the one you're probably going to choose?"

"Oh no," Margie was quick to say, then made a face as if she smelled something bad. "I already had to send him home."

"*What?*" Doreen said, shocked to say the least.

"Well, as it turns out, I had to choose one of the men from the losing team to get a second opportunity at winning." When Margie realized by the expression on Doreen's face that she had no idea what she was talking about, she explained. "Today's challenge for the men, if you want to call it that, was to play each other in tennis; they played doubles. The last team of two men standing enjoyed a relaxing evening with the lady of the house." Margie pointed to herself with pride. "With Franklin having been sent home, there was an odd number. As it turns out, I had to choose one of the men from the first losing team to fill in to make things even."

"Kind of like giving one of the losers a second chance at winning."

"If you want to put it like that," Margie said, and then went to continue, but Doreen cut her off.

"Let me guess. Kent was one of the losers."

Margie nodded.

"And you gave him the second chance, and he came back and won it all. Ooooh, I love an underdog." Doreen wobbled a little and smiled. "Good for you, Kent."

Margie looked down and tucked her lips in. "Well, that's not necessarily how things played out."

"Wha, what do you mean? Kent didn't win at his second chance?"

Margie raised her head and looked at Doreen regretfully. "I, uhh, kind of didn't pick Kent to get a second chance." Margie took a breath, for this next thing she was going to have to admit was painful. "As it turns out, before I chose which man would get a second chance, Lincoln told me that the man I didn't choose would automatically be sent home."

Doreen's mouth opened wide, and she gasped. "You didn't! You did *not* send that man home after that big ole come-to-Jesus moment."

"I did," Margie nodded regretfully, but then suddenly decided that she was going to own her decision. So without wavering, she said, "Just sitting there listening to him talk that entire time killed me. The breath on that man is a killer. I mean, seriously, he should be charged with assault for hitting people with that breath of his."

Doreen hollered as she held her jiggling belly. "You did *not* kick that man off the show because of his breath. You do know all it could have taken was a Tic Tac or two."

"Or three or four or the whole darn pack," Margie said. "If my Boaz is supposed to come with bad breath, then I can do better all by myself."

Doreen started laughing harder.

"And everyone was so shocked I had picked Kent," Margie said. "I guess when they saw that Kent and I had shared such an emotional moment and formed somewhat of a bond, they figured he was a shoo-in, or would at least be one of the finalists."

"How did Kent react?"

Margie sighed, folded her hands across her lap, and looked upward with a smile on her face. "He was ever so gracious."

Doreen gave Margie a peculiar look. "Are you sure about having let him go?"

Margie looked down at her hands, thoughts of Kent still keeping a smile on her face. She nodded. "I'm positive. He wouldn't have lasted much longer. I had a feeling that he would have opted to leave sooner, rather than later, if I hadn't chosen for him to go. I was doing him a favor. He couldn't stand being away from his kids." In speaking with Kent, Margie had discerned how hard it was to be away from his students. She imagined they needed him just as much. Kent had his own assignments, so she "released" him in a sense.

"But I thought he was one of the two men that didn't have children."

"He doesn't, not biologically anyway," Margie clarified. "But I guess you could say he's more of a father to some of his students than they'll ever know. Those students, whether or not they know it and appreciate it, are that man's kids." She looked at Doreen. "Same way I feel about every last member of New Day." She rested her hand atop of Doreen's.

"Amen, because even though I'm older than you in the natural," Doreen said, "I can respect that you might have a couple of years on me in the spirit. I never looked at your years on earth. Just always felt I could come to you when I needed you."

Margie stood. "And, oh, how the tables have turned."

"Like you just realized." Doreen stood as well. "Guess you do need us just as much as we need you."

"More confirmation." Margie began walking to the door.

"Well, now that you had your big Aha! moment and know why God sent you here and all," Mother Doreen said, following behind Margie, "can we go home?"

Margie stopped in her tracks and turned around. "Do you want to give back that nice donation they made to our churches?"

Doreen looked up in thought, then looked at Margie. "Hope you got five more weeks' worth of clothes."

"Umm-hmmm, thought so," Margie said, then went and opened the door. "Hey, since we're both up and all the scheduled taping for the evening is done, do you want to do something spontaneous and go take a dip in the pool?"

Doreen thought for a moment. She actually wasn't sleepy anymore. "Why not? I need to break in my new swimsuit."

"Okay, well, let me go get changed into mine, and we'll meet over there in about, let's say, fifteen minutes?"

"Sounds good to me," Doreen said.

"All right." Margie went to walk out the door. "Thank you, Doreen."

Doreen looked a little puzzled. "For what?"

"For having that discernment for when I'm a pastor and when I'm a friend," Margie said. "It feels good to just be able to be Margie the friend and not Margie the pastor sometimes. Makes me feel . . ." Margie thought.

"Like a person," Doreen finished. "And it's sad when a leader in ministry gets to the point where they don't even see themselves as just a person, a regular ole human being who lives, loves, laughs, makes mistakes, and everything else regular folk do. And aren't you the one who once taught a sermon on having balance in one's life?"

Margie nodded. "Yeah, that would be me."

"Humph, then I guess somebody betta start practicing what they preach," Doreen winked.

"Like ReShonda Tate Billingsley's book says, 'Amen and Amen Again,'" Margie said before she headed back to her place, changed in her swimsuit, then met up with Doreen at the pool. They spent the next hour doing something neither one of them had done in some time and everybody at one time in their life needed to do, which was absolutely nothing.

Chapter 13

"So how are things going back in Malvonia?" Wallace asked Doreen through the phone receiver. "You having any fun down there on the set?"

"Tuh," Doreen spat. "For all I've been good for down here, they could have Skyped me in," she fussed.

"Still no television time?"

"Nope, but it's not even about TV time," Doreen said. "I just feel so useless." Doreen had honestly thought that during her trip to Malvonia she wouldn't have nearly as much downtime as she had. How things usually turned out was that God would send her somewhere on one assignment, and there would be other little pop-ups she'd have to tend to as well. That wasn't the case this go-round. Far from it, as a matter of fact. She had so much free time on her hands that it allowed her mind to go back to Kentucky. Not Kentucky where she could be in the arms of her man, but in Kentucky where she could have her hands around somebody's throat for pitching those evil notes into the offering basket.

"You are anything but useless," her husband said in an attempt to comfort her. He knew his wife well. If she didn't have her hands to the holy plow, then she felt she wasn't any good to God. If the good Lord wasn't using her, then it would put doubt in her mind that just maybe God had finally figured out that she wasn't usable. Then here would come ole Satan ready to slither through the cracks and pour water on the seeds of doubt, trying to get them to take root and grow through her being. Her past would begin to sprout itself in her conscience and have her to believe that she wasn't worthy of God using after all.

That's exactly why he had not shared with Doreen the situation with the notes. That would have been just one more, in her mind, piece of confirmation that maybe she wasn't fit to be first lady. What would it look like if he was married, yet the church he pastored didn't have a first lady? So maybe he'd had some selfish reasons of his own for keeping the information from Doreen. But none of that mattered now. The cat was out of the bag.

"And Margie seems to be figuring things out on her own," Doreen said. "I mean, God is bypassing me and going straight to her with all the answers. I don't even know why He bothered bringing me here. I'm just sitting around. And you know me, I like to be doing the work of the Lord."

Wallace laughed through the phone.

Doreen wasn't the least bit amused. "Honestly? You think this is funny?"

"Well, actually," Wallace said in between laughing, "I do." He laughed harder.

Doreen had never, until now, wanted to hang up the phone in her husband's ear. She thought back to her conversation with Margie on their way to the mansion. If one of her tasks there was to teach Margie how to be a wife, then that wouldn't be setting a very good example. So she bit her tongue, gritted her teeth together, and allowed her blood to come to a rising boil as she sat on the phone and waited for Wallace to finish laughing at her. It felt like forever, but finally his laughter subsided.

"Ahhh," he said, "I haven't had a good laugh like that in a long time."

"Well, good for you," Doreen said sarcastically. "And just to know that it was at my expense."

"Oh, sweetheart, you know it's all in fun. Stop being so serious. Since I've known you, you've been like one of those things folks take to the beach, hoping to find valuable metal."

"Now what in the world are you talking about?" she said. "And I hope to God you don't ever try to use such a parable when preaching."

"I'm talking about those one things," he said. "Those, uh, umm . . ." He snapped his fingers. "Those metal detectors."

"Oh," Doreen said, realizing what her husband was talking about. "But I still don't see how comparing me to a metal detecting stick makes any darn sense."

Wallace could tell by his wife's tone that she wasn't too thrilled about the comparison. "It's like the stick just floats across the land waiting to make that buzzing sound."

"Oh, so now I'm this annoying buzzing sound," Doreen said, even more offended than before. With her blood now boiling to an all-time high, like a pot on the stove about to blow its lid, she knew it was time to get off that phone. "Look, I better let you go before this conversation goes into a direction where we can't make a U-turn and bring it back to its starting place."

"Just hold up," Wallace said in his usual calming tone.

That's one thing Wallace genuinely was, and that was calm natured. No matter how much Doreen huffed and puffed about something, he would just let her do it until she was all huffed and puffed out. He had a knack for bringing people to his level instead of allowing them to take him to theirs. In his younger years, allowing someone to make him snap had been one of his character flaws. Although his short temper had never landed him in jail . . . that was only by the grace of God.

Back in the day he'd gotten most of his street credibility from being a hothead, leaving destruction all around him. He was that dude that if somebody stepped on his new shoes while out dancing and partying, he was going to tear that club up. As a matter of fact, he had, which got him banned from almost every nightclub in his town. And having that bad boy reputation not only caused other fellas to fear him, and some to befriend him so that they wouldn't be considered an enemy, it got him all the ladies as well.

With all the church girls whose virginity he was responsible for taking, it's no wonder he ended up spending his latter days in the church. But that's not what made Wallace turn from his wicked ways and go about living life the way of the Lord. It was actually when his younger brother, who had always looked up to him since the day their father left them for dead, decided he was going to be a respected thug just like his brother.

Unfortunately, the first time Wallace's younger brother tried to get in a guy's face at the club, he was shot point-blank in the dome. The day his little brother died was the day Wallace died as well. His flesh died. He died to his flesh and became new in the Lord thanks to the hospital chaplain who entered the hospital emergency waiting room to tell the family that his brother was no longer of the earth.

Wallace blacked out, his soul immediately taking responsibility for his little brother's death. He cried out how he should have shown him a better way, how he should have been a better example to his brother.

When that chaplain walked over, put his hand on Wallace's shoulder, and said, "It's not too late. You lost this brother so that you could save all the other ones out there on the street. This brother, like Jesus, had to be sacrificed so that you would awaken to your true calling in life. Like Jesus, your brother was born to die."

He'd looked to Wallace's mother who was weeping and distraught. "Ma'am, your son was born to die. There was absolutely nothing you or your other son here could have done to stop his fate." He looked back at Wallace. "And there is nothing you can do to stop yours." He placed his other hand on Wallace's shoulder, looked him dead in the eyes, and then asked, "Are you ready to walk in your calling?"

At that moment, a peace swept across the room. It came with a huge gust of wind that blew everything out the door, but yet Wallace stood unmovable. Unlike Dorothy in the *Wizard of Oz*, he didn't get swept up in the tornado funnel. He was in the eye of the storm, yet God had him covered and protected. Wallace stood in the eye looking all around him. He could see the bottles of alcohol spinning in the funnel. He could see the women, the unprotected sex, the fighting, the disrespect, the clubbing, and the partying. All of those things he'd been caught up in funneled and gushed out of the room. And after all that, he was still standing.

After such a divine experience, what else could Wallace have said to that chaplain except for, "Yes." He fell to his knees and began crying out, "Yes! Yes!"

The chaplain looked on knowing that Wallace wasn't saying yes to him, but that he was saying yes to God. And in that moment of time, Wallace had allowed God's will to be done in his life. He'd made it a point ever since to do God's will and to resemble his Heavenly Father; to be the example to other young men that he'd not been to his brother. God was giving him a chance to get it right this time, a revelation that might have never manifested had his brother not passed away.

So the same way Wallace had been able to stand strong, poised, and calm in the eye of the storm that day in the hospital, he'd been able to do such in any type of storm or turmoil man tried to put him in, including his wife. Although Doreen was a respectful woman with a beautiful spirit, she was still human and could get a little riled up sometimes. But what Wallace could honestly say was that no man or woman could pull him out of character. He was grounded in who he was and what God's Word said.

The scripture that always carried him through was Mark 4:39 from the NKJV. "Then He arose and rebuked the wind, and said to the sea, 'Peace, be still!' And the wind ceased and there was a great calm." The key word was *calm*. He was very mindful of how he responded when the storms of life were raging heavily. He refused to get overwhelmed by the vicious and rough waves. He knew that the same way Jesus spoke to the storm that day He and the disciples were on the boat, he had the power to speak to life's storms and calm them as well. But the same way Jesus showed no fear and was calm Himself, Wallace had to exhibit that same behavior. In doing so, he noticed that most of the time his behavior rubbed off on those he might have been in conflict with. And in this moment, he needed it to rub off on his wife as well.

"In no shape or form am I trying to say that you are annoying," Wallace said to Doreen. "The point I'm trying to make is that you don't always have to be scouring the earth seeing what sinner needs a rescuing. You don't always have to be on some mission from God. Have you ever thought that maybe God just wants you to be still? That maybe for once, God has put you in a secret place for a reason? This could be your vacation, a time for Him to be able to refill your virtue. A time for you not to pour out, but to be poured into. You may need this time of rest for God's ultimate assignment on your life."

Doreen was nodding the entire time. She had honestly never looked at things that way, and if by chance that was the case, she'd already wasted almost half her time worrying and trying to figure out whether she was missing something. She'd walked the grounds of the mansion, even struck up conversations with the gardeners, her spiritual antennas always up trying to sense if there was an assignment tucked away somewhere or in someone . . . anyone. She'd never thought for one moment she was just supposed to be getting some R&R. Heck, even God rested on the seventh day. Doreen couldn't recall resting *any* day.

"Honey, I believe you just might be right," Doreen admitted. "I feel like one of those people who retire, but then can't sit still, so they go back to work. Well, I'm going to sit still. God doesn't need me running ahead of Him. So I'm going to do exactly what you said," Doreen proclaimed. "I'm going to sit my tail on down somewhere, enjoy my surroundings, and wait on God."

Wallace chuckled. "Your words, not mine, but I agree."

Doreen laughed.

"She's laughing now," Wallace said, glad that the conversation had taken a 180 from where it had started.

"Thanks to you," Doreen said, smiling. "My husband, so full of wisdom. I'm one blessed woman."

"And I'm one blessed man," he said in return.

"Well, I guess I better get on off this phone. You're probably preparing a lesson or sermon or something."

"Actually, I was just about to kick back and listen to that one new rapper's latest CD."

"Oh, okay," Doreen said, not surprised to hear that her husband, the pastor, was about to listen to music that wasn't praise or worship, but instead, filled with cussing, explicit sexual innuendos, and more than likely using derogatory words to reference women.

"I'm not of the world, but I'm in it," Wallace said. "So I need to know what's going on in it. I need to be mindful of what these young people are subjected to. What they are doing, singing, rapping, and saying. And some of these older folks too." He even made it a point to watch the music awards and video shows as well. "I refuse to let Satan be ahead of me. I refuse to get in that pulpit and preach on how one is supposed to live in this world if I'm ignorant to today's times. I need to know this slang and code words these folks are using. I'm not going to be like those preachers who don't even know when folks are being disrespectful right up in the house of the Lord because they have no idea what's being referenced."

"Amen," Doreen said. "You know you don't have to explain it to me, of all people. I'll never forget years ago when those young musicians were visiting to play for their pastor who was a guest speaker at New Day. After service, while everyone was fellowshipping, they got to playing a song that went over most of the saints' heads." Doreen laughed just thinking about what happened next. "When one of the elders recognized the beat that was bumping through the sanctuary, she politely excused herself from the conversation she was in and went and shut that crap down, rebuked those musicians, and then prayed over the instruments."

Both Doreen and Wallace laughed.

"See, that's exactly what I'm talking about," Wallace said.

"All right then, well, you go ahead and listen to Kendrick, Kanye, or whoever," Doreen said. "I'm going to call and check on Deborah."

"Okay, then, honey. And remember what I said. Just relax, have fun, enjoy yourself. Don't sit around waiting for some spiritual mishap to occur so that you can put on your supersaint cape and go save the day." He chuckled, but he was beyond serious. He could only imagine how Doreen felt having to leave town the very next day after all that had gone down at the church. Just because she wasn't mentioning it didn't mean it hadn't been on her mind. He hadn't mentioned it either, but it had definitely been strong on his. Knowing mentioning would probably make things even worse for Doreen, he didn't bring it up . . . to her. But he had brought it up to God. As a matter of fact, he was waiting on an answer from God as to what to do, if anything, about the situation. Hiding the notes from Doreen was one thing when she was none the wiser, but now it was a different story.

"I won't, I won't," Doreen said in a dismissive voice. "I'll check in on you later."

"All right, babe. I love you."

"I love you too," Doreen said before she ended the call. She exhaled and just sat on the couch smiling. Her conversation with her husband had been so enlightening.

Before hanging up the phone, she wanted to call Deborah. She went to dial Deborah's number but stopped before she'd completely dialed it. She stared at the phone for a moment before terminating the call. Then she kicked off her shoes and lifted her legs onto the couch. She lay back and put her hands behind her head. She wouldn't call Deborah or anyone else. She wouldn't even go running to Margie's apartment after the day's taping to try to offer her two cents. Nope. She'd wait for someone to come to her if they needed her. It was going to be a struggle; that much she knew. But she needn't worry. The struggle would be over soon.

Chapter 14

There were just two weeks left of taping and five men still in the running. Of course, Franklin had been the first to go due to his inability to stand up for Margie. Kent was the second to go due to Margie not being able to handle his bad breath. All Rayshawn did was talk about his glory days on the football field, the past women and groupies in his life, and how he ended up bankrupt. He needed to be delivered from that past of his he was holding onto for dear life before he could begin a future. Heck, he could barely live in the present, so Margie sent him packing as well.

Although Brandon and Margie had in common the thing of them both being pastors, Margie sensed Brandon, if the two were to become a couple and ultimately even marry, had this idea that because he was the man of the relationship, that one of two things would happen. Well, actually, Margie didn't sense it. During some one-on-one time the two had shared, he'd actually said it.

"So, do you have a copastor lined up just in case you and I end up together?" he asked Margie.

Margie was confused, and it showed on her face.

"Well, with me being the man and all, I'd be the head. The head leads. So it would only be natural that you give up your position at your church and come over to mine."

His comment had immediately taken her back to the conversation she'd had with Doreen about not wanting to become a first lady. "But I've been called to preach," Margie said.

Seeing the sour expression on her face, Brandon continued by saying, "Oh, you would still preach." He thought for a moment. "I'm thinking maybe the third Sunday of every month. All your other time can be devoted to duties as first lady."

"I don't know, Brandon." She shook her head in thought. "I can't imagine leaving New Day Temple of Faith."

"Then I'd just come to New Day and take over as the senior pastor," he said with excitement—and much too quickly for Margie's liking. "I've always wanted to preach for a larger congregation." His eyes lit up as he proceeded to run down facts about New Day Temple of Faith that Margie couldn't even rattle off at the top of her head. He knew how many members attended . . . not just how many members but the ratio of men to women. Off the top of his head he knew how many ministries the church operated, as well as their average tithes and offerings. He'd definitely done his homework as far as Margie's church was concerned. It became quite evident that he was more interested in taking over the church than taking Margie's hand in marriage, so he was sent home as well.

José was ultimately sent home too. At the time of elimination, there wasn't really any particular reason, as it had been with the other four men, for Margie choosing to send José home. She had to simply ask herself out of the six men who had remained at the time, who had she connected with the least. That person had been José. Margie felt she'd made the right decision when, after eliminating the Dominican Republic native, he went on a rampage, pointing his finger and spittle flying out of his mouth as he spoke in his native tongue. Although Margie couldn't understand half of what he was saying, she knew it wasn't the sweet, gentle words he'd serenaded her with upon their initial meeting.

Security had to be called to escort him out. The producers didn't even allow him to pack his things, opting to eat the expense of shipping his belongings to him. They just wanted him off the set and out of that house. Margie thanked God she'd gotten him out of her life when she had.

Margie had a great connection with Clayton, Alexander, Richard, Fred, and Cleveland, the five men still standing. But in a matter of minutes, she would have to eliminate one more right before choosing which one she wanted to spend a special surprise evening with. The good thing about it was that now Doreen got the opportunity to give Margie her advice.

Doreen had just done some taping where she had lunch with the final five and got to interrogate them. She was then allowed to choose which man had to leave and which man got the special dinner with Margie.

As a result, the man Doreen picked to leave got to stay, and the man she'd picked to stay was forced to pack his things and go. Doreen was fit to be tied, and before she knew it, she'd found herself acting a fool on camera the same way Margie had her first night of taping when they were making her choose one of the gentlemen to leave.

"Cut from the same cloth, you two, I see," Lincoln had said in between Doreen giving the producers a piece of her mind about their trickery.

Upon hearing Lincoln's slick comment, Doreen had turned, faced him, and said, "Did you say cut?" in a half-threatening tone. "'Cause we can get to cutting up in here all right."

"You are a first lady," Margie had to go over and whisper in Doreen's ear to remind her.

"Don't nobody care nothing about—"

Doreen was in straight Madea mode when Margie cut her off by saying, "A first lady being filmed?"

Those words instantly registered in Doreen's head and resonated in her spirit. That was all it took to snap her back to reality. She couldn't even believe just how quickly she'd lost touch with it. It was crazy how, when put in this type of reality-show environment, one could so easily be taken out of character or conform to what society expected people to act like on reality shows. Yeah, the producers knew how to push buttons behind the scene and set folks up, but at the end of the day, Doreen had to take responsibility for her actions and behaviors.

"If it's in you, it's in you," Doreen had once said. "Sometimes, it don't take much to bring it out of you, but you best believe we all got it in us." She'd just proven her own statement to be true.

So just as much as Margie had needed Doreen there to be her voice of reason, Doreen found herself in a position where she needed Margie just as much.

That was all drama swept under the rug. Now Margie had to focus on her evening with Clayton, the man who Doreen had originally chosen to be kicked off, but thanks to the twist of the program, he was the one who would end up spending a special evening with Margie, and it was Cleveland and his wonderful sense of humor that was sent home.

As hair and makeup put the finishing touches on Margie, there was a wrap on the bathroom door.

"Come on in, Anya," Margie called out. By now she was used to Anya showing up a few minutes prior to taping to escort her wherever she needed to be.

"Hello, it's not Anya."

"Oh, hi, Fatima," Margie said when Fatima poked her head through the door first, then made her way inside. "I'm so used to Anya being my personal escort."

"Yes, I know. And she'll be right in," Fatima said. She walked over and stood by Margie. "I just wanted to stop in and chat for a second."

Margie raised an eyebrow.

Fatima chuckled. "Oh, don't worry. I'm not here to add any more twists for the day. Besides," she leaned down toward Margie's ear, cupping her hand around her mouth, "that Mother Doreen is scary." She pulled back. "She's a mother all right."

Margie tilted her head and gave Fatima a *don't-you-talk-about-my-friend* look.

Fatima raised her hands in defense. "I'm sorry, I know that's your girl and all, but . . ."

"Not just my girl; my *friend*," Margie said. "You know that person who you can call over at midnight or go banging on their door at midnight to share what's on your mind? And they actually let you in? Not pretend they aren't home by being quiet, even though you can see the light from the television through the crack of the curtains?"

Fatima watched as Margie went on and on as if speaking from personal experience.

Once Margie realized Fatima was staring at her like she was some kind of basket case, she snapped out of it. "Oh, I'm sorry. Went back to my midtwenties, when my so-called friend, Judy . . ." Margie realized she was about to go on and on again, so she shooed her hand. "Never mind. You don't want to hear an old lady like me go on and on about friends, present and past."

"Actually, I do," Fatima said, yearning to live vicariously through Margie. The look in Fatima's eyes didn't go undetected by Margie either.

"You got many friends?"

Fatima sighed, and then cast her eyes downward. "Nah, not really. I mean, I used to back in high school and college." A faint smile parted her lips as she reminisced back to those day. Then just as quickly as it had come, the smile disappeared. She straightened up when she realized she was about to slip into a vulnerable state. "But you know, now I'm just so busy. I don't have the time to have girlfriends and stuff like that."

"Well, what about family?" Margie asked. "Everybody has that favorite cousin."

Fatima shrugged. "Well, you know, I'm pretty busy. I've worked on quite a few shows with lots of celebrities, some of which are not so easy to please. They'll run you ragged meeting all their needs and requests. And let's not talk about their witch fits." She shook her head.

"Yeah, I Googled you. You've worked with some A-list celebrities. I saw where you've won a few awards and have had celebrations in your honor. That's awesome. We sometimes are so focused on those in front of the cameras that we forget about how talented and important those behind the cameras are."

Fatima nodded her agreement.

"I bet all your family and friends are so proud of you. And even though I'm sure they understand how busy you are with your career and all, you've got to take the time—correction—*make* the time—to let them know that you're still there for them."

Fatima let out a harrumph. Margie realized her mind went somewhere else. She paused to see if Fatima would speak on it.

When she didn't speak, Margie continued. "We have to remember that we need to be there to support the same people who were there to support us when we were—"

Whatever Fatima had been holding inside, she could no longer keep it at bay. "Support? Yeah, *right!* When I was attending my arts high school, everyone always wanted me to be on their production team when it was time to put on musicals, plays, concerts, or what have you. And then when I got that full ride to college based on a project I produced and submitted as part of my scholarship application, everyone was cheering me on and telling me how proud they were of me. Family members were calling one another up to brag about me. It was all a dream then. It was a fantasy. But once I graduated college and went to get into the business, boy, oh boy, did things change." Fatima shook her head with fury in her eyes.

Margie, being mindful to keep things calm, said, "How so?"

"I guess everyone thought I was supposed to graduate college and jump right into filmmaking, producing major projects, or whatever. But that wasn't the case. I had to work at a car dealership selling cars to keep a roof over my head while I begged and borrowed and ran my credit into the ground financing the equipment I needed to do the projects on my own." Fatima's eyes watered. "It was such a struggle. There were times I had to choose whether to buy groceries or give one of the subjects of my projects gas money." She hurriedly wiped a tear that had escaped her eye.

Margie signaled for the makeup artist, who was also engrossed in Fatima's story, to hand her a tissue. The makeup artist grabbed a tissue, and then handed it to Margie, who, in turn, passed it on to Fatima.

"Thank you," Fatima said, wiping her eyes. She sniffed, and then continued. "Trying to reach your dreams isn't always easy. It makes it even harder when it feels like you're the only one who believes in yourself. The same people who were once picking up the phone to brag on how successful I was were now picking up the phone to gossip about what a broke, loser of a bum I was. But I persevered."

"Yes, you did, sweetheart," Margie said, rubbing Fatima's arm to comfort her.

"When I put on an event to show the first project I'd done on my own outside of school, I was so excited." Fatima stared off as she went back to that moment in time. "'I'll show 'em now,' I said. I did it. I'm no bum. They'll all show up and be so proud of me, then things will be like they used to be. Everyone would be calling me up to see what I was up to, what I was working on." Fatima sniffed again. "When I walked onto the stage to introduce myself and thank everyone for coming, there weren't as many bodies out there as I would have liked there to be. I was a little disappointed at first, but then I pulled myself together and continued on with my grand speech.

"As I talked, I looked out into the crowd for some familiar faces. You know, those friends, family, and favorite cousins."

Margie gave off a compassionate smile.

"They were nowhere in sight," Fatima said. "My family is known to be notoriously late, so I kept looking toward the door, just knowing that any minute they'd be walking in the door. Well, by the time I finished speaking, they hadn't. I could hardly watch the premiere of my project I was so focused on that door. Even afterward, when people were coming to congratulate me, I kept my eyes on the door all while hugging them." She let out a chuckle. "Better late than never, huh? I didn't care if they showed up at the end of the night. Heck, I just wanted them to show up." She got quiet.

"I take it they never did?" Margie inquired.

"Ehh, maybe a couple. My mom, of course, but she had to hurry and rush back home to make sure she got my stepdad's dinner on the table," she said with a sigh. "Before I got picked up by a major network to produce and work on projects, I had many more events similar to that, and just like always, they ended up the same. I spent the night looking at the door over the heads of the ones who had shown up for the ones who said that they were going to but didn't." Fatima stood up straight and wiped her face clean. "But look at me now. One day, I'm going to win an Emmy, or even an Oscar, and when I get up on that stage and take the mic to accept my award, I'm going to thank all those naysayers, the ones who didn't show up and support me, and the ones who didn't believe in me."

Fatima had this big, gleaming smile on her face as she pretended to be holding a trophy.

Margie looked puzzled. "Why on God's green earth would you want to do that?"

Now it was Fatima who looked puzzled. "Do what? Win an Emmy or an Oscar? Every—"

Margie cut her off. "No, I meant why would you want to take the moment you dreamed about and dedicate it to the ones who weren't there for you? I don't understand."

"Because it's them not showing up for me, not believing in me that gave me the energy and motivation to want to press forward and succeed."

Margie looked disgusted. "How fair is that for all the people who *did* come out and show up? For the people who *did* believe in you?" Margie stood from her chair and went and took Fatima by the shoulders. "Hear me and hear me well. I'm sure when you had all those events it just broke your little heart when everyone who said they loved and supported you would never show up and actually do it. And then all that time you looked over the heads of the people who were there for the ones who weren't to walk through the door. How fair is that? How dare you give more energy to the ones who didn't come out than the ones who did. How dare you concern yourself with the ones who once bragged on the phone about how proud they were of you, but yet never put their bodies where their mouths were and showed up for you."

Margie took a breath and continued. "When you're on that stage accepting your awards and honors, you can't be concentrating on those who said they would show up but didn't. You have to be grateful and thankful for the ones God did bless you with to be in attendance. After all, isn't that what really matters?"

As the pastor of a church, Margie was always trying to get new members to attend. That message she'd just given Fatima, though, truly must have been for the messenger, because at that moment, Margie decided that she would try something different in ministry and focus on and get to know better the members that she already had. They deserved it.

"So when I do see you on one of those award shows accepting your award, which I know I'm going to one day . . ."

"I receive that," Fatima said with a smile.

"I absolutely do not want to hear you thanking all the naysayers, haters, and nonbelievers for giving you the energy and motivation to succeed. Don't even think twice about giving them that much power and credit for your success. Instead, choose to allow those who do believe in you, who do encourage you, and who do support you to give you the energy and motivation to succeed. Amen?" Margie said in a tone that was asking Fatima whether or not she agreed.

"Amen," Fatima said. She sniffed and began wiping her eyes. "Oh my goodness," she said, leaning to the side to look at herself in the mirror. "Thank goodness I'm behind the camera instead of in front of it. I look a mess. No man would want me to be the lady of their house."

Everyone in the room chuckled.

"Oh, darling, you are just fine," Margie assured her.

"Says the lady who is dressed to the nines and done up head to toe. Makeup flawless!" Fatima did a couple of finger snaps as she admired Margie.

"Yeah, but look how much work it took." Margie turned and looked at herself in the mirror. "Whatever man I do choose, I just hope he'll choose me after he sees the *real* me. The no-makeup-wearing me. The no fancy clothes, hair done up, nonfancy-jewelry-wearing me. The plain old me. The one whose blond hair was starting to gray before I got it dyed dark."

"Well, after all the verbal peeling away you just did, what's left?"

"My point exactly," Margie said, turning to face Fatima. "I hope you all prepared for a lawsuit for fraud." She frowned up and shifted to a deep voice. "Hey, that isn't the same lady from the reality show." Margie was pretending to talk in a man's voice.

Fatima couldn't help but holler out laughing. "Stop it. Keep in mind that I've seen you in big pink rollers, so I know it ain't that bad."

"Big, pink . . ." Margie thought for a moment, and then recalled what she looked like when she sent in her audition tape. "Oh my stars, you didn't show it to the men, did you?"

Fatima laughed at how all of a sudden Margie was so paranoid. "No, of course not. But keep in mind, we may not have a reality star sex tape to leak, but we always have that early-morning-no-makeup-pink-rollers-in-the-hair audition tape."

"You wouldn't," Margie said, lowering her head and raising an eyebrow at Fatima.

"If it means drawing attention to this show and me getting that Emmy or Oscar—try me."

Just then, Anya walked in. "We all set?"

"I don't know," Margie said with doubt. "Your boss here is trying to blackmail me."

"Well, speaking of a black male," Anya said, "Clayton is waiting in the car that's going to take you guys to your destination."

Both Margie and Fatima stared at Anya, looked at each other, and then back to Anya, all without saying a single word.

"What?" Anya asked, wondering why they were giving her such looks.

"Did she really just—" Fatima questioned Margie, "—say that?" Fatima shooed her hand. "Never mind, let's just go."

Fatima walked toward the door. Anya and Margie followed. A few minutes later, they arrived at the front of the main house where a limo was waiting with Clayton inside.

As soon as Clayton saw Margie walking toward the vehicle, he exited the car. "I'll take it from here," he told the limo driver once he got out of the car. He replaced the limo driver at the opened back passenger door while the driver made his way back into the driver's seat.

Just then, Margie arrived at the car. "Clayton, I didn't think it possible, but you look more handsome than ever."

Looking both comfortable and casual in his stiff khaki pants and crisp, white, long sleeved shirt, Clayton did a half bow. "Well, thank you. You look absolutely gorgeous yourself."

Margie felt amazing in her crimson-colored floral dress. It was ankle length and free flowing. The chiffon material was soft on her skin as the wind gently blew it. Her gold sandals shimmered under the last few moments of remaining sunlight in the sky.

Clayton assisted Margie into the car and closed the door behind her. He then walked around to the other side and got in the car. Within seconds, the limo pulled off.

"Would you like a glass?" Clayton asked Margie as he reached for the bottle of champagne that was chilling in an ice bucket.

"Haven't you noticed that every time someone asks me if I'd like an alcoholic drink that I always decline?" Margie said.

"Yeah, I've noticed," Clayton said. "But I feel it's still always better to offer someone something or invite them somewhere and allow them to decline."

"I see," Margie said. "Then allow me to decline, but thanks for the offer."

"You are so very welcome." Clayton proceeded to pour himself a glass.

Margie watched as he placed it to his lips.

Feeling that Margie was staring at him, he turned and said, "You don't mind if I do, do you?"

"Oh no. Not at all," she said, shaking her head.

Clayton took a sip from his glass. "I just wanted to make sure that my drinking wouldn't bother you."

"Absolutely not," Margie said. "Now, if we were talking about cigarettes, that would be a completely different thing."

"Oh really?" Clayton said knowingly, then took another sip of his champagne, leaving Margie to wonder just what it was that he knew. She didn't have to wonder for long. "Then I guess Richard hasn't smoked around you on any of your one-on-ones together, huh?" It was pretty difficult for Clayton to manage to hide the excitement he felt inside having dropped the bomb on his housemate.

"I, uhh . . . didn't know Richard was a smoker." She tilted her head in surprise, raised her eyebrows, let out a harrumph, and then went on as normal. To her recollection, she'd never smelled the residual of cigarette smoke in Richard's clothing. But then it came to mind that he was always pretty much soaked in cologne.

Seeing her brush it off so easily urged Clayton to keep the bombs a-droppin'. "Yeah, well, I'm sure there are a lot of things you probably don't know about all of the men," he said, dying inside for Margie to press him to elaborate.

"Oh really?" Margie said, allowing her curiosity to pique.

Clayton let out a snicker. "Oh *yeah*."

Margie thought for a minute. Clearly, Clayton knew some things about the remaining men in the house that she didn't. What she was torn about was whether she should pick Clayton for the information, or if she should allow the men to be the ones to reveal things about themselves. But then again, they'd been in the house long enough and around each other enough where they'd had plenty of time to share anything they wanted to with her . . . if they, in fact, wanted to.

Margie looked over at Clayton. He was sitting there sipping on his champagne with the corners of his mouth raised. She fought her urge for as long as she could before she began to pick.

"Well, at least Richard has the decency to not smoke around me," she said.

Clayton stayed silent.

"But I wonder why he didn't just tell me," she said under her breath. "I hope I haven't come across as someone who isn't approachable or is difficult to talk to."

"Oh no, not at all." Clayton was quick to comfort Margie and let her know that wasn't the case. "It's just that I'm a strong believer that some people only tell a person what they want them to know."

Margie chuckled. "Correct me if I'm wrong, but isn't that basically *hiding* something from a person?"

"You *could* say that." Clayton was back to his nonchalant acting self, hoping Margie would ask all the right questions.

"Makes me wonder if any of the other men are, you know, hiding something from me."

Clayton was quick to jump in right there. "Well, if you're asking me if I'm hiding something from you, the answer is no. Absolutely not. I've been one of the most up-front men here."

"I didn't mean to offend you or to make you think I was talking about you," Margie said. "I'm a pretty good judge of character, and I haven't sensed you've been lying or withholding anything from me."

"Good. I'm glad to hear that," he said, relieved. "But I can only speak for me." There was that knowing look again.

"Are you saying there are things about the other men that I might not know?" Margie was walking a thin line. She was bordering general inquiries and pulling information out of Clayton; using him, so to speak.

In ministry, she'd learned that she didn't have to fish around and pick people for information. She allowed them to tell her what they wanted to, and she'd then allow the Holy Spirit to direct her path from there. But there had to come a time when not everything was about ministry. For Margie, that time would be now. After all, it's not like she was trying to counsel or pray for anybody.

"Maybe," Clayton said. "I'm not sure what you've talked about with the other men. All I can vouch for is what the men have told me."

Margie carefully put together her words and spoke. "Well, have any of the men mentioned anything specifically that they have not shared with me? I mean, not because they were being malicious or deliberately trying to keep something from me. More so, maybe they just didn't know how to tell me something. Being a pastor can be pretty intimidating."

"I agree," Clayton said. "Not that I'm intimidated, but a few of the men did voice such concerns. That's the only reason I can think of why Richard didn't feel comfortable telling you that he smokes."

"I agree." Margie thought about her next question. "As far as you know, is there maybe something that, let's say Fred has told you about himself that maybe he doesn't feel comfortable sharing with me? I would just hate to make the mistake of picking someone who I can't talk to and who can't talk to me. Communication is key in any relationship. Wouldn't you agree?"

"Of course," Clayton said adamantly.

Margie bit her lip. "What's even worse is that I could possibly learn something after the fact—after I've already chosen the man I want to be with—about one of the men here that could have affected my decision making. I'd hate to live with such regrets."

Margie hit the right note with those last comments.

Clayton looked at her. "No, we wouldn't want that to happen. I want you to be happy with whomever you choose. No regrets." He let out a sigh as if he was now, all of a sudden, torn. He had information on the other men who currently had a chance at going home with the lady of the house. But what was there to be torn about? It wasn't like he'd voluntarily decided to sit down and share some of the conversations he'd had with the men with Margie. Margie had asked, so what kind of man would he be if he didn't tell her the truth? The whole truth. What if Margie did find out some things about the men that he'd known about all along? She might not trust him to tell her the truth anymore. That's not how he wanted to start their future together.

Margie watched Clayton ponder internally. "Are you sure there's not something you want to tell me?" She should have been ashamed that she was sounding like the serpent in the Garden of Eden when he was luring Eve to eat from the Tree of Knowledge.

Clayton cleared his throat. "You and Fred seem to have a lot in common."

"Actually, we do." Margie smiled. "It's so refreshing when someone understands a woman's feelings, emotions, and those sort of things. I mean, I think it's really

nice when a man can get in touch with his feminine side."
All those things Margie had said about Fred was true.
And then there was the fact that he was a professional
chef. If she chose him, at least she would finally be able to
ween herself from takeout food.

Clayton let out a chuckle that was blended with jealousy and just a hint of sinister. "Oh, believe me when I
say if any one of the men here can get in touch with their
feminine side, it would be Freda."

Margie quickly turned and shot Clayton a look. "You
mean Fred."

"Yes, Fred. That's what I said, Fred." Now Clayton was
looking ornery.

"No, you didn't. You said Freda. I'm almost certain."
Margie tried to read the expression on his face. And
from what she could tell, he knew darn well what name
he'd called Fred. She shifted her body to face Clayton.
"Clayton, I've been an up-front person up to this point.
That's a quality I admire in others so I try to demonstrate
it myself. So I appreciate the fact that you've been an
up-front person as well."

Clayton let off a smile that showed he was truly flat-
tered.

"Up until now, that is," Margie added, wiping the smile
that had a touch of smugness from his face.

"But, uh, I don't know what you mean," Clayton said, his
feelings and ego deflated at the idea that Margie thought
he was beating around the bush. But in all actuality, wasn't
he? Clearly, Margie was not one to play games, so it
was time he told her what she wanted to hear.

The limo began to slow.

Margie looked out the window to see them driving
toward a docking pier.

"Oh, looks like we're here." she said. She then looked at
Clayton. "Looks as if they have quite the evening planned
for us. I'd hate for our opportunity to possibly get to

know each other better for the last time before I make my decision to be ruined by us having other things on our minds."

The limo came to a complete stop, and the driver got out and walked around to Margie's door.

"I definitely wouldn't want that to happen," Clayton replied right before the limo driver opened her door.

The driver proceeded to assist Margie out of the car. Clayton let himself out, and then rushed around to meet her.

"Wow, it looks like we're going on a cruise." Margie pointed to a large yacht that was docked about fifty feet away. She could see the camera crew in position.

Clayton looked at the shiny black vessel. He imagined just how well he and Margie could get to know each other in the middle of a bed of water. He then thought about how they could possibly spend the entire time conversing about the other men instead, and what they were or were not telling Margie about themselves. He refused to risk his final one-on-one with her before she had to make her decision being consumed with any man other than himself. So whatever it was he felt needed to be said about any of the other men, he'd say it now. Those men were not boarding that boat with them in any form or fashion.

"Margie, before we get on that boat, there maybe is one little thing about one of the other men that you might not know," he said as the two walked toward the boat.

"Oh?" Margie said curiously, stopping in her tracks. "And what might that be?"

Clayton took a deep breath. He stopped and turned to look at Margie. "Well, you already know that Richard is a smoker."

"Yes," she said.

Clayton looked indecisive about coming forth. "Fred is a great guy." He was doing something he knew Margie didn't care for, which was to beat around the bush. But he wanted to be careful with his words. "He's a great guy at this stage in the game, I guess it's safe to say." He shrugged.

"*This stage?*" Margie questioned. "What do you mean by that?"

"Well," Clayton said while slowly exhaling, "you also know how Fred is so, what you would say . . . in touch with his feminine side."

"Yes," Margie said, finding absolutely nothing wrong at all with a man who had sensitivity and wasn't afraid to show it.

"That's because . . ." Clayton scrunched his face as if it pained him to say his next words. "He actually has one . . . literally." Then he immediately took off toward the boat.

Margie stood idle just a second longer as she tried to figure out what felt like a riddle. But when she noticed Clayton was hightailing it to the boat, she took off behind him. "Oh no, you don't," she said, quickly catching up with him, tugging on his arm and forcing him to stop. "You won't talk in riddles, then expect me to ponder or guess. Now spit out exactly what it is you're trying to say." Margie couldn't have cared less about the cameraman recording how desperate she was to sop up some spilled tea. She'd been eager to hear what dirt Clayton may have had on the other men and now, with that subtle hint Clayton had just thrown out about Fred, she was anxious. She didn't want to jump the gun and assume anything, but if Clayton was saying what she *thought* he was saying, then, by God, he better just say it so she could begin to deal with it sooner rather than later.

"If I tell you, do you promise we can drop all this and just focus on us, you and me and the amazing time we're going to have together?" he pleaded, taking Margie's hands into his.

"Promise," Margie said with sincerity and having every intention of keeping her word.

"Okay then," Clayton said, exhaling, "Fred has always had the advantage over all of us other men in being able to connect to your feminine side and know what you like, want, and expect as a woman. Even more than me . . . and I grew up with a house full of women."

"Why is that?" Margie braced herself for the answer.

"It's because . . . well . . . He used to be one." Clayton dropped Margie's hands, and then hightailed it toward the boat once again before she could ask him a single other question.

Margie stood there dumbfounded and in shock. A part of her had felt all along that there was just something about Fred that made him stand out from the rest of the men. She wouldn't have guessed in a million years it was his former breast that stuck out . . . pun intended.

"Pastor Margie," one of the cameramen said, then signaled with his hand for her to go catch up with Clayton so the other cameras could get them boarding the boat together.

Margie wanted to hurry up and catch up with Clayton all right, but never mind the dang boat. She wanted to hear more about Fred. That bomb that he had just dropped, and then ran off before any of the soot from the explosion could mess up his attire, had answered her question. But it had also ignited many, many more. However, Margie kept all her questions at bay and went to catch up with Clayton so that they could possibly enjoy a wonderful evening together. She'd just have to ignore all the voices in her head shouting out one question after the next for her to ask him about Fred, Freda, or whoever. As a matter of fact, she'd leave those nagging voices right there on the docking marina. After all, a promise was a promise.

Chapter 15

"So how was your date with the green-eyed monster?" Doreen said. Margie had called her over to her apartment to discuss her date with Clayton.

"Doreen, cut it out," Margie said, nodding toward one of the two cameramen. They were capturing footage of the two ladies sitting around talking like girlfriends would do when one was trying to get the details of the other's date.

"Tuh," Doreen spat. "This is a reality show, ain't it? They want us to keep it real, don't they? Well, that's exactly what I'm doing. Now, they can cut out whatever it is they want to cut out, but that man is just what I said he is, a monster. A jealous, shifty scrounger who is on this show for fame and not to find a wife. And that's exactly why, when asked, I chose for him to get the boot. He's good TV, and that's all he is. I don't know why you let the producers talk you into keeping him. That rotten apple should have long been thrown out of the bunch. Eliminated his first night here."

One of the cameramen pulled his camera away from his face, signaling to Doreen that he'd had enough of her exposing some behind-the-scenes information. The editors absolutely had the ability to edit out some of what she was saying, but there was also such a thing as "lost footage." There was always the possibility of things being leaked. It was just safer if they never existed at all.

It was true that the producers had dropped hints to Margie how someone as lively and handsome as Clayton would draw in female viewers. They made sure to mention periodically how much the cameras loved Clayton. But that's not why Margie hadn't sent Clayton home. She personally wanted him there.

"Anyway," Margie said, sipping from her teacup as the two sat at the dining table, "it was actually a pretty nice date. We went boating on the Scioto River. Not on no little *Gilligan's Island* boat either. It was a yacht. When we docked, we were greeted by a lovely outdoor setup with a seafood and steak dinner for two. A violinist played while we talked and watched the sunset. It was just beautiful."

"A violinist, huh?" Doreen said, rolling her eyes. "Beautiful music to distract you from all his ugliness."

Margie just about choked on her tea. "Ugly? Woman, you need to repent. You know darn well he's one of the most handsome men you've ever seen."

"On the outside maybe, but on the inside, he's just as ugly as all get-out. Now that Cleveland fella, he was a hoot. A sense of humor like that comes in handy when dealing with all the serious ministry business. I felt someone with a personality like his would have been just what you needed." Doreen then said, "That Clayton will have you laughing all right—laughing to keep from crying."

"You are only going by what they show you on the playbacks." Part of the process of filming the show was that some things would be played back for the cast, and they would speak on it. It was kind of like testimonials.

"What else do I have to go by?" Doreen asked. "They only gave me an hour with the men, and it wasn't even with each one of them individually. But just from the little bit of time I did get to spend with him, I knew Clayton wasn't the one, which is why I tried to send his butt home.

And if you've got good sense and don't get blinded by his eyes, you'll send him packing too."

Margie laughed about how animated Doreen was in relaying her feelings about Clayton. "Leave ole Clayton alone. He's still just got a little boyish mischief in him is all. That to go along with his boyish looks. I think it's cute."

"It's cute on boys, not grown men."

"The same way you like to have a little fun when it comes to throwing digs at the show, allow me to have a little fun as well, would ya?" Margie sipped her tea. After swallowing she spoke again. "This is a dating show. I'm dating," she reminded Doreen. "I think that's what's wrong with a lot of relationships today. People don't know how to date before getting obsessed with one single person. They don't get out there and see what someone else may have to offer. Now, I'm not talking about sleeping with a bunch of people. I'm talking about dating them. Going out and doing something fun, something adventurous. Getting to know one another. Dinner, movies."

"And rides on yachts?" Doreen said sarcastically while rolling her eyes.

"And yachts," Margie said without shame.

"I agree that whole dating thing might be true when it comes to the younger generation," Doreen said. "They go out with a person once and want to be exclusive. Want to start going through each other's phone and all that type of mess. Get mad if the other person does try to date other people, when that's what being young is all about. Exploring."

"Exactly," Margie said, in 100 percent agreement with her friend. She was glad to hear that Doreen agreed with her about something.

"But not when you're old like us," Doreen stated.

Margie frowned. "Pardon me, but I'm *not* old."

"You know what I mean. By the time you're our age, you know what you want. Don't nobody have time for all that dating a zillion people and being engaged for two years. Do you know what can happen to someone up in age after two years?"

"I hear what you're saying," Margie said, "but this dating thing does make me feel like an ole girl again." She blushed and got all giddy.

"Look at you. You really are enjoying this, aren't you? Humph, maybe I got this thing all wrong. Maybe you being here isn't about anybody else, but all about you."

Margie looked puzzled. "What do you mean by that?"

"I mean, maybe deep inside, you've wanted a little companionship. You've just never sat still long enough to really ask yourself that question, let alone think about it."

"I'll be honest with you. I was thinking that same thing myself. Even when some of the members at New Day go on their tangents about me being single, I never stop to really ask myself if I enjoy being single. I'm rarely alone, so I don't deal with being lonely. Heck, if I get five minutes to myself, I marvel in it. I can't say I've missed having a man in my life because I can't miss what I've never had."

"Never had in a long time anyway," Doreen chuckled.

Margie remained serious. "No, I had it right. I can't miss what I've never had."

Doreen stared at Margie for a minute. "Do you mean to tell me that never, not even before you got saved, have you ever had a boyfriend?"

Margie shook her head. "No boyfriend. No elementary school crushes, no high school sweetheart, college love— none of that."

"But . . ." Doreen was at a loss for words. She had to admit that in all her years of knowing Margie, they'd never talked about the past men in their lives; just one man, who was Willie.

Prior to Wallace, Willie had been the first and only man Doreen had ever dated and/or been with. So that wasn't a very long conversation. Margie never brought up a man, and Doreen never asked about one. She didn't want to show any disrespect to her pastor by prying. She figured if she wanted to talk about it she would have. Margie might not have wanted to talk about it in the past, but she was certainly talking about it now.

"When you have an alcoholic mother you have to take care of from the age of five, somehow, boys play second fiddle to that," Margie said. "Besides, no way was I going to bring a boy to that house I was raised in. A five-year-old can only keep it so clean. When the state took my sister away after my mother's drug addict boyfriend raped her, I never saw her again."

That last part of what Margie had just said, Doreen had known about. The two had exchanged testimonies as far as their family and upbringing. Doreen even knew that Margie's mother was an alcoholic for as long as Margie could remember. But Doreen never knew that Margie's mother being an alcoholic had affected Margie having men in her life, or rather *not* having men in her life.

"Of course, as you know, the state had no problem leaving me in my mother's custody." Margie thought for a moment. "I never could figure out why they'd take my sister and not me. If my mother had let something bad happen to her, what made them think she wouldn't let something bad happened to me as well?"

"Nothing bad happened to you, did it?" Doreen asked. "I mean bad as in what happened to your sister."

"No," Margie replied, thanking God that it hadn't, "but it could have."

Doreen nodded in agreement. "But let's just thank our Lord in heaven that it didn't. Having to deal with, overcome, and be healed with the things that *did* happen is enough."

"Yeah, and getting over it was no easy feat. I honestly had hated my mother for being what I thought was a bad mother. I blamed her for the choices I made to sell drugs and eventually use drugs. Had I not allowed Jesus into my life, and then given Him my life, I honestly don't ever think I would have forgiven her."

"Didn't you say it had been something like ten years since you'd talked to your mother before you decided to forgive her?" Doreen tried to recall the talks she and Margie had shared, as well as the testimony Margie gave the church every few years.

The Holy Spirit led Margie to give her testimony to the congregation every so often. Some members needed to know that their spiritual leader had overcome some trials and tribulations in her life. It made members of the congregation feel more comfortable coming to the pastor with their own issues. Talking to someone who wasn't so perfect and who members knew had endured struggles of her own allowed them to open up more. Testimonies heal and save lives, so if people hold their testimonies hostage, someone could miss out on their breakthrough.

"Yes, ten long years," Margie said. She shook her head. "And even then, we didn't just pick up where we left off. And that was okay with me, because my mother was still the same way I remembered her, which was fussy, mean, and hateful, for a lack of better terms." Margie chuckled. "So I only went around her when I absolutely had to. I just couldn't bear the way she'd talk to people, especially when she took ill and began receiving in-home nursing assistance." Margie let out a laugh. "Man, if you'd heard the way my mother spoke to some of those aides."

Doreen chuckled. "Then I'd understand why some folks abuse the elderly, huh?"

Margie gave Doreen a scolding look. "You're wrong for saying that. Elderly abuse is wrong. But my mother had that kind of mouth ever since she was young and in her right mind." She looked down. "I used to think she hated me. I really did. Why else would she be so mean and treat me the way she did? I didn't want to forgive her for that. As long as I remained in unforgiveness, I felt it justified in not calling her, taking care of her, or going by to see about her as often as I should have."

"So she was sick already when you finally went to forgive her?" Doreen asked.

Margie nodded. "Real bad off." She held back tears. "She had diabetes that she hadn't taken care of. She had congestive heart failure. She had neuropathy. She started losing her balance and falling. We figured it was because she was addicted to those oxycodone pills and she wasn't taking them correctly. Once the nurse who took care of her started using that medical lock box, we got her pills under control and she was doing pretty good there for a minute. Then I swear, Doreen, it was like in the time span of just a week she went downhill. She went from being able to wash herself, dress herself, do minor cooking and eating, to not even being able to get up from the kitchen table."

Doreen walked over and put her hand on Margie's shoulder. Doreen had heard this part of the testimony before, but allowed her friend to speak on it whenever she wanted and as many times as she needed.

"I just remember the EMT calling me because Mom had called the squad to help her get up from the table after eating dinner. I . . . I didn't understand." Margie wiped a tear that had escaped her eye, and then continued on. "Then the very next day, her aide called the squad again because her ears were bleeding. The doctors at the emergency room ran tests, and come to find out, she'd had a urinary tract infection. And it was causing all of those issues. I didn't believe it at first until I did my own research." Margie recalled how she'd gone home that day after leaving the hospital and researched urinary tract infections in elderly people. She learned that a urinary tract infection happens when bacteria in the bladder or kidney multiplies in the urine. Elderly people are more vulnerable to UTIs. UTIs in the elderly are often mistaken as the early stages of dementia or Alzheimer's.

"Then there was that sore on her back we thought she got from one of the falls, that turned into a bedsore, had been a bedsore all along . . . I don't know." Margie started to get anxious.

Doreen pet her shoulder. "It's okay."

"I should have been there and paid more attention earlier."

"You were there when she needed you most, and that's all that matters," Doreen said.

"Yes. And as Mom got worse, I hoped and prayed that my sister too would find forgiveness in her heart and be there for Mom like I was. Then when Mom passed, I imagined that my sister would read the obituary and come pay her final respects and at the same time, maybe start up a relationship with me. That didn't happen, but I don't hold it against her."

"I can't say the same about my siblings and me when our mother took ill and passed away," Doreen said. "We fought about who wasn't pulling their weight, who could have been doing more. We'd call each other up and talk smack about the other one. It didn't take me long to figure out that who cares what the next person is or isn't doing as long as I'm doing what I'm supposed to be doing and what is required of me by the Bible, which is to honor thy mother."

"Amen to that," Margie said, raising her right hand and waving it. "I thought forgiving my mother had been hard, but having to stand at the funeral home that day and give her eulogy topped it all."

Margie allowed her mind to travel back to that very day, that very moment she stood behind the podium and spoke into the microphone at her mother's funeral. This was before she had been called to pastor and was used to speaking in front of others. Her nerves were getting the best of her, but she pressed through.

"I'm not a wordsmith. Not a master of words, but instead, I have been known as someone who has a way with words. But today, I must admit that I have been at a true loss for words altogether.

"Those of you who knew my mother may find it unbelievable that any offspring of Joanne could ever be at a loss for words considering she was a woman of many, many, and plenty of words. Some of those words I heard her repent of quite often in church." Margie smiled thinking about how blessed she'd been to take her mother to church those last few months before she fell so ill she was wheelchair bound.

"I know at most funerals or memorial services we usually hear all the good things, pleasant memories, and wonderful characteristics about the person being honored that make us smile, laugh, or nod in agreement. So when I put pen to paper to begin to try to sum up my mother's almost sixty-three years in five minutes, I was bemused, and honestly, a little uneasy. The Holy Spirit took things in a totally different direction than expected.

"With that being said, for the next words I'm about to say, some of you will gasp and some of your spirits will concur. But nonetheless, here it goes: I am so glad my mother is gone.

"My selfish flesh would want to keep her here on earth forever. Her pain would then become my pleasure. Never mind that she was weak, in pain, fragile,

lethargic, and hurting. 'Mommy, I want you to be here for me no matter how much it hurts you.' That's a selfish act, one that some of us might carry out daily with people in our lives who are strong and healthy. 'I want you here for me no matter how much it hurts you.' Folks, sometimes, we just have to let things and people go. Because without even knowing it, holding on to something that needs to be let go of could ultimately hurt and hinder us as well.

"But, see, thank God for my spirit man, for He is selfless, and as long as I stay prayed up and have people in my life praying for me, my spirit man will always dominate my flesh and prevail. My spirit man is glad that my mother is gone, for on this earth the pain and suffering she endured is no more.

"I'm sure you've all seen the pictures of my mom in the program ranging from her being a baby until her recent years. For most, they are just memories and images that might bring a smile to your face or even tears of sorrow, because, now, that's all we have left is a picture. Initially, when I was picking these pictures out, all I could do was cry . . . not just tears of sorrow, but tears of pain . . . This isn't about me, though, so I'm not talking about my pain, but my mother's pain. Not the pain of her physical ailments that she suffered from the last few years . . . the pain that we all knew she was in just by looking at her. But the internal pain that you never knew about unless she told you. The pain I can see in the eyes of her pictures because I know her story. I just learned in church last week that there is a name for it. It's called 'Soul Pain.'

"I look at one picture of my mother and wonder, was this when she was being touched by her uncle? Was this when she was raped? Was this when she was beat up, hit, called out of her name, robbed, lied on, stolen *from, cheated on? These pictures are placed to tell you her story, and it is my aspiration today to interpret it to you. Yes, I'd much rather be sitting on one of those chairs, mourning, crying, and allowing someone else to eulogize my mother, but this is the very final task God has assigned me in honoring thy mother. I must be obedient.*

"There was pain my mother carried for so many years that she was never quite able to let go of . . . not completely . . . not in the natural. But I believe God's Word, and I know in my heart that now all of those soul pains, memories, hurts, regrets, guilt, shame, and sorrows of this world that tried, and sometimes succeeded, at tormenting her soul lost their power and existence when her spirit was called home to be with the Lord. Not her body, not her soul; her spirit was called home to be with the Lord.

"Though she is the one who endured the aches and troubles, it was not for her or about her. It was for me, it was for my sister, it was for you. It was for each one of us. So if I don't take this opportunity on this day to share this message with you all, then my mother's life would most certainly be in vain. Her story would go untold.

"Before writing this eulogy, I researched what a eulogy was, who was to give it, and what one should say. One thing that was consistent in my findings was that in giving a eulogy, everyone doesn't have to be in agreement with what you say, but it has to be the truth. I stand here before you to tell you Joanne's truth.

"Joanne was hard, had a tongue that could slice you in half; she wanted what she wanted when she wanted it, how she wanted it, and however many times she wanted it. She was a no-nonsense person, never diplomatic with her words; sharp, a handful, and could give you the business whether or not you deserved it, and

would call you a dummy if you did something dumb. For the past few months before she passed, as long as she could walk, she went to church every Sunday and sat in the same spot. God bless the child who didn't know any better and asked her if she would scoot over so they could sit down."

Margie had to pause for a moment while some people in attendance laughed, mainly the members of the church who had seen Margie's mom in action if someone dared to ask her to vacate her seat, which was the first spot on the second pew.

"Whenever anybody asked me how my mother was doing, I always had some kind of outrageous story to tell that you usually only saw in a Tyler Perry movie. I called her Madea with a cane in her hand instead of gun in her purse. I would laugh about her little antics and shenanigans after the fact, but Lord have mercy, I'd be so embarrassed while it was going down.

"My mother had aides, and nurses would come to the house to help her with daily functions. She didn't just go through aides, she went through agencies. They'd call me and say, 'Margie, your mother doesn't like any of the aides we sent her, and we're all out.' These last few months I would actually have people calling my phone to tell on my mother. Her dialysis center would call. 'Margie, your mom is running around here asking people for twenty dollars because she said y'all won't buy her any more sausage gravy biscuits from McDonald's and she doesn't have any food.' My mother would have her best friend and me, as well as her aide, buy her enough sausage gravy biscuits to last her a week. We'd order five and ten at a time. God forbid we arrived at McDonald's and they'd stopped serving breakfast. Of course, that was before they started selling breakfast all day. But realizing we weren't helping my mother's *health or diet, we had to cut her off . . . and risk getting cut by her. I'm glad to say, though, that a couple of days before my mom passed, I bought and fed her a sausage gravy biscuit from McDonald's.*

"But as I received those phone calls about my mother, I'd say to myself, 'How are people going to call me to tell on my mother? I'm the child, she's the parent. What do they want me to do? Put her in time-out?'

"But that's when it hit me. Roles had reversed. Was this normal? Not only was it normal, but was it natural? Parents take care of children. The children don't take care of the parents, do they? My mother was tough, strong . . . No matter how sick and weak she seemed to the rest of the world, through the eyes of the child she had nurtured, raised, and taken care of, I did not see her that way. Back then, I couldn't accept or acknowledge the state she was in. I had a blind eye that refused to see her helpless.

"In the early stages of me seeing my mother sick, when she would want me to do something, I would just think she didn't want to do it herself. The mother I knew could do any and everything. Some things she'd ask me to do I did, and some I didn't, again, not receiving that they were truly acts my mother could no longer perform without assistance. I figured once she realized I wasn't going to jump every time she asked, she'd just do it herself. But she really couldn't. So I thank God for that ram in the bush, for those people that were there to make sure everything my mother wanted or needed got taken care of whether or not she really could do them . . . her church family, her best friend especially, who ended up moving in with her to help care for her. Her aides and nurses, of course. Her neighbors Michael and Dana. Michael's mom, Vergie

and Michael's brother Brian, who picked up where Michael and Dana left off when they moved away. All rams.

"I stayed on the road traveling for my job. I'd tell my mother about all my trips all over the world, the places I'd seen and the people I'd met. She would sit there, listen and smile. She was proud of her daughter. But then it dawned on me while writing this . . . while I was sitting there telling my traveling stories and my mother was sitting there taking it in . . . that might have been the one time in her life that she ever bit her tongue. Because if I know Joanne, in her head, she was probably thinking, 'Who cares about traveling all over the world? Tell stories about the people right here in your own town—in your own community—who you went to see, visit, talk to, and spent time with. Took a meal to. Heck, you could have spent some of that time with me!'

"So let me say this one thing that you have all heard a million times: Tomorrow is not promised. My mother's death is proof positive. I can't tell you how many people were going to go visit her tomorrow, and when they did, she was gone.

"I had done work for the same company since 2006. It took up so much of my time, but I loved it. It was because of that job I got to do a lot of my traveling. Then earlier this year, out of nowhere, the department I did work for dissolved. It was gone, just like that. I was confused, but deep inside, I had peace. I didn't fix my lips to question God. That was unlike me, because I've questioned God about a lot of things, but not this one. No sooner than I stopped working for that company did incidents start to occur with my mother. She fell, she caught an infection, she caught pneumonia, she got admitted to the hospital, and then the nursing home. The bad thing was that I didn't want all of this to be happening to my mother.

The good thing: I was able to be there. God closed a door financially, but opened one so that when the day my mother passed came, I could have peace spiritually. The day my mother passed, I had peace that I had honored her.

"There was a time when I used to think my mother was mean and hateful. But as I mentally reread her story, I realized that she was none of those things. What my mother was in was pain. Going back to what I said before, the person I was dealing with back then was not a mean and hateful woman, but a young girl whose uncle violated her. That young girl who didn't have an active relationship with her father. That young girl who got pregnant in tenth grade and got kicked out of school for being pregnant. That young girl who was abused horribly by some of the men in her life. That young girl who turned to alcohol to ease the pain . . . But that was before she knew that Jesus was the ultimate healer.

"So, heck, yeah, there may have been times she was mad, angry, hateful, and bitter. The Bible says we can be angry, but sin not. And what I can stand here and say before you is that she sinned not. She might have told you off real good, but wasn't no sin in it.

"Regardless of what our relationships were like with our mother, grandmother, aunts—whoever raised us—we have absolutely no power to manipulate it into something other than what it was. A person's perception is their reality. Therefore, we have to accept it for what it is. We don't have to walk around feeling heavy or wishing we had the kind of relationship someone else has. But what we do have the power to do is choose what we want that relationship to be today. So on this day, I pray love, peace, blessings, deliverance, and healing to every mother and child. May God keep our minds to remember all those wonderful things and traits about

the women who raised us and all they sacrificed in order for us to make it this far. I pray for the strength that we may forgive and forget those things that serve no purpose but to vex our spirits, so that we may walk forward in a future untouched by past hurts designed to keep us bound.

"We watch on the news and we see how an elderly person was found dead in their home after two weeks. That they were survived in death by children and grandchildren, and we ask ourselves, 'How does that happen? How does someone not know their mother has been dead in a house for two weeks?' Let's not let that be any of our testimonies or anyone we know.

"Honor thy mother the same way Jesus honored His. I don't care if your mother wasn't a Mary; most mothers aren't Marys to their children. In caring for our mothers, if we too are mothers, we should always be sure to bring our children along with us. We need them to see with their own eyes the demonstration of the scripture. The Bible says that we reap what we sow. In our days, especially our final days, we want to know that our children will reenact what they see in their own mother. It doesn't matter how many people I bless, love, help, or care for on earth if I couldn't do it for my own mother. If your mother has since gone on to be with the Lord, honor someone else's mother. You be that ram in the bush for someone else.

"My mother has already lived her life. Her story has already been told. What will yours be? Your mother's, your grandmother's or your friend's mother, your friend's grandmother. For as long as we breathe on earth, we are on assignment. Be obedient to your assignment, for we know that on the other side of our obedience is someone else's blessing.

"Proverbs 31:28 says, 'Her children arise up, and call her blessed.' My mother was honored, and she was

blessed. May she rest in peace, and may each of your lives and stories be filled with honor and peace as well. God bless you all."

It always blessed Margie's soul and gave her peace knowing that God had softened her heart and she'd hardened it not at His command to go to her mother. She'd been ten years out of the woman's life and was able to be there for her last days on earth.

Margie looked at Doreen. "You know the producers asked about my mother and if she'd be willing to meet with the men and help me out in this process," Margie said. "I told them she'd passed, and that's when God put you in my spirit."

"If your mother is all who you say she was," Doreen added, "you know you wouldn't have had to eliminate anyone."

"Right," Margie agreed. "They all would have run packing."

Margie and Doreen burst out laughing. They'd never laughed so hard in their lives. Doreen's sprit sensed a sudden shift coming on in Margie's laughter, and she hugged her as Margie's laughter turned into a wail.

"I miss my mommy!" Margie cried out.

"I know you do," Doreen said to her. "But no matter how much and how hard you and I sit here and cry, nothing would ever make your mother want to leave the right hand of the throne to be back here on earth. The fact that she is no longer in pain and is with the King, these tears should be tears of joy."

Margie sniffed. "You are so right. I should be rejoicing."

"You darn right. Hallelujah. Glory! We are so lucky our mothers are with the King, yes!" Doreen began shouting, and Margie joined in right with her.

The two women had forgotten about the men, forgotten about the cameras, and took this moment to celebrate and honor their mothers.

After a few minutes, Margie told Doreen she felt it was time to retreat to her apartment because she had a lot to think about. She was down to only four men. She was eliminating them one by one. It hadn't been as difficult to do as she'd initially thought. But as the number of men dwindled down, she was getting anxious because she'd been absolutely certain that by now God would have shown her which of the men were to be her lifetime helpmate. But He hadn't.

For the first time since she could remember, was God putting this entire choice in her hands? Of all the times He'd decided to do so, did it have to be now? Sure, Doreen was there to put in her two cents, but that wasn't enough. It wasn't Doreen who would have to spend the rest of her life with the man.

"If you ask me, there's not too much to think about," Doreen said. "Clayton doesn't have a chance in the world. That Clayton fella may talk right, walk right, sound right, and look right, but he don't smell right," Doreen said, pinching her nose closed with her index finger and thumb.

"Clayton hasn't done a thing for you to feel that way about him."

"Oh yes, he has," Doreen said.

"And what was that?" Margie asked, curious to find out if something had gone down between Clayton and Doreen that she should know about before she sees it when the show airs. "What exactly did Clayton do?"

Doreen looked Margie straight in the eyes and without stuttering or blinking, she said, "He breathed."

Chapter 16

"So what if being on a reality show was a more worldly way of reaching people," Margie said as she and Doreen were poolside, stretched out on two cushioned lounge chairs. "Am I not, in fact, supposed to reach the world? I mean, I'm all for preaching to the choir. I'm all for continuing to, every Sunday, reach the same saints who already know God. Because trying to stay saved is not always easy. Some saints need to hear that word and be reminded of the goodness of the Lord over and over and over again just so they can get powered up to make it through the week to next Sunday."

"I agree," Doreen said. "Used to bother me when I'd hear pastors saying that they are tired of preaching to the same people every week, the ones who are already saved and know God. But those people are often just a Sunday away from backsliding or from never stepping foot in the church again. But to go back to what you were saying, if you want to reach the world, then you have to go in it. I commend you for that, Margie. Plenty of saints will holler out, 'God, I'll go where you say go.' Then if God tells them to go on Facebook, they won't even go there. Can you imagine if the saints took over social media how many lives and souls could be saved?"

"You gon' get a million amens from me on that one," Margie said. "Or should I say, a million likes?" She laughed. "I remember one time one of the church members who writes Christian fiction books was invited to attend some type of vendor bazaar. Come to find it was being held at a strip club. This member was highly offended that the host of the event, knowing she was a Christian who sold Christian books, would have the audacity to invite her to such a place. She assumed she absolutely would not sell out of her Christian books at a strip club. After relaying the situation to me, she wanted me to be just as offended and upset as she was."

"You weren't, I take it."

"No," Margie said. "I asked her if she'd ever considered for one moment God had put it on that woman's heart to invite her because she was a Christian. Because she did have a product that could truly bless someone in attendance?"

"That's good right there." Doreen nodded her head and held her right hand up to the Lord.

"Yep, and she ended up doing very well at the event. Sold out of books and two folks who she met that evening she invited to church and now they're saved."

"Praise, God!" Doreen shouted. "Yes, Lord." She shook her head.

"That same author came to my office and said, 'Pastor Margie, when I first started writing books, my prayer was to become a famous New York Times bestselling author. My prayer was to sell one million copies of my book. My prayer was to be sold out of books after every book signing event. But now my prayers have changed. My prayer is to be a blessed selling author. My prayer is to save one million souls. My prayer is not to sell out of books, but for my books to lead to people being sold out for Christ. I no longer write to become a famous author. I write to make God famous.'"

"Glory!!!!" Doreen shouted. She then managed to wriggle her way up off that lounge chair and give God a praise dance.

Margie clapped her hands, laughed, and shouted, "That's right, sister. Give Him all the glory."

A few moments later, Doreen was able to contain her praise and return to her chair.

"And that's exactly what I did when she stood there in my office and testified," Margie said. "So you see, you never know which vehicle, avenue, platform, or source God is going to use to get people to know who He is. You just have to sit back and trust that He will."

"And that's exactly what you did when it came to this reality show," Doreen told her. "I know I might have sounded like doubting Thomas at first, but I was just messing with you."

"I know," Margie said. "And you're still messing with me."

"Yeah, but you gotta admit, it's livened things up a little," Doreen said. "And who knows? I just might get my own spinoff show after this."

"Be careful what you ask for," Margie was quick to say.

"You are so right." Doreen looked up to the sky. "God, I hope you didn't hear that."

The women laughed, then paused when they heard footsteps nearing them.

"Wine, ladies?" One of the butlers approached Margie and Doreen while they were lying under the moonlight at the pool. He was carrying a tray that held a bottle of red wine and two wineglasses.

Neither Margie nor Doreen were known to drink. Not because it didn't seem like the Christian thing to do. It had more to do with personal issues. Margie had grown up watching her mother turn into a mean drunk. Doreen had watched her ex-husband drink himself to death, and do a whole lot of sinning while he was alive and drinking. So ordinarily, they wouldn't have hesitated to decline the offer of any type of libations, but this time around, both women looked at each other.

"You thinking what I'm thinking?" Margie asked Doreen.

"That depends on what you're thinking," Doreen responded.

"I'm thinking that for years, you and I both have been on assignment, whether or not we knew it. We've spent so much time making sure that everybody else's lives came together, that we never took the time to enjoy our own lives."

Doreen nodded. "I agree." She'd felt that way on more than one occasion, but here lately, more than ever.

"Being here, at this beautiful place," Margie looked around, "it truly was just what the doctor ordered. Or should I say, God ordered?"

"Amen to that," Doreen agreed. Even though this had surely been one heck of a ride, it had also included a slice of paradise as well. For almost six weeks, she hadn't had to lift a finger. Sure, she had to lift her holy hands to the heavens a few times, but that was different.

"In a couple of days, this will all be over with. We'll be back to life as usual."

"The vacation will be over."

"I won't even say that," Margie said. "Because you know what . . . You have to admit that even though life is rough at times and our plates get full, we live a pretty good life." Margie smiled.

Doreen thought for a minute. "You know, you are absolutely right. I receive that. Truth be told, we live a life that is a vacation, not one we need to take a vacation from."

"You hit the nail on the head, which takes me back to what I was thinking . . ."

"Which is?"

"Which is, we should toast to that . . . And not with sparkling grape juice, but with wine. Real wine, and if it makes you feel any better about it, we can do it in memory of Jesus and this grand life of ours He paid the price for."

"If you think you have to convince me, you thought wrong." Doreen stretched her arm up and grabbed a glass from the butler, who had been standing there patiently waiting for the women to make a decision about his inquiry.

"That's what I'm talking about," Margie said excitedly.

The butler handed Margie a glass, and then poured both women a half glass of wine, which is what they'd specified, not wanting to go overboard.

"Will that be all, ladies?" the butler asked.

"Yes," the women replied in unison.

The butler started to walk away as the women clinked their glasses.

"To us," Margie said.

"To us," Doreen repeated.

Each woman then took a sip of the delicious wine. They shot each other a surprising look. Neither had expected the wine to be so refreshing, sweet, and tasty.

"You thinking what I'm thinking?" Margie asked Doreen for the second time that evening.

"I don't know. Depends on what you're thinking," Doreen replied once again.

"I'm thinking exactly what you're thinking," Margie said, certain she'd seen in Doreen's eyes exactly what she'd been thinking after sipping the wine.

"In that case . . ." Doreen said, and then both women shouted out simultaneously to the butler. "You can leave that bottle here." Both women burst out laughing, enjoying what was to be their final evening by the pool together, and some long overdue girlfriend time.

***

"Well, today is the day," Doreen said. "You get to pick the man you want to be your husband. The future first man of New Day Temple of Faith. The man of your house."

Margie exhaled as she looked at herself in her bathroom mirror. Hair and makeup had only moments ago finished her up for her final taping. Just earlier that morning, she had to let one of the final three men go. Richard had been the unlucky man. Margie hated to say it, but she would have much rather smelled the cigarette smoke lingering on his clothing, rather than that bucket of cologne he threw on. Not only that, but when Margie questioned Richard about his smoking habit, he denied it. At that point it was Clayton's word against Richard's, so she had no other choice but to give Richard the benefit of the doubt.

But then, on a trip through the property on the golf cart, she rolled right by Richard who was standing out in the garden just a puffing away. That evening when it was time for elimination, Richard had already had his clothes packed. He knew his fate the moment he locked eyes with Margie while she rolled by him, cigarette to his lips. He hadn't gotten eliminated because he was a smoker. He'd gotten eliminated because he'd lied about it.

Now it was just down to Clayton and Fred.

"I can't believe the show has come to an end," Margie said.

"Yep, that was a quick six weeks, but just think, you're going to be the most famous preacher in the country once it airs."

Margie turned from the mirror to face Doreen. "I didn't do this show to become a famous preacher," she said. "Just like that member of New Day I was telling you about who is an author, I didn't do this show so that I could become a famous preacher. I did the show to make God famous."

"Well, was it worth it?" Doreen asked the million-dollar question.

Margie thought for a moment, and then began nodding her head as a smile spread across her lips. "As a matter of fact, I think it was."

She turned back to the mirror and began puckering her lips together. She used her pinkie fingernail to scoop away some lipstick that had smeared just above her lip. "One day I was at a conference. There were so many prominent pastors there, ones whose reputations proceeded them. People knew who they were just by hearing their names and not even having seen their faces. I remember saying in my head, 'God, one day I want it to be so that everyone in the room knows who I am.'" She looked to Doreen who was hanging on to her every word. "He said, 'Me too, Margie. Me too.'"

Doreen let out a giddy harrumph. "And that right there will shut anybody up."

"Oh, and it did," Margie said, turning to face Doreen again. "But I'll be honest. I can't say that I haven't sat back and watched one of those Oprah spiritual specials where she has T. D. Jakes and other world-renowned pastors filling stadiums. And in doing so, that I haven't wished God would give me a platform as such." Margie thought for a moment. "Joel Osteen. Creflo Dollar. Joyce Meyer." She shook her head. "Whew weee." She exhaled. "But then I realized that God still needs a gimper like me out here for the ones who can't get in to fill those stadiums. For the ones who can't afford to pay for my team of armor bearers and security to come to them to give them God's Word. We all have assignments from God on different levels. And you know what, Doreen?"

"What's that, my friend?" Doreen asked.

Margie looked around in admiration. "I'm good right where God has me. Be it a stadium or a hole-in-the-wall church above a barbershop."

"Or on a ratchet reality show hoping the name of Jesus and your anointing will cover up the ratchetness," Doreen said. "They are taking the whole blood-of-Jesus-covers-everything a step too far," she chuckled.

Margie threw her fists on her hips. "You just had to get one more dig in, didn't you?"

"Of course. It's our last night here." Doreen shrugged while Margie shook her head at her friend.

"Well, I'm going to go commune with God one last time before I head to the set."

"All right, missy," Doreen said. "You sure you don't want to throw me a hint about which man you're going to choose to spend the rest of your life with? I mean, I know we haven't really talked in-depth about it, but we really haven't had the chance. Besides, there is only so much you can learn about ten men in just six weeks. I've been with Wallace all these years and I'm still learning!" Doreen threw her hands up.

"You know darn well I signed on the dotted line and can't tell a soul about my final choice," Margie said. "Plus, aren't you the one who told me that one time by the pool that whatever I do, do not tell people about me and my man's business?"

Doreen thought for a moment. "Yeah, that is true. It's something I tell all the new wives. But come to think of it, you would kind of be the exception since the whole world is going to know you and your man's business." Doreen let out a hearty laugh.

"Another dig, huh? Okay, I see how you are," Margie said, playing as if she was upset. Everything was all in fun though. "Anyway, you and the rest of the world will have to wait until the season finale airs. How about that?" Margie nodded her head forward with closed eyes, then opened them.

"Smarty-pants." Doreen rolled her eyes. "I guess while you put a ring on it, get a ring put on it, or however y'all done figured out how to put a spin on this she-who-finds-a-husband thing, I'm going to go get me one last dip in this pool."

"Have fun," Margie said.

Doreen exited the bathroom, and Margie found herself standing there. No hairstylist. No makeup artist. No Fatima, Anya, cameraman, or even best friend. "Alone at last," she said, feeling as though for the past six weeks she wasn't even alone when she slept, with sometimes cameramen there to watch her fall asleep.

Ironically, even though Margie seemed to be marveling in the fact that she was finally alone, in a matter of time, all that could change.

Chapter 17

"I imagine you probably didn't get much sleep last night," Lincoln said to Margie as the two stood out in the mansion's garden. He seemed to be even more excited than she was. His voice was louder and more chipper than ever before. Margie even thought that for some strange reason, his accent sounded heavier.

The set was beautifully decorated, almost as if a wedding was going to take place right then and there. There was an arch with roses and vines weaved through it. About one foot in front of the arch was where Margie and Lincoln stood. Surrounding them were pedestals with different flower arrangements resting on them. And there was a long, red carpet that led from the mansion entrance to the spot where Lincoln and Margie stood.

"To be honest with you, Lincoln, I slept like a baby," she said.

"Oh really?" he said with disbelief.

"Absolutely," Margie confirmed. "Once I finally went to sleep . . . which was just three hours before I had to get up for hair and makeup at eight this morning."

Lincoln laughed. "Aha, I knew it. With such a life-changing and -altering decision that needs to be made, I didn't think you'd get much sleep through the night."

"I could barely stay awake during hair and makeup," Margie said. "I'm surprised my makeup isn't smudged and didn't skid all over the place as much as I kept nodding off."

"Well, you look wide awake right now. As a matter of fact, you look so fresh and renewed, as if you actually had the best sleep of your life."

"And I did, like I said, once I finally went to sleep. God restored all the time I lost tossing, turning, praying, and pacing. Once God showed me the decision I had to make concerning this man, I was filled with peace."

"So you've made your decision?" Lincoln said. "And in the eleventh hour, no less."

"I have."

"Good, because the two final gentlemen are waiting to see you. I've spoken with them both, and I can assure you that neither one of them slept like a baby. They've been on pins and needles and are very anxious to know if they are the one you've chosen to be, what would one call it, a first man?"

Margie put her head down and blushed. "And I'm eager to speak with each of the two men."

"Then let's do this," Lincoln said, clasping his hands together. "I'll go inside, and the first gentleman will be out shortly."

"Thank you, Lincoln," Margie said as he walked away toward the mansion.

"Cut!" Fatima called out. She then walked over to Margie. "I'm so excited for you. I'm sure the viewers won't have an inkling of who you chose. I know I don't." She turned and pointed to the crew in the swoop of her hand. "None of us do."

"But we've got a lot of money riding on it," Anya walked up and said.

"I just know you all have not been betting, gambling, and whatnot with my fate," Margie said in a playful yet scolding manner.

Anya, not realizing Margie was completely joking, got real serious and said, "Oh no. Is that a sin?" She looked at

Margie, then Fatima for a reply. "I'm not trying to go to hell. I mean, I repented for doing a show like this in the first place. Hooking a pastor up with—"

"Anya, Anya, dear," Fatima said, cutting her off. "Really?" Fatima kept her head stiff and straight at Anya while she allowed her eyes to dart toward Margie.

Margie noticed the little interaction going on between the two women and decided to let them off the hook. "No worries, Anya. Trust me when I say I thought the same thing. And I don't have to tell you what Doreen thought."

"No, you don't," Fatima jumped in and said. "She's made it more than clear how worldly she feels this endeavor is."

"Even stamped a cross on my forehead with holy oil," Anya said. "But when she walked away I tasted it." Anya whispered, "And if you ask me, I think it was olive oil."

Margie and Fatima shot each other a look.

"It *was* olive oil, Anya," Fatima said, rolling her eyes.

"Why would a person draw a cross on someone's forehead with cooking oil, unless they were about to make stir-fry on their forehead." Anya thought about what she'd said for a moment, and then a little chuckle slipped out. She hurried to cover her mouth to keep it tucked in, but she wasn't fast enough. Soon after, another slipped out, and then another, until she found herself having a laughing fit.

Margie shot Fatima a look that said, "What the heck?" then the two joined Anya in laughing.

Margie laughed harder and harder just watching Anya laugh. It was nice to know that the young girl had it in her. "You should laugh a lot more, Anya," Margie told her. "It's good for the soul."

"Is it really?" Anya said, trying to get her laughter under control.

"Absolutely."

"Good, because I really like to laugh," she admitted.
"It's just that, you are a pastor and all. Religion is a very
serious thing, and I wanted you to be able to take me
seriously."

"Is that why you've been walking around here like some
old church mother with a stick in her butt, even though,
by the looks of it, you're only in your twenties?"

"Actually, it is," Anya said, once again with a serious
tone and face. "My great-aunt who raised me was very
into church. As a matter of fact, she *was* the church
mother." Anya bit down on her nail. "Come to think of
it, I can't recall ever seeing her smile. And she kinda
did walk like she had a stick up her a—"

"Anya!" both Margie and Fatima yelled out.

"Just kidding," Anya said, looking at Margie. "Just
wanted to make sure you were still, you know, holy."

Margie exhaled with relief.

"Come on, let's get back in position and finish up taping
before this little icebreaker between the two of you goes
completely left," Fatima said, putting the earpiece in
her ear and making sure it was in position. "Did Lincoln
finish briefing you?" she asked Margie.

"Yep, I'm all set," Margie assured her.

Anya scurried off from in front of the cameras, but
stopped and turned to Margie. "And by the way, Pastor
Margie. You and Mother Doreen's Lucy and Ethel act . . .
hilarious!" Anya busted out laughing as she walked away.

Margie smiled on the outside seeing Anya make up for
lost laughs. She smiled on the inside knowing she'd had a
hand in helping Anya see that God had a sense of humor,
and so did His people.

Fatima looked to Margie as she walked backward to
her position behind Danny and his camera. "Fred is coming out first." Fatima crossed her fingers, then mouthed,
"Good luck."

The entire set was truly excited to see what man Margie would choose. That was something Margie never had to disclose to anyone; what man she'd choose as the one she wanted to be with. They knew from past experience that a person could change their mind right up until the last moment. On one dating show, a bachelor had picked a woman, gave her a ring, but then had regrets about letting the woman before her go. He took the ring back and decided to go with the first woman after all. It was a horrifying experience for the woman who thought she was the chosen one, but the whole incident got the show superb ratings and an Emmy.

It turned into such a tear-jerking finale because the viewers had such pity for the woman's heart who had been broken. The bachelor was voted the most hated reality star, and the woman was loved by brokenhearted and empathizing women all over America. She ended up getting her own show where this time around, *she* was the person doing the choosing instead of the one fighting to be chosen. When she married the man she'd chosen on her show, she ended up with her own reality show wedding special as well. Since then, she and her husband are four seasons into their reality show together, which has aired and celebrated the birth of two children.

It was things like this that gave Margie hope and confirmation as far as her appearance on such a show.

"Thank you," Margie said to Fatima, then positioned herself on the marker she'd previously been told to stand on. A few seconds later, Fred came out of the mansion heading down the red carpet toward her.

He was decked out in a black tuxedo with red accessories. He was carrying a single rose, and his cheeks were just as red as the flower. He couldn't have hidden his nervousness no matter how hard he tried. Margie was surprised, because typically, Fred's confidence level seemed to supersede that of Clayton's—which was no easy feat. But considering the situation he was currently in, Margie could imagine how he might feel less than sure of himself. It was any man's game at this point. Both Fred and Clayton had genuine cause to be nervous.

Margie, on the other hand, wasn't the least bit nervous. Her decision had been made, and she had true peace with it, which, in her book, was a confirmation from God that her decision was of Him.

"If you don't have peace in your decision, then it's not of God," she'd once told a couple during marriage counseling. "You have to know that you know that you know and be confident in the choices you make that will affect your life as well as others."

Margie's confidence showed as she held her head up high, admiring Fred as he got closer and closer to her. A mental montage of Margie's encounters with Fred rolled through her memory. A smile appeared on her lips and her eyes when she thought about when he'd stepped out of the limo on the first night they'd met. His smile was so contagious. She thought about later that same evening how he'd stolen her away from the rest of the men and the two talked in the den of the mansion. He'd been the first one assertive enough to pull her aside and get to know her.

What really stood out to Margie was when she'd picked him for some one-on-one time and he got free reign on how they would spend their three hours together. Margie was delighted when Fred escorted her into the state-of-the art kitchen and gave her a cooking lesson. That's when she learned that Fred had started off his cooking career as the head chef at one of the casino hotels in Las Vegas. At least every other day, a guest would be so delighted by the cuisines he crafted that they'd ask to personally meet the chef and give him their compliments. Most of the guests were A-list celebrities who would ultimately invite Fred to prepare meals for their own personal taste or for private parties they were having.

Margie watched the way Fred's eyes lit up when he spoke of the honor and compliments. She imagined that's when and where his confidence took root.

Fred should have been proud of himself, his skills, and talents, because the final dish the two prepared had been phenomenal. The way that Beef Wellington with mushroom sauce melted in Margie's mouth, she wouldn't call his ability anything other than a gift from God. That said a lot, considering Margie had a hand in it, and she considered herself the worst cook on this side of the map. Only the power of God could cover up the mess she made out of a meal.

Fred had fed Margie her first bite of the dinner they'd prepared together. She'd closed her eyes and imagined that type of treatment from Fred every day. And now, as she stood in front of him, that dream could become a reality.

"For the lady," Fred said when he arrived at the foot of the red carpet where Margie had been standing waiting for him. He handed her the long stem rose.

"Thank you." Margie accepted the rose. "You look totally stunning." She checked him out head to toe. "No pun intended, but you look groom ready."

He laughed and blushed at the same time. "Only if you were the bride," he said, which made Margie, in turn, blush.

"Well, you'd make an excellent husband, that I know for sure," she said, completely serious.

"You think so?" Fred was full of doubt, and therefore shocked that Margie thought he would make an excellent husband.

"Of course you would, and you know you would," Margie said. "If you didn't think you'd make a good husband, then why would you have even come on this show?"

He put his head down, thought for a moment, and then lifted it back up. "Confirmation, I guess." Even though he'd lifted his head, he wasn't looking Margie in the eyes; more like over her shoulder.

"From me or from God?" Margie said with furrowed eyebrows.

Margie's knowing question made Fred snap his head and lock eyes with her. "Well, I, uhh . . ." Even though weeks with cameras in their faces following their every move had gone by without them being even the slightest aware of them, at this very moment, it was evident that Fred was very much aware. His eyes looked right into one camera. When Fatima began waving wildly for him to focus on Margie and not the camera, he turned his attention back to Margie, but didn't speak.

Margie could see in Fred's eyes that there was so very much he wanted to say. There were probably feelings he'd wanted to express, feelings he'd never expressed before or had probably even known how to. Feelings he'd probably kept deep within, afraid of what others would think of him. Margie sensed that as long as those cameras were going, he wouldn't speak the words he was truly longing to. She wanted to yell "cut" so badly in order to have a private conversation with him. But she'd learned her lesson about that and knew it would be in vain.

Holy Ghost, direct and order my steps, Margie prayed. She paused, then began to speak. "The same confidence you have in your trade, skills, craft . . . your gift . . . you should have in yourself as, not just a husband, but a human being," Margie began. "I get you wanting validation.

Sometimes all it takes is the right kind of validation from the right people. Yes, God's validation trumps all, but some people still need encouragement from their fellow man."

Fred nodded that he was listening and was willing to continue to listen. That was another characteristic about him that Margie admired; his ability to listen without interrupting or trying to overtalk others.

"In life, we will make a plenty of mistakes," Margie said, being very mindful not to speak anything God didn't put in her spirit to say. "While driving, we might make the wrong turn and end up lost. We might choose the wrong color to paint the walls of our new home. We might even choose the wrong mate to marry. These things can make us feel like we're the mistake. So it feels good when someone taps us on the shoulder and tells us that we've done something right. Gives us hope that we're not a complete mishap," Margie chuckled.

Fred joined her in the laughter, nodding that he completely understood.

"But I know one thing for certain and two things for sure," Margie told him. "God doesn't make any mistakes. He didn't make a mistake when it came to you." She took Fred's hands into hers and shook them for affect while she made her last statement. "You, Fred, are not a mistake. Nothing about you or how God created you is a mistake. You are good. You are a good chef. You are a good person, and I believe you would be good at anything you set your mind to, even if that included being a husband." Margie smiled.

Fred returned the smile as he looked deep into Margie's eyes. There was something about Margie's eyes that spoke volumes. All the men had discussed and agreed on that. Something about the sincerity, love, and hope in Margie's eyes made the blow of being sent home that much more bearable for the men. But that didn't mean Fred wanted to be sent home.

There was something else Fred was seeing in Margie's eyes; something he hadn't seen before. It was compassion on a much deeper level than he ever knew existed. Her eyes were looking deep within him; beyond the Fred she'd been introduced to. Beyond the shell of a man, but to the core of him instead. *She knew.* Fred knew she knew. Her eyes told him so.

"Mistake." Fred allowed the word to softly fall from his lips.

Margie didn't find it hard to believe that out of everything she'd said to him, the only word that truly resonated with him and penetrated his being was "mistake." Her spirit told her that growing up, he'd probably thought that was his name. He'd probably been told more times than he could count that he was a mistake, that he did nothing but make mistakes, that every choice he made would be the wrong choice, therefore leading to a life of mistakes.

"We live in such a critical world," Fred said. "We criticize things we don't even understand. We talk about how ugly and worn-out someone's shoes are without having walked in them, without knowing the long hard steps on the rugged path. Because, trust me, there was no yellow brick road, or even a blueprint, for that matter, for me to follow in life."

Margie paused to make sure Fred had said all he'd wanted to say at that point. She then spoke. "I know often in life we are told that criticism should be welcomed, as it helps us to grow," she said. "That might be true when it comes to some people criticizing you. But with some people, they use criticizing others as a means of complimenting themselves; therefore, you should take it with a grain of salt, or let it go in one ear and

out the other." Margie, upon the direction of the Holy
Ghost inside of her, used her hands to cover Fred's ears.
She whispered a soft quick prayer. "Dear Lord, protect
Fred's ear gates." She then dropped her hands to his
shoulders. "I rebuke anything you might have been told
growing up that affected or affects you in your adult-
hood in a negative way. I rebuke the spirit of confusion."

Fred tensed up with Margie's last statement. Margie
sensed such, and then was quick to clarify something.
"And don't get me wrong, I'm not saying you are confused."

"Then what are you saying? Because I've talked to a lot
of spiritual people in my lifetime, and *confused* tends to
be the label most of them use."

Again, Margie was certain to think before she spoke.
She wanted to be 100 percent in tune with the Holy Spirit.
Perhaps killing that bottle of wine last night hadn't been
the smartest thing to do. Wine and the Holy Spirit didn't
mix, so she could only pray that all of the alcohol had left
her body and she was operating in pure sobriety.

Margie also wanted to be careful with her words
because she wasn't sure how much of Fred's story the
show would air. Truth be told, she honestly had no idea
whether what Clayton had told her about Fred was true.
God had not permitted her to confront Fred with words
someone else had delivered about him. She couldn't
imagine Clayton would have made it all up, risking a
defamation of character suit just to walk away with the
lady of the house. But then again, Margie had to admit
that she was one fine lady of the house. Who knew what
extremes the men would go through to make her theirs?

Being at the house and being the center of attention of
so many men had definitely given Margie's self-esteem a
nice boost. In the process of feeling better about herself,

she didn't want Fred to walk away from the experience feeling exposed and bad about himself.

"You are who God says you are." Margie looked Fred dead in the eyes and said, "Nothing you do in life will ever change that." She spoke with strong conviction. "Do you understand that? You will always be who you were born to be, for God knew you before you were even conceived in your mother's womb. He knew your story. He knew what mistakes you might make in life, but He knew that you," she pointed to Fred's chest, "were no mistake. And you know what? Just for fun, let's say you were born a mistake. Because of our Lord and Savior, Jesus Christ, you can be born again. Do you hear me? I don't care how you were born and which way you were born, but you, my friend, can be born again!"

Fred's jawbones tightened. He was biting down so hard trying to hold in his tears. He was so moved by the passion, compassion, and love of Christ Margie was showing him that he was overwhelmed. This is what love felt like; the love of God. Because this was not the lady of the house speaking into Fred's life. This was God speaking through the lady of the house.

Certain her words were registering with him, Margie continued. "We all sin, we all make mistakes, and we all get confused. God knows this, and God also knows our hearts. We can cover up our hearts with designer bras, T-shirts, suit jackets, and blouses, but He knows what's in there. He knows who we are and what we are. There is nothing medical or scientific that can change the fact that we are born a child of God. And I strongly believe with all of my heart if we just focus on that single fact, if we don't worry about race, sex, religion, nationality, color, complexion or creed, but focus on the God in us and the God in each other, then we'll all know and be who God called us to be."

Fred took in Margie's words, then swallowed. He gathered his composure and was finally able to speak. "Thank you so very much for those words you have just spoken. I believe I just received what I came here for."

"Your confirmation?" Margie asked.

"Yes, my confirmation," Fred confirmed. "And actually, it was confirmation from both you and God."

Margie looked puzzled. "Confirmation from me?"

"If I'm not mistaken, in so many words, did you not just say without saying it that God did not say I was your husband?"

Margie couldn't help but laugh. "Oh my. I just gave you a ten-minute monologue and not once did I mention anything about the real reason you came here, huh?" She covered her mouth in embarrassment.

"I hope you don't find it rude that I'm correcting you, but I beg to differ," Fred said. "I think everything you just said is exactly what I came here for." He smiled at her.

"To God be the glory," Margie said, sniffing away her tears of joy she was storing inside. It always overwhelmed her whenever she felt a move of God.

"So, to make it official, I guess you might want to just say it," Fred said. He nodded toward Danny, then whispered, "For the cameras and all."

Margie nodded her agreement. "Fred, I'm sending you home," Margie said with a huge smile on her face. She never really enjoyed sending the men home. This was usually something she hated doing, knowing that it might hurt someone's feelings or make them feel unwanted. As a servant of God, Margie felt it was always her job to make people feel welcomed, wanted, and like they belonged in the Kingdom. But at the end of the day, she truly felt that's what she'd done for Fred.

Fred planted a kiss on Margie's cheek. She gave him a hug, and while doing so, whispered in his ear. "God has all the answers. Seek Him, Fred. He can and He will make you whole if you ever feel a piece of you is missing. Form a relationship with Him. Call on Him. And for the record, there is a blueprint for you. It's called the Bible." She pulled away and winked at him.

Fred nodded. "Thank you, Pastor Margie. I will call on God. Before now, I wasn't sure whether God could even hear my voice, or if He would listen to me. But now I know that He will."

Margie nodded. "Yes, He will," she said. She pulled away from Fred and watched as he turned to head back up the red carpet. "Fred, wait!" Margie called out.

Fatima, Anya, and the rest of the crew were filled with anxiety. Was it possible that Margie was about to make for really great television by changing her mind and actually choosing Fred?

Fred stopped and turned to face her. "Yes?" he said.

Even the cameramen were eager, each camera zooming in to make sure they didn't miss a single word, gesture, or expression.

"How do you know?" Margie asked.

Fred shrugged with confusion. "Know what?"

"That God will listen to you?"

Fred relaxed his face, glad Margie had asked him something he could easily answer. Knowing that, Fred replied, "Well, He spoke to me, didn't He? He spoke to me through you. So why wouldn't He listen to me?" On that note, Fred turned and made his way back into the mansion.

Margie's eyes filled with tears that she now couldn't control. Fred entering the mansion was symbolic of the mansion he may one day enter after his life here on earth. That place Jesus had prepared for all. It was just a matter of whether one accepted the key that would unlock it.

Chapter 18

"That had to be the happiest man to ever be sent home yet," Fatima said as the makeup artist hurried to touch up Margie's face before the final man was to exit the mansion. "And if my ears weren't deceiving me, I swear he was speaking in tongues by the time he walked back into that house."

Margie and Fatima laughed.

"Man, you are good," Fatima said to Margie.

"To God be the glory," Margie said, pointing upward.

"Oh no, you've been giving God the credit for every single thing since you've been here," Fatima said. "I know one is supposed to be humble, but, Pastor Margie, I think you are in complete denial. You freakin' rock. And as Prophetess Nicole Ross Byrd would say, 'you got the Holy Ghost for real."

Margie laughed at the line she'd often seen the prophetess post on her Facebook page.

"But seriously though," Fatima said, "you've got to own up to your part."

Margie thought for a moment. "Yeah, you're right, and my part is obedience. Operating in the sheer obedience of the Lord is everything."

"I guess I can't argue with you there," Fatima said. "I'm going to run to the bathroom real quick before the green-eyed monster comes out." Fatima winked before she headed off toward the mansion.

Margie figured she must have viewed or been told about some of the footage with Doreen referring to Clayton as such.

"Folks are so hard on poor Clayton," she said.

"I bet it's safe to assume that he's not hard on himself at all," the makeup artist said.

Margie looked at her. "You too?" She couldn't understand for the life of her why everyone thought Clayton was this man who was stuck on himself. Since when wasn't it okay to be confident without being labeled as something negative? "Now, just how in the world did you manage to come to that conclusion?" Margie was curious to know.

"I do all the men's makeup too," the makeup artist reminded her.

Margie hadn't even really thought about the fact that the men had to get a puff of powder or two as well for the sake of being on television. With the way Clayton felt about Fred being in touch with his feminine side, Margie could only imagine how funny acting he might have been when informed he had to wear makeup. Margie laughed at just the thought. "I'm glad I wasn't there to see that fight."

"Oh, it was awful," she said. "He refused to just let me do my job."

"You have to take into consideration that it's probably tough for a man to have to sit there and allow someone to put makeup on him."

She stopped messing around with Margie's face. "That was not what the fighting was about. Far from it." She looked Margie in the face. "He wanted to apply his *own* makeup. He knew all the names of the shades and everything. Coffee Creamer Tan, Olympic Bronze, Caramel Cane Copper. For a minute there, I thought there was some funny business going on with him, if you know what I mean." She raised her eyebrow, and then laid her hand flat out and began fanning it. "You never know these days."

"Hmmm, you never know, now, do you?" Margie knew that to be the truth, but what she didn't know was how Clayton was so well versed on theatrical makeup. "Sweetie, do you happen to have your cell phone on you?"

"Sure." She pulled her phone out of the pocket of the smock she was wearing. "You need to make a call?" She extended the phone to Margie.

"Not quite." Margie took the phone. "Is there a pass-code?" Margie was glad that the staff wasn't prohibited from using their cell phones.

"Oh no. I don't play no passcode stuff. As much as Reggie and I have been through—Reggie is my fiancé—but as much as we've been through with the cell phone business," she said, sucking her teeth . . . "You know, crazy text messages, mysterious phone numbers popping up, walking out of the room to take a call. No sir, no ma'am. We nipped all that in the bud by just not even putting passwords to get into our phones."

"Oh, I see," Margie said, her head spinning just think-ing about all that drama. "I think I might know something that works even better than that," she offered.

"Really?" Her eyes bucked, and she got so excited.

"Yes. It's called trust."

Her lips spread into a smile. "I hear you, Pastor Margie," she said, "loud and clear."

Margie launched the Internet on the cell phone and began her Google search.

"There, all done," the makeup artist said as she tucked her blush brush into her pocket.

"All right, everybody ready on the set?" Fatima shouted out as she exited the mansion.

"Perfect timing," the makeup artist said.

"Yeah, perfect," Margie said with a furrowed eyebrow as she handed the phone back to the makeup artist. "Thank you." Margie exhaled and stared off.

"Everything okay, Pastor Margie?"

Margie looked at the young woman. "You know what? Actually, everything is beyond okay."

"All right then." She put her phone in her pocket and went to walk away.

"And don't forget what I said about the whole trust thing," Margie called out to her. "These days, it's getting harder and harder to trust anyone, but you have to at least give people the benefit of the doubt . . . Until they prove you wrong. Like Oprah Winfrey loves to quote her mentor, the late great Maya Angelou, 'when someone shows you who they are, believe them.'"

The young lady nodded and walked away. She then stopped and turned back to Margie and said, "But what if they don't show you who they are, I mean *really* are?"

"Well, unfortunately, you typically have to wait on God to pull the covers off of them," Margie said.

"But what if He doesn't?" There was a worried expression on her face.

"God won't allow you to be ignorant to Satan's devices," Margie told her. "Just keep your eyes open, and if the writing is on the wall, don't paint over it with your favorite color. Clean house, and when you're finished, throw out all the dirty water. You hear me?" Margie winked.

"I hear you. Thank you, Pastor Margie. It's been amazing working with you, a pleasure to know you, and a true blessing to have been a recipient of your wisdom these past six weeks. Because even when you didn't know I was listening, I was." She smiled and walked away.

If Fatima hadn't yelled, "Quiet on the set," Margie probably would have gotten emotional. But she knew it was showtime, so she got herself together and waited by the arch.

"Here he comes . . . and action!" Fatima took her usual place behind the cameraman.

Clayton floated down that red carpet like he was on skates. He was smooth. When he smiled, if Margie wasn't mistaken, his shiny, white teeth caused a sparkle to bling against the camera lens. He looked like a million bucks. He walked like a million bucks. He had such an air about him that Margie guessed he probably felt like a million bucks. Once he approached Margie, why, heck, he even smelled like a million bucks. And from experience, she knew that as soon as he opened his mouth, he'd even talk like a million bucks.

"You look absolutely amazing," Clayton said, handing Margie a red rose with one hand while the other rested behind his back.

"Thank you." Margie accepted the rose.

"Actually, I have two for you." Clayton whipped his other hand from behind his back and extended another rose to her. "Twice the lady deserves twice the roses."

"How sweet," Margie gushed. She quickly pulled herself together. She did not want to seem like putty in this man's hands. That's one of the reasons why she couldn't get into the *Scandal* series. Initially, she admired her some Olivia Pope. She came across as if she was going to be a powerful, strong willed, independent woman. Then she turned into this weak, adultery fool. That was not inspiring to Margie. So as interesting as she thought the show was going to be, she couldn't stomach them making viewers think she was going to be this superwoman, then her kryptonite came in the form of some other woman's husband. Same went for the show *How to Get Away with Murder*. There was nothing glamourous about a woman appearing weak and making careless decisions when it came to a man.

"Not as sweet as you." Clayton was pouring it on thick, like Margie was a big ole stack of pancakes.

Margie giggled. "Thank you, and by the way, you look stunning." She gave him the once-over. "Looks like you came right off the cover of a magazine." She gave Clayton a knowing look. "But I guess that's possible, considering . . ."

Clayton cleared his throat and loosened his bow tie. "Before you say anything, Pastor Margie, I just want to tell you what an honor it has been to have made your acquaintance. No matter what man you choose to be with tonight, please know that you'll always be a part of me."

"Part," Margie said in a mocking tone. "I imagine you always get the part."

"Pardon me?" Clayton said, loosening his tie even more as his cheeks turned red.

"Never mind," Margie said. She'd alluded enough to the fact that Clayton had been dreaming of being in front of the camera since he was eight years old. At least that's what his IMDb bio she'd pulled up on Google had read. When she'd first Googled his name, Clayton Farmers, she came up with nothing. She came up with nothing when she Googled Clayton B. Farmers, adding his middle initial. When the name Clayton Benton popped up on the lower page of the search, she was led to click on it. She'd recalled Clayton mentioning his middle name when they'd first met. She was almost certain it was Benton. After clicking the link, there popped up a headshot of Clayton himself. Looks like the D-list actor was going by his first and middle name only.

He'd been in several commercials, had done some print ads, and was even an extra on a few television shows. He had speaking parts twice in two major film productions, but *Lady of the House* had been the most camera time he'd gotten in his almost six decades of wanting to act. So

Margie couldn't help but wonder if all of this, everything he'd said to her, everything he'd done, had all been an act. Was he really an engineer like he'd told her he was? The good thing about it, though, was that none of that had even mattered. God had given her the answer to who she'd choose today long before she'd Googled Mr. Clayton. It wasn't about what Margie wanted or didn't want; it was all about God's will for her life. Just imagine how Hosea must have felt in the Bible when God told him he had to marry Gomer—a harlot!

It really would have made for great television if Margie had outright confronted Clayton about her findings, but she was operating under the direction of the Holy Ghost, and the Holy Ghost wasn't into embarrassing people.

"Clayton, you are a wonderful man," Margie said. "You are handsome, kind, and a loving father, it seems."

Clayton seemed to relax somewhat at Margie's words. He smiled and nodded. His confidence was climbing. "Thank you so much, Margie. You are an awesome, lovely, and kindhearted woman that any man would be blessed just to know, let alone have you as their possible future wife."

"Thank you," Margie said, looking down to blush, then looking back up at Clayton again. Margie had to admit that she could stare off into this man's eyes for days. The blueness gave the deepest blue ocean a run for its money. However, she put on her life jacket, and then dived back into his eyes. Prayerfully, she wouldn't drown. "I was so smitten by you on the first day I met you. I was attracted by your confidence, openness, and honesty. And I hope I don't sound too shallow by admitting that I was first attracted by your looks. I mean, seeing someone as handsome as you step out of that limo like that . . ." Margie began to fan herself as Clayton laughed.

She got herself together, and then continued. "I want to thank you for taking time out of your life to spend the last six weeks with me."

"You are more than welcome," Clayton said. "The pleasure, indeed, has been all mine. And I'd do it all over again if I had to." This wouldn't be the first time Clayton had captivated a woman with his looks. In past years, his charm had made women overlook some of his flaws, or make them invisible altogether. His looks; those were his superpowers.

Margie felt her head about to go under. It was hard to keep her head above water when it came to Clayton and all of his kind words of flattery and compliments. She caught her breath. "Every time there was an elimination that had to be made and I had to send one of the men home, I just couldn't let you go," Margie admitted. "It was so difficult. I think it was my curiosity that was getting the best of me. I wanted to know more. I wanted to learn everything that I could."

"Well, I hope I didn't disappoint," he said, now totally convinced that even at this final elimination, Margie still wouldn't be sending him home.

"And you didn't," Margie assured him. "I think, thanks to you, I know all that I need to do in these final moments. You've told me everything I needed to know."

Nothing could have wiped the huge smile of victory off of Clayton's face—Nothing except for Margie's next words.

"Which means I don't need you here anymore. And for that reason, I'm sending you home."

Technically, the smile didn't exactly get wiped off of Clayton's face. It was actually just frozen there. His facial muscles hadn't yet caught up with what his brain had heard Margie say.

Not only was Clayton confused as all get-out, but so was the crew. Lincoln stood off to the side looking as though a goldfish was stuck in his throat. Just as soon as he could come out of his cloud of shock, he looked at Fatima. She was already staring at him. She stood off behind Danny, whose mouth was opened to the floor. She was waving her arms frantically for Lincoln to interject.

"Do something! Say something!" Fatima mouthed frantically to the show's host.

Lincoln eagerly nodded his head, letting Fatima know he was on it. He tugged at the bottom of his deep violet suede suit coat, took a fist, and beat it on his chest. That must have loosened the goldfish up, allowing him to swallow it, sending it swimmingly on its merry way downstream. He gulped, cleared his throat, and straightened his bow tie that matched his suit jacket. Then he stepped over to Margie.

"Umm, excuse me, Pastor Margie," Lincoln said, "but, uh, you do realize that Clayton is the last man standing. You, uh, already sent Fred home. They were the last two."

Margie stared at Lincoln the entire time he spoke. "Yes, I know," she said just as nonchalant as she could have.

"But, uh, we asked you if you had made your decision," Lincoln continued. "Which man you wanted to spend the rest of your life with, the man who would be . . . well . . . your first man, and help you run New Day Temple of Faith."

"Umm-hmm." Margie nodded, confirming to Lincoln that everything he was saying was true.

"But—"

"And I did make my decision," Margie said just as plain. Again, she was so nonchalant that it was starting to drive poor Lincoln crazy.

Lincoln exhaled. "Pastor Margie, for weeks you've spent time with ten wonderful men. You narrowed it down to just two. The whole goal was to come out of this experience having found the perfect mate to be your helpmeet."

Margie nodded. "Yes, and I did." Again, she was so imperturbable that Lincoln couldn't stand it. He wanted an explanation for all this, and he wanted it now.

"Oh, for Christ's sake, woman!" Lincoln exclaimed, throwing his hands in the air, and then letting them fall to his side. "Is this some kind of payback for all the little tricks and twists we threw in? Huh? Is that what it is?" Lincoln was so animated that even though he seemed to be defending Clayton somewhat, Clayton had to pull his head back and look at Lincoln like he was crazy.

"Hey, now wait a minute," Clayton said, grabbing Lincoln by the shoulder to calm him down. "This *woman* has a name. Show some respect."

"Man, you betta get yo' hands off of me," Lincoln said, snatching away from Clayton and wiping off the spot on his jacket that Clayton had touched. "I will whoop an old man," Lincoln said to him. He then looked at Fatima. "Tell 'em, Fatima. I will whoop an old man's a—" He was stomping his foot with the pronunciation of each syllable.

Margie, Clayton, Fatima, and everyone else looked on in shock. They weren't so much in shock that Lincoln was ranting and raving, but all of a sudden, he was doing it without his English accent.

"Ha! I knew it!" Clayton said, pointing an accusing finger at Lincoln. "I could sense that forced, phony accent a mile away." He began laughing while pointing at Clayton. "I might not speak with an English accent, but my parents did, and I know an authentic one from a trumped-up one."

Lincoln's eyes shot fire at Clayton. Sensing that this was probably not going to end well, Fatima stepped from behind the camera to grab hold of Lincoln.

Margie's mouth was wide open. She couldn't believe this Lincoln was the same bourgeoisie-acting Lincoln who had displayed nothing but the epitome of class since being on set. He'd always been decked out like a sharply dressed, classic man. He'd talked with an English accent even though he was black, like Idris Elba. Margie had even seen him sipping on tea with a raised pinkie finger while the directors went over scenes with him. And now, all of a sudden, he was raising his fist and talking as if he'd never learned to speak proper English in his life.

"No, back up off of me!" Lincoln yelled to Fatima while he tried to take his jacket off as if he was going to fight.

"Is this young man for real?" Clayton said while Lincoln still struggled to get at him. Clayton watched Lincoln act a fool for a moment longer, and then grabbed his bow tie. He'd already loosened it as much as he could, so this time, he just yanked it off. He proceeded to take his jacket off too. "Don't let the age fool ya," Clayton said. "I do still know how to work these hands." He balled his fists and began showing them off to Lincoln. "Think a pretty boy like me didn't have my share of fights? I fought over a plenty of women. And I'm going to fight over one more, if need be."

"Clayton, no!" Margie shouted out. "There is no need for you to do this."

Clayton put up his fists and mean mugged Lincoln. "I was raised to defend a woman's honor, and that's just what I'm going to do." Clayton was not going to be like Franklin, who didn't stand up to Lincoln the last time he got fresh at the mouth with Margie.

The next thing Margie knew, Lincoln had broken away from Fatima and "accidentally" slammed into Clayton. Clayton unexpectedly got Lincoln in a headlock and began giving him a knuckle sandwich. "Say 'uncle.' Say 'uncle'," Clayton began to demand of Lincoln.

"Dear Lord, will one of you men get from behind those cameras and do something?" Margie shouted.

Danny looked at Fatima for permission.

"You heard her. Do something!" Fatima screamed at him.

With the person he took his orders from granting him permission to put down the camera, Danny did just that and went to break the two men apart. He managed to pull Clayton off of Lincoln and hold his arms to keep him from giving Lincoln any more knuckle sandwiches. Unfortunately, with Clayton being restrained, Lincoln was able to get in a good blow that laid Clayton out flat.

"Oh, God!" Margie yelled, and then raced over to Clayton's side. She kneeled down on the ground. "Clayton, are you okay?" She didn't get a response from him. He was out cold. "Call the paramedics," Margie yelled frantically. She looked over to no one in particular. All she saw was silhouettes. Everything was in such a blur. "Someone help him." She looked back at Clayton. She slapped him on the cheek to try to bring him to. That didn't work. Margie didn't know what to do. It was true that she had been in this position before; kneeled down beside someone who was laid out. But usually they were laid out in the spirit, and she was praying over them. So even though that wasn't the case in this situation, she did what she always did, which was to pray.

It wasn't long before the set's first aid team arrived. Margie moved out of their way so that they could tend to Clayton.

"He's totally out of it," Margie said after Anya helped her to her feet.

Fatima and Danny had escorted Lincoln to another room. Margie stood there, with Anya embracing her, watching as Clayton was examined. She'd been so thankful that they'd gotten through the entire season's recordings without a single physical altercation, which is what viewers expected of almost every reality show, whether or not God's name was attached to it. Just five more minutes and the show would have been a wrap and perhaps gone down as the first reality show where no one got physical. Why, why, why?

Margie felt so guilty because it was her own little twist that had caused all the drama. She knew her actions had nothing to do with how someone else reacted. People needed to learn a little self-control. But still, she couldn't help but feel bad about the entire situation.

"That nose is broken, that's for sure," one of the people assisting Clayton said as they pointed to his slightly bent snout.

Just then, two paramedics came in rolling a stretcher.

Margie put her hand over her mouth as she gasped at the sight of the paramedics coming to take Clayton away. She began praying harder in her head as she watched the paramedics lift Clayton onto the stretcher. They secured him, and then went to roll him away.

"Just a moment," Margie called out. She ran over to the stretcher and stood over Clayton. She placed a hand on his chest, closed her eyes, and continued praying. She'd just felt the need to lay healing hands on him. "Thank you," Margie said to the paramedics after she finished praying and opened her eyes.

One nodded as they went to roll him away.

As Margie walked away, she heard one of the paramedics say, "Hey, I think he's coming to." They'd put smelling salts under his nose. They'd called out his name and had tried to bring him to. But Margie had simply gone over and laid hands on him.

Margie turned and rushed back over to Clayton. His head was slowly moving from left to right. His eyeballs were fluttering under his closed lids as if struggling to open. He moaned, and then finally opened his eyes.

"Praise God," Margie said under her breath.

"Pastor Margie?" Clayton asked, trying to focus. His vision was a little blurred.

"Yes, yes, it's me," Margie said, rejoicing that he'd come to before her very eyes. She would have been worried sick about him otherwise.

"Did I win?" he asked.

Margie couldn't believe that after all that had been said and done, on top of the butt kickin' he'd taken from Lincoln, that his only concern was whether he'd won the reality show. Whether he'd been the last man standing.

Sadly, Margie would have to tell him yet another time that he was not the chosen man. He hadn't been the last man standing figuratively or literally. Telling him once hadn't been too difficult. Having to tell him twice, this time while he was laid out on a stretcher, wasn't as easy. Margie took a deep breath. "I'm sorry, Clayton, but you didn't win. I didn't choose you."

"Pshtt," Clayton said, twisting up his lips as if he couldn't have cared less about not being chosen as Margie's first man, so to speak. "I meant, did I win the fight?"

Margie was taken aback and suffering from a slightly bruised ego. Guess that answered her question as to whether he had been serious about maybe someday being her husband or whether he'd been acting all along. "You're lying on a stretcher, for Pete's sake," Margie said not totally unsympathetic. "Of course, you didn't win." She continued. "As the young people would say," she put her hands on her hips, "you got knocked the—"

"Is Clayton okay? Did he come to? Is he going to be all right?" Fatima came back outside frantic with concern.

"He'll live, I'm sure," Margie answered as Fatima walked up next to her.

"Thank God." Fatima let out a sigh of relief.

"So I didn't get picked by the Lady of the House, but I got into a fight that's landing me in the hospital?" Clayton reiterated all he thought was taking place.

"I don't know about the hospital," one of the paramedics jumped in and said. "But we'd at least like to put you in the back of the ambulance, check some vitals, ask you a few questions, and maybe observe you for a bit. Does that sound okay to you?"

Everyone looked at Clayton for a response. They all watched as his stoic face spread into the hugest grin ever.

Fatima and Margie looked at each other with concern. Had Lincoln knocked the sense out of the poor man? This was no laughing matter, yet, he looked as if he was going to bust with joy.

The next thing anyone knew, Clayton hollered out, "Yes!" and pumped his fist in the air. "This is sure to get me lots of attention, camera time, and maybe even eventually my own spinoff show. I'll be Clayton #thatmanwhogotknockedthe—"

"Guys, can you take him away!" Fatima said to the paramedics with disgust.

They nodded and began to roll Clayton away.

Clayton was chattering with excitement the entire time. "I have some great ideas, Fatima," he yelled. "Don't pitch it to your people without my input. As a matter of fact, have your people call my people!"

Just as they rolled him out of sight he looked up to the heavens and pumped his fist one last time while yelling out, "Thank you, Jesus. It only took you over fifty years, but I'm finally going to be a star. My being on this show was destiny, true destiny."

Everyone was in complete silence and total awe.

Margie was the first to speak. "And just think, I was actually feeling bad for him."

Fatima shook her head. "I guess I have to be a better judge in character when deciding on cast members in the future."

"And don't just do a background search, but a Google search as well, like I did five minutes before he walked out of the mansion this evening," Marge said.

Fatima shook her head. "I can't believe I dropped the ball on that. But they were all old men."

Margie cleared her throat, reminding Fatima that they were all around her age.

"I'm sorry," Fatima apologized about the age comment. "We expect some of the younger people we cast on our shows to be fame seekers and not genuinely down for the cause. But who knew a man Clayton's age would be playing those types of games?"

"Hey, you're never too old for love, and you're never too old to reach your dreams," Margie said with a smile.

"Yeah, you're right," Fatima agreed. "But I'm so sorry about all this." Fatima was racking her brain over how she didn't see this coming with Clayton. "He seemed so honest and sincere during the interviews. I mean, who would have thought someone would use God for fame?"

No sooner than the words had come out of Fatima's mouth did she realize exactly what she was saying.

She and Margie looked at each other and laughed. "Who doesn't, nowadays, try to use God for fame, would probably be the simpler question to ask," Margie said.

"You've got that right, Pastor Margie."

Margie got serious as the Holy Spirit dropped words into her being to share with Fatima. "Because you do know that's what folks are going to accuse you of with this show? You and me both?"

Fear cast a shadow across Fatima's eyes. "But—"

"I know that was not your intention or mine, but don't get sidetracked or distracted with what other people say,"

Margie said. "Sometimes, you just have to sit back and say nothing. Let God fight your battles."

"I agree," Fatima said. She looked at the mansion entrance. "Although God didn't do a really good job of fighting Clayton's for him." Fatima put her hand over her mouth and made the oopsie face. "That wasn't so nice, was it?"

"Fatima, darling," Margie said as she put her arm around the show's producer, "we all, at one point or another in our lives, do or say something that's not so nice. But fortunately, we serve a forgiving God. Amen?"

"Amen, Pastor Margie," Fatima agreed.

Margie removed her arm from around Fatima and the two looked around at the destruction. A pedestal had been knocked over. There were bow ties and suit jackets on the ground. And it looked as though Clayton had even been knocked out of one of his shoes.

"I guess this is a wrap," Fatima said, sounding exhausted and discouraged.

"Yes, I guess so," Margie said as she continued to look around. "For now, anyway."

"What do you mean by that?" Fatima asked, confused.

"Well, sometimes things aren't always what they look like," Margie said. "And even though this looks like the end of the road, and probably not the happy ending you expected, you never know what else God might have in store. And you know something?" Margie said to her.

"What?" Fatima replied.

"Something tells me that when it comes to *Lady of the House*, God is not finished."

And Margie couldn't have been more right.

Chapter 19

"Everybody's pretty upset with me, huh?" Margie said as she and Doreen rode in the limo that was taking them back to her house. Doreen's flight back to Kentucky wasn't scheduled for a few more days, so she was going to stay with Margie and do some visiting while in Malvonia.

"Margie, my friend, it's one of those moments when you have to say the heck with what everybody thinks about you; it's what God knows about you," Doreen said. "And God knows you did what He told you to do. Period, point-blank. I don't have to tell you that."

"I know," Margie said, "but it's always so disappointing when other people don't understand it." She turned from staring out of the window to look at Doreen. "I heard one of the crew members say they think that's what I was up to the entire time. I was just a preacher trying to hustle money for the church in the name of Jesus. That I was using God's name in vain." Margie shook her head and looked back out of the window again.

"You and I both know that's the furthest thing from the truth."

"Yeah, but everybody else doesn't know it. I just never want society to think I'm a phony, a fake, a hustler, or some two-bit preacher lady. I know many people say that they don't care what people think of them. Well, they should. It matters. There are sixty-six books in the Bible, and we're number sixty-seven. People read us every day. And I don't want people reading between the lines about me when all is said and done." Margie shook her head. Then suddenly she remembered the message she'd given Fatima the evening before. *The message is always for the messenger first*, she told herself, then figured she'd better start operating in the same words she'd given Fatima to operate in.

"When all is said and done, it will be God with the final say," Doreen said. "Let the crew, producers, network, and whoever else behind *Lady of the House* get over it. If they can't see God and the ministry in this thing, then that's their fault." Doreen was bothered by the fact that the crew had been upset, murmuring and complaining about Margie not having picked a man on the show. Doreen had to bite her tongue quite a bit, but now what she hated even more is that it was really starting to bother Margie. She didn't want Margie to think all she'd done had been in vain. Being obedient to the Lord was never something done in vain, and as a pastor, Margie should know that first. But just like the message they'd been wanting to portray all along, Doreen had to remember that Margie was not only a pastor, but she was human. Humans always had to be reminded of biblical things, no matter how well versed in the Bible they were.

Doreen quickly turned her body from the straightforward positon to face Margie. "Every time you had to kick one of the fellas off the show, you said you tried to do it in an encouraging manner."

Margie nodded. That was usually the case. She knew rejection wasn't a good feeling, so she made sure she always had kind words for the men she'd sent home. She made sure to let them know rejection from one person was so as not to block them from being accepting of what God really had for them. One example she'd given one of the men was that sometimes a person had to be told "no" in order to make way for the "yes" God had for them. Margie keeping them there was keeping them from what God really had for them.

"In a sense, you ministered to each and every man on this show and the whole world is going to get to see it," Doreen said excitedly. "At least, all the parts that aren't edited out anyway. But just imagine, someone out there is going to hear a word that is meant for them too."

"You're right. It's like when you're sitting on the pew in church and someone is being prophesied to, but you feel like it's a word for you. Well, sometimes it is. All God needed was for you to be in earshot," Margie said, now getting just as excited as Doreen.

"Now we're on the same page," Doreen said. "There won't be one person, after seeing this show, who will see you as anything other than a servant of God. I don't care how much editing out they do."

Margie closed her eyes and shook her head. She then opened them and looked at Doreen. "Look at you, right down to the last minute you still have my back and have to talk the good sense the Lord gave me back into my head."

"Did I get through to you at least?" Doreen wanted to know.

"Absolutely."

"Good, then now I can say my famous last words," Doreen said with a confident look on her face. "My assignment is over."

She and Margie then both said in unison, "It is finished!"

Doreen was wise enough to know, though, that God always got the last word. It was never finished until God said it was finished. It was just getting started . . . for her anyway.

Chapter 20

It was ten in the morning when Margie returned home from dropping Doreen off at the airport so that she could catch her flight home. As soon as Margie walked back in the door, her cell phone rang. She looked at the caller ID, smiled, and then answered the phone.

"Fatima, how are you?" Margie said into the receiver, setting her purse down on the table by the door.

"I'm actually pretty stoked," Fatima said excitedly.

"Well, you sound it, that's for sure," Margie said. "What's got you so geared up?"

"We put together some clippings of the show and sent them to the network, who, in turn, forwarded them to some of their reviewers and bloggers in order to get the buzz started about the show."

"Oh really? Wow. I didn't know the public would get to see parts of the show before it actually premiered."

"Not the public, per se. Well, just any bits and pieces that any reviewers or bloggers might share. Like I said, just enough to get folks talking to really generate an interest for the show. Now remember, per your contract, you can't talk about the show, especially the outcome. You or Mother Doreen. No one needs to know who you picked, or in your case, who you didn't pick, which was none of the men. It would ruin everything. No one would watch the show if they already knew how it ended."

"Doreen and I both understand," Margie assured her. "But trust me when I say that you didn't have to have her and me sign a contract in order to not talk about this show." Margie let out a harrumph.

"That bad of an experience, huh?" Fatima asked.

"Actually, I'm just being dramatic," Margie said. "Doreen helped me to see that the show was a true blessing to so many people in so many ways, and that God's will truly was done."

"I'm glad to hear that," Fatima said.

"But anyway, I don't want to bring down your lovely hot air balloon," Margie said, trying to pick the conversation back up. "From the sound of your voice, I guess the reviewers and bloggers had all good things to say about the show."

"Wellll, I wouldn't necessarily say that," Fatima said in a whiny voice, "but for the network it's all good. Things that will definitely make people want to catch some episodes."

"Then I can't wait to see what they had to say."

"Good, because I e-mailed you the links to the clippings and comments. E-mail me back or call me and let me know what you—" Fatima's words had started to trail off while she was saying her last sentence, as if something was preoccupying her, then she just abruptly stopped speaking. "Look, Pastor Margie, I just got an emergency text. I have to run to a meeting. But I'll talk to you later, okay?"

"All right. And thanks for—" Margie didn't even get the rest of her words out before she heard a clicking sound in her ear. "Hello? Fatima?" She pulled her phone away from her ear to see that the call was no longer in progress. "Oh well," she said.

She couldn't wait to read what had been said about the show, but she'd have to. She wanted to get nice and comfortable in front of her computer screen. So she headed to the kitchen to fix her a cup of tea first. A few minutes later, she was sitting in front of her computer reading her e-mail from Fatima.

"Well, here goes nothing," Margie said as she clicked the link in the body of Fatima's e-mail. "Pastor Margie is proof that God has a sense of humor," Margie read out loud. "That's the truth," she agreed with the reviewer. As she read on there were some not-so-nice reviews. "No true woman of God would ever go on TV to meet a man. She'd trust God enough to send her Boaz." Margie shrugged that one off. The negativity of it hadn't even stung since Doreen had already more or less voiced such. Come to think of it, Doreen had already said just about anything negative the rest of the world could come up with. Unbeknownst to Doreen, she'd prepared Margie for any blows that might come her way. Margie smiled, because something told her that it wasn't unbeknownst to Doreen at all. The woman of God knew exactly what she was doing all along. Her hard comments softened the blow for any Margie would receive from outsiders.

Margie was finding that most of the negative comments didn't really sting her as much as she thought they would. She was already immune because Doreen had injected her with the immunization shot that wouldn't allow the words to kill her spirit. The words might have hurt just a tad initially, but when you are immune to something, it won't kill you.

"Thank you, Father," Margie looked up and said, "for using friends and even family as immunization shots. That way, when we go out in the world and are put into contact with poisonous tongues and the people they belong to, we won't die. Our spirits will not be killed. Amen."

Margie had taught on that very same subject once upon a time. Who knew that eventually that message would come to pass in her own life?

As she read on, she giggled at some of the trending hashtags people were using. "Hashtagassaultwithbreath," Margie read out loud, and then laughed. During the preview clippings they'd shown her sharing her comment about Kent's breath with Doreen.

"Hashtag greatestahamoment" Reading that made Margie smile.

Overall, there were probably equally as many negative comments as there were positive. There would always be people who found the bad and people who found the good in things. Some reviewers vowed they would never watch the show. That was fine with Margie. Everything wasn't for everybody. If people didn't like the show, then they had every right not to watch it. But what Margie hoped didn't happen was that people who claimed not to like it didn't set their schedule to watch it just to dog it out on social media. Instead, she would pray for those who God meant to receive a message from the show would watch and receive.

Margie exited off the page with the reviews, but didn't shut down her e-mail account. She opened up a new document so that she could begin working on next week's Bible study lesson. Before getting started on that, though, she heard the notification letting her know she had a new e-mail.

"Oh, wow!" Margie said out loud when she saw that Fatima had sent her another e-mail. She clicked it open and began reading it. The first couple of lines were the standard greetings and pleasantries. Margie smiled as she read them. But then, all of a sudden, the smile faded as she continued to read on. She couldn't even finish the entire e-mail before she found herself questioning it out loud. "But I . . . But why?"

Margie was so baffled and confused by the news Fatima had just informed her of in the e-mail. A part of her was disappointed and just a tad angry. However, she finally gathered her composure, and then continued reading the message, hoping she'd get her answer, which she did.

Once she finished reading the e-mail in its entirety, all Margie could do was shake her head and look up. "If you say so, God, then so be it."

She read the e-mail one more time, and then hit the reply button and generated an e-mail to send to Fatima.

Hi, Fatima. I very much enjoyed watching the clippings and reading the reviews from Lady of the House. I just got the e-mail of you letting me know that somehow the cut footage was sent to the networks along with some of the edited footage. I guess that's why you raced off the phone with me earlier. I'm sure you felt just awful to learn of the error. But who knew the powers that be would actually find the cutting-room floor footage of the crew members more drama filled than the actual show itself? So, congrats on serendipity allowing you to get the job as head producer on the new reality show called Reality Show, which will, unfortunately, take the place of Lady of the House that will now never see the light of day. I can't blame them though. I'd have to agree that Lincoln and his antics compared to mine will be far more entertaining.

Margie had to take a break from writing to laugh out loud herself. She replayed in her head some of the behind-the-scene lines the crew members said and did, right down to the hairstylist and makeup artist. As much as she wanted to, she couldn't forget about when the two of them got into it after she had said the word "hunky." Then, of course, there was Lincoln's tantrum on final elimination night. Margie realized then there was no need to get upset; what those crew members did behind the cameras absolutely made for better TV, at least the kind of TV that society was used to viewing when it came to reality shows. So on that thought, Margie continued typing.

I have to admit that at first, upon reading your e-mail, I was a little disappointed. I'd really hoped we could prove the naysayers wrong by introducing the world to clean reality television. But, like I told you, it's never about the naysayers anyway. I'm just glad you were able to be elevated at the end of the day. It was truly an honor to be a part of your vision, and I wish you nothing but the best.
Pastor Margie

Margie switched over to her Word program and began working on her Bible study lesson. About an hour in, she heard that same chiming sound again, letting her know she'd received a new e-mail. She clicked over to her AOL e-mail account and saw that Fatima had replied to her e-mail. She cracked it open and began to read it.

I'm so glad you understand the executive decision that was made. I don't want you to think for one minute that your being here was in vain. And just to show you such, please click the link below and you will see for yourself.
Thank you for everything, Pastor Margie.

Margie smiled and after reading Fatima's e-mail, said, "Well, I guess they say if you've touched one life, then you've done your job." But if she were to be honest with herself, she didn't want to just touch one life. She wanted to touch lives by the droves. Jesus didn't do all He'd done just to touch and save one life. He did it to save a nation of people. By no means was Margie comparing herself to Jesus, but heck, as farfetched as it sounded, she wanted to save the world. And even if realistically she couldn't, was there anything so wrong with trying?

Margie had honestly felt that through this whole reality-show experience, she was being provided a platform to tell and show the world who God was. Though thwarted by the final outcome of it all, she still knew that she had to trust God.

Margie was about to delete the e-mail when she realized she hadn't clicked the link that Fatima had provided. She did so and up popped a clipping from one of the scenes on the upcoming reality show titled *Reality Show*.

Margie put her hand over her mouth as she watched the clipping. Within moments, tears settled on the rim of her bottom lids.

She went to type Fatima another e-mail, but this time, decided she'd just pick up the phone and call her.

"Fatima Swanson speaking," she answered the phone.

"Fatima, you are truly an angel," Margie sniffed into the phone.

"I take it you clicked on the link I sent you."

Margie nodded, so overwhelmed by joy.

"Isn't it amazing that they decided to use some of the scenes with you comforting and ministering to folks; I mean, right down to the makeup artist. I had no idea all of that was going on behind the scenes."

"I guess I have Danny to thank for all that."

"Danny?" Fatima asked.

"Yes, apparently he keeps those cameras rolling at all times unless he hears you yell 'cut.' There's no way he would have gotten some of that footage had he done otherwise."

"That's my Danny," Fatima said proudly. "So just to confirm, you're okay with the new twist and us showing you pretty much in just your pastoral role, even though at first, my intention was to do just the opposite?"

"I love it," Margie said, wiping her spilling tears away.

"So you know those couple of times we filmed you teaching at New Day, I think they are going to show some of that too." The producers had kept their promise in allowing Margie to go back to church so they could get some footage of her preaching.

"Awesome," Margie said. God truly was having His way in all this, and all she could do was smile.

"And, Pastor Margie, I was wondering if whenever I'm in town you wouldn't mind me dropping by New Day."

"What? Are you serious?" Margie exclaimed.

"Yes, you heard me right. After so many years of not being in the church, for some reason, when we went to your church to film, it didn't feel like I was on the job at work."

"Really?" Margie said. "What did it feel like then?"

Fatima let out what sounded like a sigh of relief. "It felt like home."

Even though Margie couldn't see Fatima, she could sense her smile through the phone.

"And there's no place like, home, dear. No place like home," Margie said.

"Well, I better get going," Fatima said. "With all the sudden changes there is so much work to be done and so little time to do it. Thanks again for everything, Pastor Margie."

"No, thank you," Margie said as the call ended. She leaned back in the chair, crossed her arms, and then looked up to the heavens. "Well, God, it doesn't surprise me that we did all that for one sheep." Margie shook her head and went back to working on her Bible study lesson; the subject she would teach popped into her head and out of her mouth: "the prodigal daughter returns home."

Chapter 21

"I missed you, sweetie," Wallace said as he walked up to Doreen and kissed her.

Doreen stood at the passenger pickup area of the airport. One large and one medium suitcase was parked next to her. One of the skycaps had assisted her in carrying them out. She held her carry-on bag in her arms.

"I missed you as well." Doreen threw her arms around her husband, glad to be back in his loving, comforting, protective arms. She was glad to be home period.

"How was taping? How did things turn out? Is your work done, Iyanla?" Wallace said, jokingly.

Doreen laughed. "I do feel like God be sending me to help people fix their lives," she said. "Now if He'd only send me someone to help me fix mine." One thing Doreen could attest to was that those six weeks on the set helped her keep her mind off of the situation at her church. And even when it did enter her mind, there was plenty around the mansion to do to help get her mind back off of it again. But now she was back . . . where the problem still existed.

Her husband and Melanie might have been able to throw away those envelopes with those vicious messages on them, but until they figured out who was behind the act, the problem itself was not going to go away. Whoever was doing it felt comfortable enough to return to the church Sunday after Sunday and be right up in Doreen's face.

"Funny you should say that," Wallace said. He retrieved Doreen's larger suitcase, and then took it to put in the trunk. After doing so, he came back to retrieve the medium-sized one.

"I'm waiting," Doreen said.

"What?" he replied, looking up at her with a clueless expression.

"Oh, Lord," Doreen said, sensing that her husband had something up his sleeve. "What's going on? How come when I said I wished God would send someone to fix my life you said, 'Funny you should say that'? Then you marched off like you ain't said a thing." She grabbed her husband by his arm before he could run off toward the trunk. "What's going on, Pastor Wallace Frey?"

He stopped and looked at his wife. "I guess you could say that God answered your prayers." He winked, and then proceeded to put the suitcase in the trunk.

Doreen raised an eyebrow and gave her husband a suspicious look as he unloaded her carry-on from her arms and placed it in the back of their SUV as well.

She folded her arms and shook her head. Even though she knew they couldn't sit idle outside the airport passenger pickup location much longer without being asked to move, ticketed, or towed, she wasn't stepping foot in that car until her husband told her what was going on.

"Pastor Frey?" The questioning voice came from behind Doreen.

Both Doreen and Wallace turned to see a woman clearing the automatic glass doors of the airport. The heavyset woman was dressed to the nines wearing a large brim church hat that hid most of her face. She was toting a single suitcase and a carry-on.

"Right on time," Wallace said. He walked toward the woman to whom the voice belonged.

"My partner I told you about missed her flight," the woman stated. "She's going to have a car bring her to the hotel."

"No problem." Wallace took the woman's suitcase as Doreen stood off in the background confused as all get-out. He turned to his wife. "Honey," he said to Doreen as he walked toward her, "I'd like you to meet someone." He stopped once he reached Doreen. The woman in the big hat who had been following behind him stopped as well. "Honey, this is First Lady Arykah Howell." He turned to the woman. "Lady Arykah, this is my wife, Doreen."

"First Lady," the woman said, extending her hand toward Doreen. "Your husband has told me quite a bit about you. It's a pleasure to meet you."

Doreen's mouth dropped in awe. She didn't know the face; heck, she couldn't see the face, but she knew the name well. If this was the same Lady Arykah some of the pastors' wives had been talking about, she had been making quite the name for herself. Doreen might have been the Iyanla Vanzant in the Kingdom, but Lady Arykah was known as the Oliva Pope of the Kingdom.

First ladies were known to take a lot of flak from their congregations. If things got too out of hand, were beyond the first lady's control, or there just needed to be a neutral party involved to resolve certain issues, they could always call upon Lady Arykah to come handle it. In this case, that's exactly what Wallace had done. He figured he'd sat on this situation long enough and he owed it to his wife to get it handled and not just sweep it under the rug.

"And I've heard quite a bit about you," Doreen said, shaking Lady's Arykah's hand.

"All good I hope," Lady Arykah said as she flipped her hat up so that her face was now revealed.

Both women's hearts nearly stopped.

"It's you!" they each exclaimed simultaneously while pointing to each other.

"Oh, so you two *have* met before?" Wallace said.

"Honey," Doreen said to her husband, "this is that first lady I think I told you about." She spoke in a loud whisper and was bucking her eyes. "It was years ago. The one Margie and I thought we were going to have to . . ." Doreen's words trailed off.

"Beat down," Lady Arykah said with a snuffle. "Funny we should meet again. I didn't recall the name when your husband mentioned it to me. You're right; it was some years ago when we first made each other's acquaintance at your former pastor's home over macaroni and cheese. It was back in Ohio, so I didn't make the connection. It was back when I was just getting into the groove of being a first lady. But let me assure you that I've matured in Christ since then."

"Oh, I don't doubt that, Lady Arykah," Doreen said with no intentions of holding Lady Arykah's past actions against her, especially not when the first lady's more recent actions and works for the Lord superseded it. If folks did that to Doreen, she'd never finish her assignments for the Lord. "Your reputation precedes you, Lady Arykah. I see God is now using both you and your husband mightily. I actually feel honored that you are here."

"Well, to God be the glory," Lady Arykah said. "So glad He's giving me this opportunity to make another impression on you."

"I too am glad that God has allowed us to reconnect." Doreen looked down. "I just wish it was under different circumstances."

"I hear you," Lady Arykah said. "But right now, from what your husband told me, you're just getting back to town, and I'm getting in town. I'm sure we're both a little jetlagged. So why don't we relax today, get a good night's rest, and then discuss matters in the morning?" She looked from Doreen to Wallace, then back to Doreen.

The husband and wife looked at each other. Wallace shrugged that he didn't mind while Doreen shrugged that she didn't mind.

Doreen looked back at Lady Arykah. "Sounds good to me."

"Good, then it's all settled," Wallace said. "Lady Arykah, I'll get you to your hotel. There is a credit card on file so order room service, whatever you'd like."

"Hotel?" Doreen said, shocked. "But we've got an empty guest room she can stay at."

"Oh no!" Lady Arykah shook her head and shook her index finger. "I've been around long enough to know that there is only one queen that should sleep in the throne. There can only be one lady of the house."

Doreen looked at Wallace, and they both chuckled that Lady Arykah had unknowingly cited the name of the reality show Doreen had just spent the last six weeks taping.

"I hear you loud and clear," Doreen said to Lady Arykah. "Loud and clear."

"Alrighty then," Wallace said, then made sure the women and their luggage were loaded into the vehicle.

As they drove off, something came to Doreen's mind; something she'd heard Lady Arykah say to Wallace.

"You mentioned something about your partner," Doreen said. "So someone else will be joining us?"

"Yep," Lady Arykah said while she finished up reading a text. "She just sent me a message. She'll be all set to meet with us in the morning."

"Good." Doreen smiled. "I can't wait to meet her."

"And just who is this partner again?" Wallace asked.

Doreen and Lady Arykah gave each other knowing looks.

"Let me just put it this way, honey," Doreen said as she placed a hand on his shoulder. "God's sending us a real live angel." She looked back at Lady Arykah. "Not to say that you aren't an angel as well."

"Oh, I know exactly what you meant. But an angel can't fly with one wing, so it's good to know that my other one is on the way."

"Good to know indeed," Doreen said, then turned around and looked out the window as they drove. All her worries and concerns were as good as gone. Doreen knew that with Lady Arykah in the house, so to speak, some feathers at Living Waters Living Word might get ruffled, but by the time Lady Arykah and her partner in crime were finished up in that place, just like Olivia Pope's, Doreen was 100 percent sure that her parting words would be, "It's handled."

NOTE FROM AUTHOR:

If you want a hint as to who Lady Arykah's partner is that is coming to assist her with Mother Doreen's issue at Living Word Living Waters, be sure to read *She's No Angel* by E.N. Joy and Nikita Lynette Nichols, releasing December 2016.

Joylynn M. Ross now writing as BLESSEDselling Author E.N. Joy (Everybody Needs Joy)

BLESSEDselling Author E.N. Joy is the writer behind the five-book series, "New Day Divas," the three-book series, "Still Divas," the three-book series, "Always Divas," and the three-book series, "Forever Divas," which have been coined "Soap Operas in Print." She is an Essence Magazine Bestselling Author who wrote secular books under the names Joylynn M. Jossel and JOY.

After thirteen years of being a paralegal in the insurance industry, E.N. Joy finally divorced her career and married her mistress and her passion: writing. In 2000, she formed her own publishing company where she self-published her books until landing a book deal with a major publisher. Under her company, she has published New York Times and Essence Magazine Bestselling authors in the "Sinner Series." In 2004, E.N. Joy branched off into the business of literary consulting where she provides one-on-one consulting and literary services such as ghostwriting, editing, professional read-throughs, write behinds, etc. . . . Her clients consist of first-time authors, Essence Magazine bestselling authors, New York Times bestselling authors, and entertainers. This award-winning author has been sharing her literary expertise on conference panels in her hometown of Columbus, Ohio, as well as cities across the country.

Not forsaking her love of poetry, one of E.N. Joy's latest poetic projects is an ebook of poetry titled *Flower in My*

Hair. "But my spirit has moved in another direction," E.N. Joy said when she decided to make the transition from secular writing to Christian fiction. Needless to say, she no longer pens street lit (in which two of her titles, *If I Ruled the World* and *Dollar Bill*, made the *Essence* magazine bestsellers list). *Dollar Bill* appeared in *Newsweek* and has been translated into Japanese. She no longer pens erotica or adult contemporary fiction either, where her title written with New York Times Bestselling Author Brenda Jackson, *An All Night Man*, earned the Borders bestselling African American romance award.

You can find this author's children's book titled *The Secret Olivia Told Me*, written under the name N. Joy, in bookstores now. *The Secret Olivia Told Me* received a Coretta Scott King Honor from the American Library Association. The book was also acquired by Scholastic Books and has sold over 100,000 copies. She also has a middle grade ebook titled *Operation Get Rid of Mom's New Boyfriend* and a children's fairytale ebook titled *Sabella and the Castle Belonging to the Troll*. Elementary and middle school children have fallen in love with reading and creative writing as a result of the readings and workshops E.N. Joy instructs in schools nationwide.

E.N. Joy was the acquisitions editor for Urban Christian, an imprint of Urban Books, for ten years. In addition, she was the artistic developer for a young girl group named DJHK Gurls. She penned original songs, drama skits, and monologues for the group that deal with messages that affect today's youth, such as bullying.

You can visit BLESSEDselling Author E.N. Joy at www.enjoywrites.com or e-mail her at enjoywrites@aol.com. Be sure to join "E.N. Joy's Readers' Lounge" on Facebook where her number one fans get comfy on the virtual couch to discuss the author's works.